RIP TIDES

PARADISE CRIME MYSTERIES BOOK 9

TOBY NEAL

D1255294

Print ISBN-13: 978-1-7337517-4-2

Psalm 46:2-3
Therefore we will not fear, though the earth should change, and the mountains slip into the heart of the sea; though its waters roar and foam, though the mountains quake at its swelling pride.

CHAPTER ONE

OCEAN THE COLOR OF GEMSTONES—TURQUOISE and lapis, with a few emeralds thrown in—seemed to mock Detective Sergeant Lei Texeira with its beauty as she pushed through the ring of spectators on the beach at Ho`okipa, Maui. A couple of uniformed officers she was familiar with were holding back the crowd, and Lei gave them a nod. "Push them back farther. Put up some scene tape."

Before she looked at the body she'd come for, Lei's eyes swept the crowd. The onlookers were subdued—all but one, a young brunette woman wrapped in a towel. She was sobbing into the arms of a blonde friend. Lei made a mental note to come back to the woman, and turned to her partner, Pono Kaihale.

"Can you start getting names and contact info? See who we can get statements from before these witnesses start drifting off?" The first officers on the scene were busily trying to isolate witnesses and take statements, but they had their hands full as the crowd ebbed and flowed.

God bless Pono. Her longtime friend and partner never had a problem with her taking the lead. He nodded, whipped a notepad out of his pocket, and waded back into the crowd. Lei pulled her radio off her belt and called for reinforcements to help their team grab anyone who might be a viable witness.

She swiveled to take in the whole scene. Ho`okipa Beach Park was a crescent moon of coral beach tucked inside rugged, black boulder-strewn bluffs. Fifty to a hundred yards from shore, she could see three different areas where surfers clustered in the water around breaking waves.

Finally, Lei turned to face the famous victim.

Makoa Simmons lay on his back on the golden, large-grained coral sand of the beach, deep gouge marks showing where he'd been dragged up from the aqua waterline. Doing a quick visual, Lei couldn't see any sign of injury other than the foam that had bubbled from his lungs and dribbled from slack, bluish lips. The young man's eyes were shut, skin grayish, his tan lying over its surface like paint. Wet hair, strands of blond and brown, tangled to muscled shoulders. His body was magnificent, wide shoulders tapering to a narrow waist, sun-bronzed as a surf god.

Even Lei, who didn't follow surfing closely, knew Makoa Simmons was Maui's rising surf star and had been looking good to take the prestigious Triple Crown of Surfing this year, with two of the three Oahu events in the contest already won.

Now he lay on the sand in front of her, dead as a piece of driftwood.

Lei felt a clench in the area of her heart. She hoped she never got used to this, no matter how many years she worked as a cop. The death of someone so young, the waste of potential reminded her of how much she herself had lost in this past year. It was too much to think about now, but the familiar yawning hole of grief sucked at her.

One of the paramedics stood up from where he was organizing his lifesaving equipment, and Lei turned to him. "What can you tell me?"

"Got the call from the lifeguard tower." The paramedic pointed to the bright yellow, two-story metal structure at the end of the beach. "Said they had a drowning. Didn't know it was Makoa Simmons until I got here. Lifeguards brought him in from the surf lineup."

Two lifeguards were standing, hands on hips, their heads close together as they talked, their faces somber. Lei caught the eye of the taller of the two and gestured for him to come talk. He and his partner, younger and slighter, came across the beach.

When Lei had their attention, she said, "I'm going to need to interview each of you. I've called the medical examiner, Dr. Gregory, and he should be here any minute to examine the body."

The lifeguard, a muscular Hawaiian man in traditional red shorts and a bright yellow rash guard shirt, nodded. He extended his hand to shake hers.

"I'm Sam Napua. I saw the surfers waving for help in the lineup and went out. Two of them were holding Makoa up. Soon as I signaled my partner, he joined me in the water and we got him in to the beach as fast as we could. Started CPR, but he was never responsive."

Dr. Gregory, the ME, pushed through the crowd, which had swelled as the news of the surf star's death spread via "coconut wireless" gossip. The portly doctor, whom she knew from various cases, was wearing one of his trademark aloha shirts, this one decorated with menehunes doing hula. He waved to Lei with a gloved hand as he signed in with the patrol officer on the log.

"These are the paramedics who tried to revive the victim," Lei told the doctor as he approached. Dr. Gregory, usually talkative and good-humored, sobered at the size of the crowd and the celebrity of the victim. He nodded, and with his assistant, Tanaka, knelt in the sand beside the body to begin their assessment.

"Can you help me identify the rescuers who were helping Makoa in the lineup?" Lei asked, turning back to Sam Napua.

"Sure. I thought you'd need to take statements once we saw

Makoa wasn't reviving, so I asked them to wait on the steps." He gestured to where two surfers sat on the metal stairs of the lifeguard tower. Lei hadn't noticed them before because the lifeguards had been standing in front of the steps, blocking them.

"Thanks. I'll talk with them next. Did you know the victim?"

"I did. Great kid." The lifeguard blinked his eyes hard, and Lei could see moisture in their dark brown depths. "Always friendly and down-to-earth. He's been surfing here for years."

"Tell me what you saw when you first approached the victim in the water."

"Well, I was using ol' Kelly here." Sam pointed to a huge white surfboard with a red cross on it. "This is our rescue board. We use it as our primary rescue device at this beach, with all the surf we deal with here."

"Kelly?"

"After Kelly Slater. Best all-around surfer in the world." Sam's teeth flashed in a brief smile as they both looked at the cumbersome board propped against the metal stairs of the tower.

Lei and her husband, Michael Stevens, had been beginner surfers for some time now, so she knew the riders were gathered around wave peaks that broke regularly in a certain spot, a predictable point where surfers could "line up" with a geographic marker of some kind on the beach and be positioned to take off. A good deal of the skill of surfing was being in the right place at the right time to get an optimal position on a wave, and that was rarely accidental.

"Which peak was he at?"

Sam pointed. "Over there."

Lei saw he'd been at the Point, the first of the peaky areas. Today the surf was coming in at around six feet in wave height from trough to crest. Even as Lei looked, a surfer took off, making the drop and pulling up to position himself for a "tube," where water covered him and he traveled inside the wave.

Another rider dropped in on him, spoiling the ride by blocking

4

his passage. The wave closed over the first rider, and Lei saw him disappear, wiping out. She frowned, watching the surfer who'd stolen the ride, on a green board, pump his way down the wave as it broke and finally kick out at the end.

"Did you see that?" Lei asked Sam. Getting caught inside a barrel, hitting another surfer's board or the bottom, even tangling with your own board in a wipeout were all common hazards that could cause death—but it would be highly unusual for a surfer of Makoa's ability to drown in such relatively minor water conditions.

"Yeah. There's been a lot of bad manners in the water lately," Sam said. "I've had to break up quite a few beefs on the beach." Even as they watched, the first surfer who'd lost the wave was yelling, pumping his board through the water toward the man who'd stuffed him. He smacked the water and cursed when he reached the other surfer. The drop-in surfer on the green board shrugged and moved off.

"So tell me what you saw when you got to Makoa and his rescuers," Lei said.

"They were holding him on one of their boards. They said they'd found him facedown, floating. They saw Makoa take off on a wave, and they were watching him because they were paddling back out. Then another surfer dropped in on him, and both of them wiped out. Or at least, that's what it looked like to them. But the other surfer paddled away, and Makoa's board came back up without him."

"Where's that other surfer?" Lei focused on Sam's face. She saw worry and suspicion in his weathered brown features—a tightening of the lips, a narrowing of eyes bracketed by fans of wrinkles from squinting into the dazzle of sea and sun.

"They said they didn't know. He paddled back out, and by the time they got Makoa up and out of the impact zone where the waves were breaking, they couldn't see him anymore."

"So he's not that guy that just snaked somebody again?" Lei

asked. The aggressive surfer they'd been watching had just dropped in on another rider.

"No, but dat buggah goin' get in scraps when he come in," Sam said, lapsing into pidgin, frowning. "Okay if I call him out of the water?"

"Yeah. That's dangerous, what he's doing. I want to see if he's the guy Makoa tangled with."

Sam jogged to the lifeguard tower, said something to the surfers, retrieved a bullhorn and an air horn, and climbed the steps of the tower. He blew the air horn, and everyone on the beach jumped.

"Surfer on the green board, exit the water," he bellowed into the megaphone. Lei started at the loudness of the bullhorn. She turned to look out at the man who'd been violating surfing etiquette—and was surprised to see that, instead of exiting the water as he'd been ordered, the man was paddling downwind toward the next break as fast as his arms would propel him.

Sam repeated his direction.

"Stupid," Lei said to Pono, who'd materialized at her side. "Where the hell does he think he's going?"

"Out to sea, looks like."

Sam returned, dark eyes flashing with irritation. "Want me to catch him on the Jet Ski?"

"Yeah. Bring the fool in," she said. "Where does he think he can get away on a surfboard?"

Lei walked toward the lifeguard tower and the two men who had rescued the victim as Sam and his partner ran back and drove a quad with a Jet Ski already trailered on the back, across the beach. Sam's partner turned the quad and backed the vehicle into the shifting sand lapped by surf as Sam guided the Jet Ski off the trailer and into the water.

Sam then jumped aboard, flipping down a floating rubber tow mat, and throttled the engine, turning the craft to zoom across the choppy inside of the bay toward the fleeing surfer. The man had made it all the way past the last Ho'okipa break.

Backup patrol officers had arrived, and Pono was organizing them to canvass the crowd. Dr. Tanaka and Dr. Gregory had erected a privacy shield, a pop-up metallic-looking tent, over the body to screen out the sun and prying eyes as they did undignified things to what remained of Makoa Simmons.

Lei refocused her attention on the two rescuers. "Tell me what happened," she said.

LIEUTENANT MICHAEL STEVENS sometimes wished he wasn't so good at his job. If he weren't, he wouldn't have been given new duties. Stevens rubbed a knot of tightness between his brows. He'd gotten the unwelcome news that, due to budget cuts, his little station out in Haiku was being reabsorbed into bigger Kahului Station. He was keeping his rank, but he'd been reassigned by Captain C. J. Omura to be head training officer for new detectives.

Stevens sighed as he set his station's expenditure report down. Glancing out the door of his office, he could see his men packing up—at least he wouldn't have to work on budget reports anymore, *and* he'd gotten a raise. But he didn't like the idea of not having his own active cases.

He took one of a stack of cardboard boxes he'd picked up behind Foodland and began cleaning out his desk.

"Boss." Detective Joshua Ferreira, closest thing he had to a partner, knocked on the doorframe. "Want I should get some guys to bring their trucks to move all this furniture?"

"I have to check with the captain, see how much of it is already down at Kahului and how much we're going to have moved into the state storage facility," Stevens said. "Thanks for reminding me." He picked up the phone and rang through to Omura's office.

"Yes." Omura always sounded clipped and in a hurry. It kept

calls short and made her more efficient, he realized, but he never looked forward to calling her.

"Hey, Captain. What do we do with the furniture here? Are you putting all the men in with other details, or will we have our own corner in the building?"

"In with the rest. You can tell them their reassignments," Omura said. She rattled off the six men's names and their new assignments. "Just take your personal things out of the building. We'll have to squeeze you guys into the existing space, and we'll have Buildings Division move the Haiku furniture into the big storage facility."

"Okay," Stevens said. "What about where you're putting me?"

"You're going to share an office with the recruiter and new officer trainer, Eric Tadeo. I told him you're coming."

"Great," Stevens muttered.

"Excuse me?"

"I said, great. Whatever works for the department," Stevens said louder.

"Good." Omura hung up with a *click*.

Stevens sighed again and stood up. Ferreira was still waiting in the doorway. "We're all being reassigned and the stuff goes into storage," Stevens said. "I have everyone's assignments. Tell the guys to come in."

He continued to gather up and sort the files in his desk drawer, his mind going, as it often did, to the bust on the Big Island that he and his wife, Lei, had made three months ago. Their house had burned down as collateral damage of that case, and Lei had lost their first child four months into the pregnancy.

The new house they were building, a simple three-bedroom in concrete block, was almost finished. He couldn't wait to be done with spending every non-working moment laboring on the house. The insurance hadn't paid out enough to rebuild, so they'd had to rely on the help of friends and coworkers, which didn't make for speedy construction.

Stevens felt like he'd been slogging through molasses ever since that Big Island case. Complicating things was a nagging worry that the shroud killer, an enemy who'd targeted those closest to them, might not be the one they had in custody. He hoped they'd seen the last of the shroud killer's relentless attacks, but there hadn't been enough evidence to prosecute the man they'd arrested for those particular crimes.

Every day seemed to take superhuman effort to get through, and he wondered if he could be suffering some sort of depression or if it was just grief over the fire and losing their baby. He'd begun to look forward to that daily belt of Scotch at the end of the day, because it seemed like they'd both been operating on autopilot.

The only person who really made him and Lei smile was his son from his first marriage. Kiet, at seven months, was happy and active, always crawling to grab something and put it in his mouth, jade-colored eyes sparkling with curiosity and humor.

Stevens wasn't looking forward to developing a training program when he wasn't enthusiastic about the changes or sure they would work. In the past, candidates for detective studied, passed the test, and then worked closely for six months with a "mentor" senior partner until they were ready to take their own cases.

Now the dictate had come down from central on Oahu that they needed to have more procedural standardization to reduce variability in case write-ups and other errors that had plagued departments statewide. He'd been given the assignment to develop that program and work with all new detective trainees.

Stevens finished his sorting and looked up as his small team filed into his office.

"Hey, guys. I have Omura's new assignments for you." He read off their names and new assignments, allowing the groans and teasing that erupted at some of the assignments. "Just pack your personal stuff. Department furnishings are going into storage."

The group was returning to the main room, grumbling side conversations going on that Stevens pretended not to hear, when Brandon Mahoe, one of his trainees now doing a turn at the watch desk, knocked on the doorjamb.

"Someone here to see you, sir. Says she's your mother."

CHAPTER TWO

L<small>EI JOTTED DOWN</small> the names of the two rescuers in her spiral note-book: Barrett Sharkey and Ipo Gomez. They were both mid-twenties, muscular and tan, and had known the victim for years.

"We were stoked Makoa was home for the weekend," Sharkey said. "He lives on Oahu now, on the North Shore. Lives with some other team riders at the Torque house at Pipeline."

Lei noted this. "So he was home for the weekend. I take it he stays with his parents when he's home?"

"Yeah, or at his girlfriend's." Sharkey pointed at the girl in the towel, whom Lei had already noticed. The girl had collapsed in the sand, her head on arms looped around her knees. Her friend was pressed close to her next to the plastic barrier tape. "Her name's Shayla Cummings."

Lei made another note. "Okay. Why don't you tell me exactly what happened."

Gomez took the lead this time. "We were both paddling out, so we saw Makoa take off on a big set wave. Then this kook dropped in on him. Guy we've never seen before."

"Not the guy on the green board? The one the lifeguard's chasing?" Lei asked, frowning.

"No. He was short and dark like that guy, but he was on a white board," Sharkey chimed in.

Could the aggressive surfer have changed boards somehow?

"Anyway, that guy dropped in late, and they tangled. Looked like a mean wipeout. And then the white water from the set hit us, and as we were trying to get through it, I saw the guy on the white board paddling in. Makoa's board was floating." Gomez pointed to it, a white board with red stripes and a lot of sponsorship decals, set on the beach. "But Makoa never came up. So I yelled to Bear, and we paddled for the board. I got it, and Bear used the leash to follow it down to Makoa. He was underwater."

"Was he stuck on something?"

"No. He was just deep underwater. Must have had his lungs really full, and he's got just about no body fat, so..." They all looked over at the surf star, now being lifted by Dr. McGregor and Tanaka into a long black bag.

Sharkey hung his head and rubbed his eyes. "Damn," he whispered. "Never thought it could happen to someone like Makoa."

Gomez shook his head. "Neither did I."

With the help of the remaining lifeguard and a couple of the uniforms, McGregor and Tanaka carried the bagged body up the beach. The group carefully lifted the young man into the back of the ME's van. The girls wailed, and Lei saw friends try to comfort them.

She pulled the witnesses' attention back to her. "Did you see any sign of foul play?"

"No. Unless you call dropping in on a guy and crashing into him foul, which I do," Gomez said. "That bastard bagged out of there because he knew he did wrong."

Another disruption pulled their attention away as the lifeguard arrived back at the beach on the Jet Ski with the runaway surfer dragging behind him on the flotation sled. Lei and the two rescuers watched as the lifeguards both lectured the guy as he got out of the water. Lei, following a hunch, held up a hand to Sharkey and Gomez. "Wait here a minute."

She gestured for one of the uniforms to follow her and walked down to the water, her black Nikes sinking into the soft, deep yellow sand, the sun hot on her hair. Sam Napua had a hand on the surfer's shoulder as he said, "You're off the beach for a week."

"Whatevahs," the man said. "Plenty of other places to surf."

"I wonder if you could explain what you're thinking when you drop in on somebody," Lei said. "It's not just rude. It's dangerous. Someone drowned here today after getting stuffed in a wave."

The young man, lean and dark with well-defined muscles moving easily, picked up his board from the water's edge and raked her with a contemptuous glance. He couldn't miss the badge on her belt and her weapon in the shoulder holster, let alone the uniformed officer beside her.

"I'm born and raised on this island, and if I want a wave I'm going to take it. My family been here longer than all these *haoles*."

"So you think being a local entitles you to something." Lei narrowed her eyes at him. "I think it entitles you to a citation for disturbing the peace. With a side of reckless endangerment." She gestured to the officer beside her. "Ticket him, please." She didn't usually carry a ticketing pad but had learned that there was often a need when responding to calls at the beach. The officer wrote the ticket and ripped it off, holding the slip of paper out to the angry surfer.

"Happy to meet you in court," the officer said. "I saw the whole thing. And you disobeyed the lifeguards and cost the county money and time bringing you in. I can write you up for that, too. You can take me to your vehicle so we can check your ID."

Lei saw the young man's eyes flicker and his jaw tense as he bit back angry words. He took the ticket, daring a "stink eye" glare at them as he broke into a trot for the parking lot with the officer behind him.

"Glad you cited him. Guy like that needs a smack down. He

just doesn't get it," Sam Napua said. "Those kind of attitudes are no way to live *aloha*."

"Thanks for all you do," Lei said sincerely to Sam. She'd always felt lifeguards were underpaid and under thanked. Sam glanced at her left hand, and she was glad she was wearing the simple, channel-set wedding ring from her wedding to Stevens not so long ago. Pono rejoined her with a stack of witness statements, and they went back up to the two young men she'd been interviewing.

"You did what you could to save Makoa," Lei said to them. "I may need to talk to you again." She handed them each cards. "I'm sorry you weren't able to get to him in time."

"He must have hit his head or something," Sharkey said. "I don't know why else a guy with skills like Makoa would have drowned from a simple wipeout."

"I'm sure the medical examiner will have more on that. Now, since you know her, can one of you introduce me to his girlfriend?"

Gomez knew the girlfriend better, so he led Lei over to the distraught young woman crying with her friend. Lei felt the grief pouring off the girls in palpable waves and tried not to let it activate her own emotions.

"Shayla. This is Detective Texeira," Gomez said, his hand on the girl's shoulder. "She's trying to find out what happened to Makoa. Can you talk to her?"

Shayla lifted huge brown eyes to look at Lei. She was one of those women who simply couldn't look ugly, even with a red nose, eyes streaming, and hands filled with hair she'd pulled out of her own head.

"I'm sorry to have to ask you questions right now," Lei said, feeling her hands prickle with sweat as she thought of her own extremity of grief not so long ago. She knew she'd been ugly in it: her freckled, olive-skinned face blotchy, eyes swollen to slits, curly hair matted. No, she wasn't one of those women who looked pretty crying.

"It's okay if it helps you find the man who did this," Shayla rasped.

"So you don't think it was an accident?" Lei asked, adding, "Can we go into the shade a bit?" A nearby beach naupaka tree cast lacy patterns over the yellow sand, and the girl, her friend, and Lei moved into the pool of shade.

"I think that bastard who stuffed him might have done something." Shayla groped for something to wipe her face with. Her blonde friend pulled off a T-shirt, revealing a tanned, toned body in a fuchsia bikini. The blonde handed the shirt to Shayla, who wiped her eyes and blew her nose on it. "He's been getting threats at the Oahu house."

Lei's attention sharpened. "Did you see where the guy went when he came in?"

"Yeah. I was watching Makoa surf. I always do when he's home. So I saw the whole thing. I didn't realize Makoa was in trouble, but I watched that guy come in because I've been concerned about the threats. He was maybe five-eight, and tanned with dark hair. Wearing black Quiksilver board shorts and a black rash guard. He got out of the water, grabbed his board, and ran up to the parking lot. I thought he was leaving because Makoa's so popular. The guy knew he'd have the boys after him for dropping in on Makoa."

Shayla sat up straight, golden-brown eyes flashing, and pulled waist-length, sun-streaked brunette hair back and braided it quickly as she spoke. "He got in one of the Sports Maui rental vans. You know the ones they rent in Kahului for windsurfers? He had one of those." She straightened the strings of her bikini, a cream-colored crochet that revealed as much as it concealed. "He roared out of here. Then I looked back out and saw that Bear and Ipo were looking for Makoa in the water."

Her eyes filled again as she looked out at the turquoise ocean, the breaking waves. The scene was timeless and unchanging, as if her world hadn't just been shattered.

Lei knew that feeling too well. Shayla was bright and observant, in spite of her grief. A credible witness.

"How long was it between when the guy took off and when he drove away?" Lei asked gently.

"Maybe ten, fifteen minutes."

"Did you get a license plate?"

"No. I stopped looking when the van began pulling out. I just noticed it because I could tell the guy was in a hurry to get out of there."

Lei's mind was already clicking ahead to the next steps. With Makoa's high profile, any allegation of foul play had to be definitively ruled out before a statement was released to the public, and they were a long way from that with this kind of testimony.

"What can you tell me about the threats he was getting?"

"They were e-mails from different addresses. Telling Makoa to throw the contest or 'we'll make you pay.'" She made air quotes with her fingers. "He had some threatening letters in the mail, too. And someone called his cell phone, left messages from a blocked number telling him to go home to Maui. Makoa just thought it was other competitors with sour grapes."

"Anyone in particular?"

"Yeah. He has some rivals." She gave Lei three names, all pros Lei recognized from the circuit. "You should also check out the guys he lived with at the team house. Makoa said Bryan Oulaki was especially bitter when he won the last event. Thought it should have gone to a North Shore guy like himself."

"Thanks." Lei took down that information as well. "If I need to question you further, what's a number I can reach you at?" Shayla gave her a number.

"I need to talk to his parents," Lei said. At the mention of that, Shayla hung her head. "What are their names? We need to speak with them as soon as possible."

16

Shayla had begun to sob again, and this time the friend, barely controlling her own tears, gave Lei the names and address of Makoa Simmons's parents.

Lei stood, brushing sand off her black jeans, and tucked the notepad into her back pocket. There was pretty much nothing she hated more than going to break the news of a child's death to parents, but it was an important interview that couldn't be passed on to others. She walked over to Pono, who was gathering witness statements from the other officers who'd helped with the canvassing.

"Ready to go on our favorite kind of home visit?" Lei asked.

Pono put all the witness statement papers he'd gathered into a file folder. "I wish we could fast-forward this part," he said.

"Me too." Lei sighed.

STEVENS STOOD SLOWLY, feeling his face freeze into an expression he hoped was socially acceptable as he turned to the door. By the puzzlement in his subordinate Brandon's expression, he didn't think he'd quite pulled it off.

"Send her in." His lips felt stiff. He hadn't seen his mother in five years. Not since he'd left the LAPD and transferred to a series of posts in Hawaii, in fact. And there was good reason for that.

His mother, Ellen Rockford Stevens, stepped into the doorway. "Hello, son."

Of course she led with reminding him of his obligation to her. Her voice was sanded with years of drink and smoking, but he'd have known it anywhere. She'd made an effort to clean up. Her hair was bottled blonde and brushed, and she'd been a good-looking woman in her prime and still stood taller than most. But her once-bright blue eyes were faded and watery, and she was so thin that skin hung off her bones. She'd always been slim, but this was alarming.

"Mom." He came around from his desk and hugged her. It felt like gathering a bundle of sticks for firewood. She smelled of stale cigarettes and the alcohol making its way out of her pores. She clung to him, hiding her face.

"I have nowhere to go," she whispered. Her voice was a rasp. He had to tilt his head to hear her even as he shut his office door on the silence that had fallen over his staff out in the front room.

Stevens's stomach hollowed as he led her to one of the plastic chairs in front of his desk. "How'd you get here?" he asked, walking back around to sit behind his desk, taking the last few items he'd been packing and setting them in the box, finding comfort in the simple little movements.

"Took a plane, of course." She gave a snort of a laugh. "One-way."

"Oh." Stevens pulled out a drawer, rechecked that it was empty, gathering his thoughts.

He'd known this day might come. His mother was a progressive alcoholic, and when he'd moved from Los Angeles five years ago, she'd already spent time on the streets after being kicked out of bars. He'd gotten so sick of being called to come get her or bail her out he'd come all the way to Hawaii to get his own life going.

She must have run through everything their father had left her.

"I can tell you aren't happy to see me. Haven't had so much as a Christmas card from you this year."

"I gave up after you couldn't make it to our wedding," Stevens said, narrowing his eyes at her. "I sent the ticket and everything."

"I wasn't feeling well."

"Well, it looks like you still aren't feeling well."

"I'm ready for a new start. I think being here could help."

"That's good, Mom." He swallowed all the things he wanted to say. "Where are you staying?"

"I don't know." She blinked, and her eyes overflowed. He continued packing so he wouldn't have to look at her. "I was hoping to stay with you."

"Have you contacted Jared?"

"He didn't leave me any numbers." She sounded hurt. "What kind of sons are you, moving six thousand miles out across the ocean? Not even letting me know where you are."

"We wanted to have our own lives, Mom." Stevens dropped a pile of manuals off a shelf into a box with a *thud*. "You have your life, and it's in a bottle. Until that changes, we don't have much in common."

She sputtered indignantly. It sounded like an angry kitten.

Sorrow sliced through him in a way that stole his breath. He owed Ellen life. He owed her respect, whatever her addiction. She was his mother, and she was desperate. He looked up at her.

"I'll take you out to our house. You can spend the night, but you'll have to be in the tent in the yard. We're squeezed into a tiny cottage with Lei's dad and my son while we work on our house. It's not the best time for guests."

"You have a son?" Her face brightened, eyes widening. She smiled, and he glimpsed the beauty she used to be and felt that sadness again. "I have a grandchild?"

"His name is Kiet. He's my son with my ex, Anchara."

"Oh. You didn't invite me to that wedding."

"No, I didn't. I'll call Jared and let him know you're here." He didn't want to get into any of this painful history. He reached for his phone and pressed a number for Jared.

His younger brother, a firefighter at Kahului Station and recent transplant to Maui, picked up right away. "Hey, bro!"

"Jared, Mom's here."

A long pause. "Shit," Jared said.

"That was my thought." Stevens cut his eyes over to his mother. She was groping through a backpack on her lap. He could tell by the trembling of her hands that she needed a drink or a cigarette—maybe both. "I'll put her in the tent at our house tonight, unless you have a better idea?"

"You know I only have a one-bedroom apartment." Jared had

taken over the lease on Stevens's bachelor apartment in Kuau. It was close to the ocean and work, he'd said, and so far he'd seemed happy there.

"Well, she's gonna have to be out in the tent," Stevens said. "We're tight as sardines in the cottage, and the house needs another couple of weeks before we're ready to move in. Anyway, can you come over tonight? Join us for dinner?"

"I don't think so." Jared's voice was bitter.

Stevens turned away from his mother and hissed into the phone, "Come on, bro. You can't leave me holding the bag on this."

"Like you left me holding the bag when you went to Hawaii five years ago? I dealt with her shit with no help for years after you left."

"Hey, now. It was time for you to step up, and if I were there, she'd always hit me up first." Stevens's voice was rising along with his emotions. Things had been so great since his brother had moved to Maui. Trust his mother to bring old tensions with her.

"I'll think about it. You don't know what went down between us before I moved." Jared hung up abruptly. Stevens slid the phone into his pocket and stood.

"Jared's not sure he can make it. I'll take you home, Mom, if you don't have any other plans?"

"No plans," she said, a note of relief in her voice. "That sounds lovely."

Stevens called Wayne briefly to let him know he was coming home early with his mother. Finally, he held down the intercom button, calling Brandon Mahoe at the front desk. "Taking the afternoon off. Getting my mother settled," he said.

"No problem, boss," Brandon replied, and Stevens heard sympathy in what he didn't say.

He picked up his weapon and personal items as his mother stood, smoothing a tunic top she wore over skinny jeans and battered, cuffed boots that had been good quality at one time. She still managed to look classy, if a little run-down. He took her arm, and she leaned on him gratefully.

He had a flash of memory: him on one side of her, Jared on the other. A big copy of *The Jungle Book* open on her lap. He and his brother had loved that story. She'd been stroking the hair off his forehead. Her voice was husky and hypnotic as she read. He remembered how happy he'd been. He could still see the curve of his brother's forehead across from him, Jared's mouth plugged with a thumb.

They'd been happy, once, and she'd been a good mom before the drinking started, and escalated dramatically with his father's death when Stevens was sixteen.

He walked her through the room, acknowledging the nods from his men. He paused at Ferreira's desk. "This is my mother, Ellen. I'm heading out. See you tomorrow."

"Mrs. Stevens," Ferreira said, rising with old-fashioned gallantry to shake Ellen's hand. "Nice to meet you."

"Likewise," she said. "Got a smoke?"

Ferreira's face froze in surprise as she went on. "I know Michael doesn't smoke, and damn if that plane flight wasn't a long time without a cigarette."

"That's the worst. Sure." Ferreira dug in his chest pocket for the square pack and shook out two. "Can't smoke in the station, though, ma'am."

"Of course." She took the cigarettes. "I thank you."

Stevens endured this and walked his mother through the building. As soon as they got outside, she put one of the cigarettes to trembling lips and flicked the old silver Zippo their father had been awarded for ten years of service in his firehouse. Stevens could still glimpse his father's well-worn initials in the soft glow of the metal between his mother's thin fingers. Her cheeks hollowed as she drew hard on the cig, and he lost patience with her and the stab of grief he felt at that tiny reminder of his dad. He took her elbow and gave a tug.

"My truck's over here."

"Hey!" he heard someone call, and turned to see a minivan with a lighted taxi emblem on top. "That lady owes me for a ride!"

Stevens turned to his mother. She shrugged, making a go-ahead gesture with her cigarette. He shook his head as he walked back and paid off the driver. He then settled his mother in the passenger seat of the brown Bronco he'd been driving for years. He set her backpack behind the seat.

"Smells like dog in here," his mother said.

"Yeah, a bit. We have a Rottweiler, Keiki. She's one of the family. She rides back there with the baby sometimes. Wayne Texeira, Lei's father, watches Kiet for us during the day," he said, turning on the vehicle.

"That's nice," Ellen said without interest. She rolled down her window and leaned her head out. "It's so beautiful here." Palm trees lining the main thoroughfare flicked by as Stevens merged onto Hana Highway, heading out of Kahului into the sugarcane fields and farther north.

"Just wait until you see where we live." Stevens felt his spirits lift as the road took them out of town and they faced the great shadowy purple bulk of Haleakala, wreathed in afternoon clouds, the sky a brilliant blue above. "It's out in the country. Really green and peaceful."

"I could use a little peace." His mother rested her head on the jamb of the door. He looked over a few moments later and could tell she'd fallen asleep by the slackness of her jaw. Her thin blonde hair fluttered in the wind.

He called Lei, but she didn't pick up. He left a message. "My mom's in town and going to stay with us a few days. I'm putting her out in the tent, and hopefully Jared's coming to dinner. Hope you're feeling up for company."

CHAPTER THREE

Lᴇɪ ᴀɴᴅ Pᴏɴᴏ pulled up a round, curving drive planted with decorative areca palms and parked in front of a large plantation-style home at Makoa Simmons's parents' address in Wailuku Heights—a newer, upscale area. Pono was driving his beefed-up purple truck, and Lei reached up to tap the tiny replica Hawaiian war helmet that hung from the rearview mirror. "For courage," she said.

"We're going to need it," Pono agreed, gathering his handheld recorder and a notepad.

Lei opened her door. The truck was jacked up on big tires, so she used a chrome step to hop to the ground. She straightened her clothes and shrugged into the light khaki jacket she wore to conceal the shoulder holster. She liked to use her smartphone for recording, and as she slipped it out of her jacket pocket, she saw that Stevens had called and left a voice mail.

Lei listened to the message as they walked up wide, gracious steps to a carved wooden Balinese-style front door. She grimaced at the news that Stevens's mother was on-island. She'd never met the woman, but what he'd told her hadn't impressed her.

"They don't seem to be hurting for money," Pono observed, doing a survey of the well-groomed yard in the exclusive neighborhood. This side of the valley had sweeping views of the sugarcane fields, the town of Kahului, and the rising purple bulk of dormant volcano Haleakala. Clouds crowned the summit today, and as she often did, Lei had a sense of the mountain looking down at her benignly. She slid the phone back into her pocket.

"I'm finally going to meet my mother-in-law after work today," Lei said as Pono rang a brass bell inset in the door.

He raised thick black brows. "Good luck with that."

"Yeah. Gonna need it." Lei reached up in a familiar gesture to touch the white gold pendant she wore at her throat. Footsteps echoed, and the door opened. Lei could tell by the woman's swollen, tear-streaked face that someone had already told her about Makoa.

"Hi. I'm Detective Sergeant Leilani Texeira, and this is my partner, Pono Kaihale, from Maui Police Department. I can tell you've heard the news, and I'm so sorry for your loss." Lei and Pono held up their badges. "I know this is tough, but can we come in? We have some questions."

"Okay." Gail Simmons's blue eyes filled again as she stood aside, holding the door open for them. She was dressed simply, in a floral tunic and leggings. "My husband is on his way home from work. I called him."

"We're so sorry." Pono's rumbling bass added pathos to the words as the distraught mother covered her face with her hands.

Lei stepped inside a stone-flagged entry with large ceramic pots of ruffled orchids on either side of the door. A sunken great room opened before them with a floor-to-ceiling swath of windows framing a view that led the eye down a grassy field to the cobalt sea. Whitecaps flecked the surface of the ocean, reflecting clouds scudding by.

Lei wished she were anywhere else other than in this elegant room as the grief of Makoa's mother battered at her own emotions. "Come sit down."

She put her hand on Gail's shoulder, and with Pono on the other side, they guided the woman to a beige suede couch facing the windows. Lei felt anxiety tighten her chest as Mrs. Simmons gave way, sobbing on Pono's bulky shoulder.

She got up and went in search of tissues, her eyes taking in the glossy kitchen, hallway with rooms opening off it, a bathroom lined in shells and coral-embedded tile. She grabbed the box of tissues she found on the back of the toilet and returned to sit beside Mrs. Simmons with a glass of water from the kitchen. Finally, when she had wound down a bit, Mrs. Simmons mopped her eyes and straightened up.

"My husband should be here soon. I also called our daughters on Oahu. They're both students at University of Hawaii. They're going to come home as soon as they can get flights."

"So Makoa wasn't in college?" Lei asked.

"No. He never went. His pro surfing career began as soon as he turned eighteen, so that was his priority."

"Did he live here? With you?"

"Yes. He wanted his own place, but I argued that this house was so big, and empty now, and he was on the road so much with contests, that it was no trouble for him to stay in his old room when he was home. Though he often was over at his girlfriend's. Shayla Cummings." Gail's mouth tightened.

"Tell me about his relationship with Shayla," Lei probed gently. She wanted to get a little more background on the striking young woman who seemed so devoted to Makoa.

"She's a bikini model. Works at a surf shop when she's not doing modeling." Mrs. Simmons blew her nose. "The girl is nice enough, but I wanted more for Makoa. Now there won't be more. Of anything."

Mrs. Simmons gazed out the window, balling the tissue in her hands. It was like a switch had been tripped, and she fell silent and still, all animation gone from her face.

The front door flew open so hard it banged against the wall. Mrs. Simmons jumped as Lei and Pono stood, turning to face Makoa Simmons's father.

"Who's this, Gail?" Rory Simmons had a booming cannon of a voice and the bright red face of someone with high blood pressure. His thinning brown hair was disordered, and he was panting with emotion.

"Detectives Kaihale and Texeira of the Maui Police Department," Pono answered smoothly, coming forward with his hand outstretched. His burly presence projected calm authority, and the agitated man—a leathery, heavier version of the young man whose body they had found on the beach—took his hand and shook it automatically. Lei hung back a bit as he came down into the seating area, leaning over to embrace his wife.

"My God. Our son," he said brokenly. She clung to him, weeping, as he sat beside her on the couch.

Lei and Pono took a couple of soft, suede-upholstered chairs across from them. The light from the bank of windows cruelly lighted every wrinkle and gleam of wetness on the faces of the older couple in front of her.

Lei tried to imagine the magnitude of losing a young-adult child in the prime of his life, when she'd been so recently felled by the grief of a miscarriage. She didn't even know when she'd be ready to try getting pregnant again. There was no greater risk for the heart than having a child.

Finally Rory Simmons turned his attention to them. "Why are you here? Makoa drowned surfing, right?"

"Yes. We're here to officially notify you of his death—and to find out anything that might be relevant to it." Lei spoke carefully, recognizing an alpha-male personality in the bluff, barrel-chested man.

"We always want to talk with families when there's been an unexpected death, even if ultimately it turns out to be accidental," Pono said. "What can you tell us about Makoa's activities in the last few days?"

"I don't see how that's relevant to Makoa drowning in the surf," Simmons growled. "I always told that boy surfing would be the death of him."

Mrs. Simmons pulled away from her husband. "Shut up!" she screamed. "He loved what he did. He was a world champion! But nothing he did was ever good enough for you!"

Lei scrambled mentally for the information on the Simmons parents she'd quickly gathered on the way over. Rory was a contractor, a self-made millionaire who'd made his money building large housing tracts in Hawaii. Gail, his wife, was a former teacher who was busy with various charities. Apparently there was a long-standing disagreement about their son's choice of career. Lei helped Gail get up and go to a separate chair.

"You two are in shock. Please take a little time to pull yourselves together," Lei said. "Is there anyone who can come over and keep you company?"

"I called my sister and my best friend, Sally," Gail said. She straightened her blouse and narrowed bloodshot eyes at her husband. "I don't want to hear you say one more negative thing about Makoa's surfing again."

"I'll say whatever I like," Rory said. A cord stood out from his cheek; Lei could see he was clenching his jaw. "He was my son, too, though you always spoiled him."

Lei looked helplessly at Pono just as the door opened again and two distraught women, Gail's sister and friend, arrived.

Rory got up and stomped away down the hall. Pono followed him, trying to talk to him as he headed for some inner sanctum. Lei went back to the kitchen for more glasses of water.

She wasn't able to get anything useful or coherent from the

women, so she took herself back down the hall, only to meet Pono exiting Rory's home office.

"We need to come back later," he said briefly, and she nodded and followed him out. Taking charge of this interview wasn't going well, and she wondered if it was because of her own grief. Sitting with the extreme emotions around her had her stomach in knots, and even though initial statements should always be taken right away, she just didn't have the heart for it when they weren't sure that this drowning was anything more than an accident.

Acknowledging that she was still hurting from the events three months ago was hard, but they'd had a lot to deal with. Their house burned down, a violent firefight raid, a hijacking—and worst of all, her miscarriage. She'd carried on, but didn't feel the same. Coming up soon, she had to go to the Big Island to testify in the trial of her enemy. Her stomach clenched at the thought.

Pono's truck had almost been blocked in by other vehicles, but with some creative maneuvering they got out of the driveway and headed back toward Kahului.

"That went about as good as could be expected," Lei said.

"Yeah."

"Did you get anything off the dad?"

"Not really, nothing more than was obvious in the living room. He didn't agree with his son's choice of career and the mother supported it." Pono rubbed his lips under the short, bristling mustache he sported, a habit he had when troubled. "We need to go back when they've settled down a little."

"I'll feel better taking a shovel to that shit pile when we know what the ME says about cause of death. No sense stirring all the issues if it was an accident."

"Agree."

Back at the station, Lei organized her notes, and side-by-side, Lei and Pono built the case file. Lei was happy to be back partnering with her oldest friend on the force. Captain Omura had reassigned them for a time, but continued restructuring in the department and both their continued requests had gotten them back together. Lei had liked all her other partners—Jack Jenkins on Kauai, Ken Watanabe when she was in the FBI on Oahu, and Abe Torufu while she did a brief stint on the bomb squad—but she and Pono knew each other so well that they worked smoothly and quickly on everything from paperwork to interviews.

"I'm going to call Dr. Gregory. See if he's got anything off the body yet. We need to keep working the case hard for the next twenty-four if it's a homicide. If it's not looking that way, it's not as important to chase down that windsurf van today," Lei said.

"Right." Pono was uploading the photos he'd taken at the scene.

Lei used her desk phone to call the morgue. "Hey, Doc," she said when Gregory answered. "I know it's early, but are you getting anything off the body to indicate homicide? Because if so, we've got some leads we should follow up on."

"Just a minute. I was grabbing a bite to eat at my desk."

Lei squinched her eyes shut, picturing his desk in the corner of the big, open room full of bodies on tables in various stages of dismemberment. To Gregory's credit, the doc had a folding screen separating his work area—but still, the smells alone were enough to put Lei off food for hours.

"Okay. Yeah. We haven't had time to open Simmons up yet, but I found bruising on his throat and the top of his head, hair pulled out even. The more hours that pass, the more we'll be able to see the soft-tissue damage on the body. But it looks like someone could have grabbed him by the neck and head. Probably held him underwater."

"Oh, damn," Lei said faintly. She hadn't realized until that moment how much she'd been hoping the surf champion's death was accidental. Murder was going to amplify the tragedy of the young surf star's death and stir up the close-knit surfing community even more.

"I'll know more when I open him up and check his lungs, but so far everything else is indicative of drowning as cause of death."

"Okay. Thanks. We'll move on this right away."

"I'll put him at the front of the autopsy line. I know this kid was high profile. I'll give you a call as soon as I have anything more."

"Appreciate that." Lei hung up and turned to Pono. "Possible homicide. We'd better brief the captain and find that van."

STEVENS PULLED up the driveway to their property out in rural Haiku; an area dominated by jungle and large eucalyptus robusta trees, brought over to Hawaii in a mistaken attempt to grow a lumber crop and now dominating the landscape of that area. He punched the code into the gate and the ten-foot-tall cedar edifice retracted, flush with the wall that circled their two-acre property. He drove the rest of the way through a grove of fruit trees and parked in the open garage area that had been one of the first things completed on the new house.

Keiki, their Rottweiler, greeted him with a single bark, pressing in against his leg as he opened the door of his Bronco.

"Hey, old girl." He stroked her head and played with her silky ears. Keiki hadn't been the same since the house fire, when she'd been traumatized as well as burned. Her energy just seemed lower. But now she scented Ellen and sniffed loudly, shooting Stevens a glance as if in question. "Yeah. My mom's here."

His mother was still asleep in her seat, so Stevens took a moment to look around. His father-in-law's cottage, where they were all currently residing, was a cheerful little home with a sheltered front porch and two red hibiscus bushes bracketing its steps. Beside him the harsh-looking concrete walls of their new house, built for security and stability rather than looks, were complete. They'd spent extra for a terra-cotta-colored, metal tile roof. Pretty soon, the stucco guys would come and apply exterior texture that would make the house, currently looking like a barracks, more attractive.

Stevens didn't much care what it looked like. After living through two fires, he just wanted to sleep in a place where that particular nightmare would never happen again, and if it cost more and took longer, his nightmares might at least decrease.

He reached over and shook his mother's shoulder gently. Her bones felt brittle under his hand. "Mom. Wake up. We're here."

Ellen sat up, blinking, and he got out and came around to get her backpack and open her door, surprised when he saw moisture in her eyes as he took her hand to help her out of the seat.

"Thanks, Michael," she said. "You know how to treat a woman. I'm thankful."

Keiki sniffed around her legs and slowly wagged her stump of tail as Ellen stepped out of the truck with dignity. Stevens felt a tug of soft nostalgia as she took his arm.

"Where are you putting me?"

"Well, that's the thing." Stevens gestured to the looming bulk of the house beside them. "We're still under construction here after a house fire, so we're going to have to put you in a tent out in the yard."

He led her across the smoothly mowed lawn, which Wayne kept shipshape, to a large tent, already set up with an air mattress in it, back behind a mango tree. He and Lei slept out there when they needed more privacy than the tight quarters of Wayne's cottage provided, and it was also a fun place for Kiet to play.

"This is nice," she said, looking around the interior, furnished with a patterned rug, a chair and camp table, the already-made bed, and a playpen filled with toys for Kiet.

"Yeah, this is our little getaway when any of us thinks the cottage is getting too cozy," Stevens said. "You'll have to go in the new house for the bathroom, though, but at least the plumbing is in and working there. We're a ways away from being able to move into it."

Stevens decided not to say more, wondering how long she was planning to stay and afraid to ask. He set her backpack down next to the desk and couldn't miss the longing glance she cast at the bed, like she just wanted to get in and sleep.

"Come meet Wayne. We'd be lost without his help with the baby."

Ellen followed him across the yard, silent as he pointed out the various kinds of fruit trees on the property: breadfruit, mango, Hawaiian orange, macadamia, tangerines, and a stand of coffee and cacao trees in one corner, which were Wayne's experimental project.

Wayne met them on the porch, Kiet, crowing with delight, in his arms. The older man's gaze sharpened as he shook Ellen's hand and took in her appearance.

"Pleased to have you visit," he said graciously. "This is Kiet. Our grandbaby."

Stevens took the child into his arms. His mother stared at the baby as if mesmerized. "Kiet Edward Mookjai Stevens," Stevens said deliberately, so Ellen would know that he'd given Kiet his father's name.

"He's beautiful," she breathed. Stevens knew it was true. His son gazed at his grandmother from remarkable jade-colored eyes. His thick black hair shone in the sun, and his skin was the color of taffy. The baby extended a chubby, dimpled hand to reach for Ellen, and she reached for him as well.

Stevens hadn't anticipated the emotion that would tighten his chest and clog his throat as he handed his mother her grandchild for the first time. But it was there, and it was as real as her thin arms, which encircled the child as she buried her face in his tender neck. Kiet swiveled back toward Stevens, uncertain, and then, as if deciding to sample the wares, he patted Ellen's head.

She sat down in a nearby rocker with the baby in her arms, and

Wayne cleared his throat. "I'll throw some extra food together for dinner. Jared coming?"

"Thanks, Wayne. We hope he'll make it."

"I just needed to see my boys," Ellen said. "I didn't know any of this was going on." Her voice was muffled in the baby's neck.

"Well, better late than never, right?" Gentle humor in Wayne's voice took any sting out of the words. "We've been through a rough time in the last six months."

"I'm glad to be here," Ellen said, rocking Kiet.

"Good to have you," Wayne said. "Mike, can I have a word?"

Stevens followed his tall, rangy father-in-law back into the house, and the man turned to him in the tiny kitchen, pitching his voice low as he ran a hand through salt-and-pepper curls.

"Is she sick?"

"An alcoholic, like I told you a while ago," Stevens said. "Still drinking and smoking, from what I can tell so far."

Wayne frowned, his dark eyes worried. "I bet she's got something more going on."

"Jared's pissed at her. I'm not sure he's coming to dinner tonight, but I'm sure we'll find out more. I don't know how long she's going to be staying." Stevens felt the familiar frustration and worry thinking about his mother brought. "We can put the screen tent up on the lawn so we can all sit down together."

"Got some laulau stashed in the freezer for a rainy day," Wayne said. "You better give Lei a heads-up."

"I left her a message." Stevens looked down at his phone, clipped on his belt and vibrating. "Speaking of..." He answered the phone and went back onto the porch as Wayne took a foil-wrapped packet out of the freezer.

His mother was rocking Kiet on the porch, humming a little melody that Stevens recognized in some deep place as he took the call from his wife. Her voice sounded tight with tension.

"Pulled a homicide. I won't be home until late. We have to dig in hard until we run out of leads. It's Makoa Simmons. Looks like he was drowned on purpose out at Ho`okipa."

"Oh crap." Stevens walked down onto the grass and out to the metal storage shed where they kept the screen tent and foldable table and chairs. "That's just tragic."

"I know." Lei sighed. He could picture her rubbing the medallion she wore on a chain around her neck, a habit she had when she was stressed. "How's it going with your mom?"

He'd reached the toolshed, a simple metal structure, and pushed the sliding door open, taking out the long plastic bag that held the tent.

"She's not too well. Really skinny and seems exhausted. She bought a one-way ticket over."

A long pause as Lei thought this over. "Is she staying long?"

"I don't plan for her to." Stevens blew out a breath. "But she doesn't seem to have anywhere to go."

Lei didn't question this further, and he liked that. He knew it was at least in part because in Hawaii culture, family came first. No one would put a relative out on the street who needed shelter. "Is she staying in the tent?"

"Yeah. I'm not sure Jared's coming to dinner, so it would be great if you could make it home for that, even just an hour or two."

"I'll try. May have to bring Pono, though. We're moving on in this, so we'll need to keep it short."

"That's fine. Whatever works. She's really taken to Kiet." He turned to look back at the porch. Kiet had rested his head on his mother's thin chest, and they both appeared to have fallen asleep in the rocking chair. The sight moved him. "She was surprised to find she was a grandma, but I can tell she's happy about it."

"That's good. So…Makoa Simmons." Lei was obviously still thinking about her case. "We're just sorting through the possible motives, but it seems like there was a lot of professional competition out there with the other pro surfers along with some sour grapes. Discord in the home, too. I may have to follow the case to Oahu, where he lived."

"Well, it's a high-profile homicide, so do what you gotta do." Stevens heard frustration about his reassignment come out in his voice as he said, "We're almost out of the old station. Captain put us back into the main station house like I told you was happening, and I'm now the new detective trainer for Maui."

"You're going to be great at that!" He hadn't expected Lei to sound so enthusiastic. "You are so good at teaching and getting the men to dig deeper, make their best effort. Captain's smart to put you on that."

"I suspected she was going to give me some other duties. I'm just not sure how I feel about not having active cases anymore." He hauled the heavy tent bag to the open area where they liked to set up for dinners outside. With his mother here for a while, he planned to leave the tent up so they'd have room to sit down at meals. The roof would keep the rain off, and the screen was absolutely necessary to keep mosquitoes out. With the two tents in the yard, they'd effectively increased their living space.

"Well, you know Maui. I bet you just get started and develop the program they want and then, at the same time, we'll get a bunch of nasty cases and you'll have to work those, too."

Stevens smiled. "Might happen like that."

Talking to Lei had lightened his mood. He pulled the tent out of the bag one-handed, and the metal poles clanked onto the grass.

"Times like this I just..." He dropped the bag. "I miss you being here."

"Yeah. I'd rather be there than here." He heard by her breathing that she was on the move. "What time are you eating so I can try to swing by then?"

"Probably around six-thirty, when, hopefully, Jared gets here."

"Okay. Save some for us."

"It's laulau your dad's been stashing for a special occasion."

"Laulau!" He knew Lei loved the steamed Hawaiian meat dish, slow-cooked in kalo leaves. "We'll be there for sure. I gotta go."

"I love you. There. *Pau* for today." He'd said he'd tell her that every day after they were married. Though they joked about it, he still felt good about trying to stay faithful to his promise.

"I love you more." He heard a vibration of conviction in Lei's voice as she hung up.

CHAPTER FOUR

Lᴇɪ ᴀɴᴅ Pᴏɴᴏ tracked down Shayla Cummings's home address. As they got ready to go out with the station's on-call sketch artist, Lei's phone lit up.

She saw it was her friend Special Agent Marcella Scott, on Oahu. "I need a couple minutes," she told Pono. Her partner nodded and headed out to claim a cruiser with the sketch artist. "Marcella! How are the wedding plans coming along?"

"Okay, but that's not why I called you." There was a serious note in her friend's voice. "I wanted to let you know Ray Solomon is out on bail."

"What?" Lei felt her stomach drop, her mind's eye filling with her last view of Ray's face, those distinctive golden-hazel eyes sunk deep in pouches of fat, filled with a hate that burned her as totally as he'd burned their home. She shivered involuntarily. "I think Hilo PD should've let me know he is out. I have to go there in a few weeks to testify at his trial."

"I've been keeping an eye on him for you," Marcella said. "He's in a group home type place for the indigent disabled. He doesn't seem to be doing anything but watching a lot of TV."

"Marcella, don't let his paralysis deceive you. Ray hates me for his disability, blames me for all that's gone down with the whole Chang family." The history was long, and had its roots all the way back a generation. "I'm a handy target. But finding out he's out of jail doesn't help me rest easy."

"I'm sure there's too much heat for him to do anything, even if he had the connections anymore. Without his partner, Anela, who was the legs of the operation, he seems to be totally shut down."

"Does the FBI have surveillance on Terence Chang anymore?" Lei asked, worried about the young man who had helped them with the Big Island case—but for his own, not entirely clear, reasons.

"No. After Ray was in custody, we pulled the surveillance on Terence. We had no grounds."

"Well, thanks for the heads-up. I may get to see you, sooner than later. I have a big case that may bring me to Oahu. I'm hoping Marcus can partner with me on it."

"I'm sure he'd be delighted. Call me when you get here."

"Will do." Lei wrapped up her goodbyes, and frowning with the worry of this news, trotted through the station to find Pono and the station's contracted sketch artist.

They piled into one of the station's police cruisers, as neither of their trucks had a third passenger seat. The artist, a skinny young man named Kevin with a spindly goatee twisted into a braid and gauges in his ears, leaned his head in between the seats as Pono pulled the vehicle out onto the busy traffic of Hana Highway.

"So am I sketching the guy who offed Makoa Simmons?" he asked, the late-afternoon sun winking on a little red stone in his nose piercing.

"It's a lead. Nothing more," Lei said. The department contracted with the young man and he'd signed confidentiality agreements, but Lei was always cautious of civilians' commitment. "You can't discuss it."

"Of course." The artist reached up and played with the big, metal-lined hole in his ear.

"Why do you do shit like that to your body?" Lei asked. "I'm curious. I really want to know."

"It's a style thing. An aesthetic."

Pono eyed the young man. "Those holes in your ears look like handles for grabbing in a fight, and a punch to the nose is really gonna hurt with that piercing," he said conversationally. "But that's just the way we cops think."

"Good thing I leave the brawling to people like you," Kevin said, contempt in his voice.

Lei grabbed his ear, her fingertip digging into the gauged hole and giving just enough of a tug to show the young man how easily she could rip his lobe off.

"Respect," was all she said, and let go.

He sat back and shut up.

Shayla lived in a small cottage on the property of a house in Kuau. Lei had an affection for the little neighborhood, a mishmash of expensive beachfront mansions mixed with run-down old plantation-style homes right on the ocean near Maui's best North Shore surf and windsurf spots. Stevens's old apartment building, where Jared now lived, wasn't far from the bikini model's cottage.

They pulled up at the address and got out. Shayla's house was in the back, and they went around the garage, following a path of beach stones set in the grass. A wide-branched old plumeria tree sheltered the tiny cottage, and Lei breathed in the warm, sweet scent of the big white blossoms that dotted the lawn and the porch.

The same girl who'd been comforting Shayla at the beach opened the door. "She took a sleeping pill and she's in bed," the friend said. Her eyes were red-rimmed. She wasn't as pretty a crier as Shayla was.

"I never got your name," Lei said, taking out her trusty spiral pad.

"Pippa Thomas," the woman replied, pushing long blonde hair back behind her ears. "I'm Shayla's best friend, and I loved Makoa, too."

"Well, I know this is a hard time, but we need Shayla to work with our sketch artist here on a likeness of the young man she saw drop in on Makoa," Lei said, indicating the artist, who'd followed them into the small, tidy space.

"I'll see if I can get her up. Have a seat." Pippa indicated the faded, tropical-print couch and went into the back.

"Pono, why don't you have a look around? I'll talk to her friend."

"Sounds like a plan." Pono was already browsing the pictures in the hall, looking for any with Makoa in them, when Pippa and Shayla returned. The surf star's girlfriend had hastily donned a too-short embroidered satin robe. Her long, tanned legs, loose breasts, and tumble of waist-length brunette hair caused the sketch artist's jaw to drop.

"Are you feeling up to working with us on a sketch of the guy you spotted coming in from the water?" Lei asked.

"Okay." Shayla sat in a flounce of satin on the couch. Her eyes were half-closed, her voice hoarse. Lei wished she'd had the sketch done at the beach, when Shayla was more alert.

"Hi. I'm Kevin. I'm going to ask you some questions and keep showing you what I'm working on so you can help me stay on track," the artist said. He sat gingerly on the couch beside Shayla with his pad and pencil.

Lei pulled Pippa aside. "Can I speak with you privately?"

"Okay." The girl's eyebrows rose in surprise, but she followed Lei back outside under the plumeria tree.

"We're not ready to tell Shayla yet, but Makoa's death is looking suspicious," Lei said.

Pippa's big blue eyes instantly filled, and she covered her mouth with her hands, hunching as if from a blow. "Oh no," she whispered. "No."

"I'm sorry." Lei let a moment go by as the girl rubbed the heels of her hands into her eyes. "I need to know of anyone close to you and Shayla who might have a grudge against Makoa."

"Eli Tadeo. He's Shayla's ex. He hates Makoa. He's threatened him plenty of times. Shayla's been really stressed about it."

Lei noted the name. "Anything else you can tell me about Tadeo?"

"Shayla's been on the verge of taking out a restraining order on him. Tadeo's never gotten over her. Leaves stuff in her mailbox, keeps calling. Trash-talks Makoa around town every chance he gets."

"Hmmm," Lei said. "But that guy you saw drop in on Makoa wasn't Tadeo?"

"I don't know. I was in the bathroom that whole time, so I missed it. I got back just when Shayla was realizing it looked like Makoa drowned."

"Well, let us break the news to her, okay?" Lei asked.

"God, I can't believe this. Give me a minute alone." Pippa turned away, and when Lei glanced back, the girl had put her arms around the plumeria tree and was sobbing, her face pressed against the rough bark.

Lei returned to the house. Shayla looked up from the face forming on the sketchpad. "Why does the other detective want to look around my house? Did this guy do something to Makoa other than drop in on him?"

"Was this man Eli Tadeo, your ex?" Lei asked, tapping the emerging sketch.

"No." Shayla's delicate, well-marked brows drew together in a frown. "This wasn't an accident, was it?"

Lei sighed. "No. It's looking like he was drowned on purpose."

"Oh my God!" the girl wailed. "No!" She jumped up off the couch, her breasts threatening to escape the robe. Pippa ran back into the house just then and embraced her friend. They sobbed together. Finally, the blonde lifted her head, frowning at Shayla.

"Shayla, you have to help the cops with the sketch. Maybe they can find him from that. You have to focus." Pippa gripped her friend's shoulders.

"You're right." Shayla gulped down her tears, pulling herself together with an effort. "Let me get dressed. I'll be right back and will do whatever I can." She strode down the hall. Lei felt like she was watching a case study in the stages of grief: denial, anger, bargaining…Lei hoped that someday acceptance would come.

Things went faster after that. Pono and Lei donned gloves and did a swift once-over search through the cottage, with Shayla and Pippa's permission, since the girls shared the cottage. They found nothing of the surf star's belongings but a few toiletries and clothes. Shayla, now dressed in a white T-shirt and cutoff shorts, worked with Kevin, and they both concentrated hard on the sketch while Pippa washed dishes and made refreshments, offering them all glasses of chilled lilikoi iced tea.

When they packed up to leave, the few things that might be of interest in evidence bags, Lei turned to the girls.

"Please don't discuss this with anyone," Lei said. "We need to have total confidentiality to move quickly and catch this guy."

Both girls nodded, and Kevin took a moment to hug each of them and leave his number "in case you need anything."

Lei narrowed her eyes at him as they got into the cruiser. "We'll drop you in Kahului. Then we need to go to the van rental places with this sketch. Not a word to anyone or we'll know who leaked this."

"Of course," Kevin said, and Lei noted the respectful change in his demeanor.

"Slick move, giving the girls your number," Pono said. "But I think they like tan, cut surfer dudes."

"There's always room for us creative types. We're good with our hands," Kevin said with a leer.

Lei rolled her eyes as Pono put the siren on to save time.

They dropped Kevin off at the station and hurried to the van rental place, only a few blocks away in downtown Kahului near the airport. The rental company was a dusty, windswept lot filled with parked vans surrounded by chain-link fence, a few scrubby kiawe trees providing patchy shade. The office building was a converted Matson container with an air conditioner chugging away and dripping condensation next to the steps. Inside, the customer service attendant hunkered over a Sudoku game on an iPad.

Lei and Pono held up their IDs. "Have you seen this man?" Pono slid the sketch across to the attendant, who set aside his game to look at it.

"Could be the guy who returned a van today."

Lei's pulse picked up. "What was his name?"

"Just a sec." He typed onto the iPad. "He gave his name as Clark. Stephen Clark."

Lei noted it. "How did he pay? Do you have a credit card?"

"No. Cash."

"Can we see the van? We need to see if he left any prints. This man is wanted for questioning in a serious matter," Pono said.

The attendant's eyes widened behind his magnifying readers. "Okay." He tossed the glasses down. "I'll take you to it. He only rented it for two days."

"Did you check the address on the license?" Lei asked as they followed him back down into the lot.

"No. I just check that they have one. It's over here." He led them to a van with racks on top. It was in a row of identical vans. "He only left an hour ago."

"How did he leave?" Lei asked sharply. Pono had gone back to their vehicle to fetch the crime kits.

"Called a taxi."

"Did you hear his destination?"

"No." The man frowned. "But I got the feeling he was in a hurry. My best guess is the airport."

"What kind of taxi?" A plan was forming in Lei's mind. If it was only an hour, they might still catch the suspect on the island.

"A-1 Taxi Company."

"Thanks." Lei made a shooing gesture. "We'll let you know when we're done."

Reluctantly, the man headed back to his trailer as Lei broke into a trot, heading over to Pono.

"Okay if I track down the taxi he took? I want to see where he went. We can cover more ground faster if you look for prints in the van. I'm betting ten to one that was a fake ID he gave the attendant."

"Sure. I'll crawl around in the hot box van on my hands and knees with the dusting powder while you chase the guy." Pono pushed his ever-present Oakleys onto the top of his buzz-cut black hair. "Get a move on, woman. You promised me laulau at the end of the day." She'd told him about their six-thirty dinner appointment on the way over, and it was four-thirty now.

"On it." Lei ran back to the cruiser and called the taxi company. Sure enough, some minutes later she had verified that the passenger had ended up at the airport. She peeled out of the lot, and only minutes later had pulled up in front of the airport and was talking to security.

It wasn't long before copies of the sketch had made their way to every security person and checkpoint in the airport, and Lei was sitting in air-conditioned comfort, reviewing security cam footage, watching a young man with wiry build, dark wavy hair, and a Quiksilver T-shirt getting onto a Hawaiian Airlines flight to Oahu.

"Did that flight land yet?" she asked.

"Yes. It's only twenty minutes to Oahu," the security chief said regretfully.

"What name was he traveling under?"

Lei was able to verify that he'd gone to Oahu under the same name he'd rented the van with, and that name had come back to a fake ID. He'd paid cash for his ticket, too.

"Dammit," Lei said to the chief, having faxed the sketch and screen-grab captures of the video footage to Honolulu PD for distribution and initiated an all-points bulletin for the man on the other island. "Just missed him."

Heading back out to the cruiser, she called her favorite detective in HPD, Marcus Kamuela.

"Lei! To what do I owe the pleasure?"

"Hot case." Lei spoke quickly, filling him in on the situation so far as she got back into the cruiser and headed over to pick up Pono. "I'll come over if I need to. Find out if this guy has any connection to Makoa Simmons in the surfing scene on Oahu."

"Makoa Simmons. Man, that's tragic," Kamuela said. He had a deep voice with a husky edge to it. "I'll check with my captain to see if I can get assigned to your case."

"That's what I was hoping for. Appreciate it," Lei said, pulling in to the van rental lot. Pono was waiting on the steps of the trailer, crime kit in hand. It was six p.m., and they would be able to take a break for dinner as she'd hoped. "I was just on the phone with Marcella this morning. Maybe I'll be seeing you both soon. I'll call tomorrow with any prints we've pulled off the van. The name the guy traveled here under was fake, so we're gonna have to see what Pono turned up in the rental."

"Hope you find his ID. That will make everything easier on this end."

Lei hung up with Kamuela as Pono got into the cruiser. Her partner looked hot and annoyed. "You didn't get him, I see," he said.

"No. He made it off the island under the same fake ID he rented the van with. I hope you were able to pull some decent prints."

"I pulled prints, all right, but there are so many, from so many different people who might have handled or been in the van, I have no idea what the right ones will be."

"Let's grab some off the attendant so we can rule him out, real quick," Lei said.

"Already done."

They got on the road. Lei put Captain Omura, their commanding officer, on speakerphone as they drove out of town through the waving expanse of sugarcane fields toward Haiku. She and Pono caught the captain up on the case as they wove along the picturesque two-lane road, passing various ocean overlooks and beach parks, the sunset blazing over the nearby expanse of sea.

"I want to go to Oahu tomorrow," Lei said. "Detective Kamuela can help me hunt this guy over there. I suspect he's going to have some connection to the pro surf circuit." Lei told Omura what the girlfriend had said about harassment threats from rivals.

"We have to get an ID on this suspect ASAP," Omura said in her crisp voice. "I can authorize that trip. Pono, you stay back. You can reinterview the family and run down this Tadeo character. Though it seems a stretch that a jealous boyfriend would hire someone to drown Makoa Simmons…"

"My best guess is that the man who drowned him was a rival," Lei said. "Another pro surfer."

"Why didn't anyone at Ho'okipa recognize him, then?" Pono asked. They had left the darkening sunset breaking through clouds over the West Maui Mountains and turned up the narrow road winding through stands of torch ginger, heliconia, and tree ferns toward Lei's property. "If he was a well-known surfer, fake ID or not, he'd be recognized. So maybe he's a small-kine surfer with a grudge, or a hired hitter of some kind."

Lei had turned on the radio, and the announcer broke in with a news bulletin about Makoa's "death by drowning under suspicious circumstances" at Ho'okipa Beach Park. She snapped off the car's stereo, agitated by the reminder of how big this case was, the attention it would get, and how tragic the loss to the whole surf world was.

"Some cojones, going surfing with Makoa Simmons and drowning him in front of witnesses," Lei said.

"How do you plan to kill someone that way? It would take perfect timing," Captain Omura said, her voice tinny in the radio feed. "Which leads to the idea that it was an opportunistic crime. But the fake ID, the cash rentals, the quick getaway all point to a calculated plan. In any case, we need to make a public statement. Circulate that sketch here on Maui, at all the airports throughout the islands."

"It's circulating already." Lei was glad they'd been able to get the artist and Shayla together and such a clear image worked up quickly.

"Good. Come back downtown and I'll call the TV station. We'll do it at eight-thirty, so they can air it on the ten o'clock news."

"Okay. We're grabbing a quick dinner at my house first," Lei said. Thank God they were home. She'd have time to eat, change her shirt, and do something about her hair, whipped into disarray as if beaten with an egg whisk by the wind at the beach. Lei hung up and punched in the gate code.

"Where are we all gonna sit?" Pono asked. He knew their situation intimately, having been at the house the night of the fire and all through the aftermath. He'd put in more than his fair share of hours working on the new house, too.

As if in answer, they spotted the screen tent erected over a folding table and chairs, nicely set with a cloth and the replacement dishes Lei had picked up at Pier 1 in Kahului. A hurricane lantern with a thick candle cast an inviting glow. Standing on the porch of the cottage was Stevens, with Kiet in his arms.

Lei jumped out of the cruiser. Keiki, her coat still rough and patchy since the fire, greeted her with happy butt wagging. She stroked the big dog's head and hurried toward Stevens, smiling, her gaze running over his tall body.

Looking at him never got old for her. His light blue eyes were intense under dark brows, shadowed with worry, as they often were, though he smiled back. The baby in his arms reached for Lei, burbling a greeting that never failed to lift her heart. "Ba-ba ba!"

"It's not far from ba-ba to ma-ma. He's going to say it any day now," Lei said. "How's my happy boy?" She scooped the child into her arms and lifted her face for the quick, hungry kiss Stevens gave her—a kiss that said he was glad she'd made it to the house, wished she was staying longer, and promised more when they were finally alone.

Short as the time was that she'd have with her family, Lei was glad they'd made it to dinner, too. She'd almost forgotten her mother-in-law was there until the woman rose from the rocking chair and came to stand beside Stevens.

Lei assessed Ellen Rockford Stevens automatically: She was taller than Lei at around five foot eight, painfully thin at a hundred and fifteen to twenty pounds. Her bottle-blonde hair had dark roots and hung lank to her shoulders. Her mother-in-law wore a shabby but good-quality tunic top in a blue that matched eyes that must have been the striking shade of Stevens's at one time but now reminded Lei of bleached sky over desert. Age showed in deep lines on a pallid face, in the loose skin of her neck, in liver spots on her hands. Her expression was pleading and sad.

"Welcome to Maui." Lei gave Ellen a one-armed hug that squished Kiet in close to both of them, feeling a surge of compassion for this fragile human being: Kiet's grandmother and the one who'd given her beloved husband life. "It's great to finally meet you."

CHAPTER FIVE

STEVENS GESTURED TO PONO, who'd been taking his time getting out of the cruiser. "Come meet my mom. Ellen, this is Pono Kaihale, Lei's partner and one of our ohana."

"Pleased to meet you." Ellen smiled and shook Pono's hand, then gave a little gasp as he took something from behind his back and draped it over her head. It was a kukui nut lei, the polished orbs glossy as black gems.

"Welcome to Maui." Pono drew her into a gentle hug. Stevens grinned at the consternation on Lei's face.

"How'd you get that, partner?" his wife exclaimed. "Showing me up!"

"The van rental place had them, and you'd told me your mother-in-law was going to be here. Had to get her lei'd," Pono said, with a twinkle in his eye that made Ellen laugh. Stevens realized he hadn't heard that laugh in forever.

Ellen smacked Pono's arm playfully. "Now, that's a proper Hawaiian greeting," she said. "Guess I needed a real Hawaiian to remember it."

Wayne came to the door, a big bowl of salad in his hands. "Looks like the family's all here but one," he said, and then the gate rolled open and Jared drove up in his truck loaded with ocean sports equipment. "Right on cue."

Stevens saw his mother falter at the sight of his younger brother getting out of his vehicle. He didn't know what had gone on between them, but he suspected it hadn't been pretty. When the transfer to Kahului Station came through, Jared had taken it. All he'd said to Stevens was, "I couldn't deal with her anymore."

Jared came to the porch with his loping walk, his blue eyes cautious as he looked at their mother.

"Mom." Jared took her hands and bent to give her a kiss on the cheek. "You made it over here." Stevens had to admire the phrase for its understatement.

"I did." Ellen let go of his hands and reached out to hug Jared. Stevens could see how stiff his brother stood. Everyone else had turned away and busied themselves with something: Pono was carrying the salad to the table, Lei was playing with the baby, and Wayne had gone back into the kitchen. "I'm sorry about what happened before you left."

"You'll have a chance to make it up to me by staying sober." Jared's voice was low and hard.

"I'm planning to." Ellen's words quavered, but Stevens could tell she meant it. He could also read that any revelations about her health were going to have to wait until they had more privacy.

Stevens put a hand on their mother's shoulder, giving her an encouraging pat. "Jared, why don't you take her down to the seat of honor. I'll help bring the rest of the food."

Soon dinner was underway. The pork laulau was delicious. It was Lei's turn to feed the baby tonight, so she'd seated herself next to Kiet's high chair and alternated taking bites of her dinner and working spoonfuls of baby food into their son's mouth with a soft plastic spoon.

He could tell Ellen was enjoying being at the head of the table with Pono on one side and Jared on the other. Lei and Stevens were across from each other, and Wayne was at the foot. The soft, warm night, filled with the sounds of conversation, leaves rustling, and crickets singing, was a balm to his spirit. He was almost glad in that moment that the house was gone and they could live so close to the outdoors.

Even with all the undercurrents and the full table, Stevens couldn't help glancing at his wife. Lei was beautiful in candlelight. He enjoyed the slender, toned lines of her body in the narrow tank top and black jeans—she'd left her weapon and jacket in the cruiser. Her tawny skin, stippled with those tiny freckles he loved, glowed in the candlelight. Tilted brown eyes picked up amber and brandy glints as the candles reflected in their depths, and her mouth stretched wide in laughter at the baby's efforts to grab the spoon. Her wild hair was a curly nimbus that made him think of angels.

God, he loved her.

He caught Jared's amused eye on him and shrugged. He knew he had it bad, and marriage hadn't changed that. Seeing Lei laugh hadn't stopped feeling good after their recent heartbreak.

Looking at his mother in the soft light, almost pretty again, he hoped being here was going to be enough to heal her. But that cynical cop voice in his head told him it wasn't likely.

Jared and Ellen finished eating first, and he offered to walk her around the yard. They got up, and she took his arm, leaning into her son as he pointed out the trees Stevens had already shared with his mother.

"I have to go to Oahu tomorrow," Lei told Stevens. "I'm sorry to leave you with all this, but the case is taking me there. I wish I could tell you guys about it, but it's too confidential. We have to go back out tonight."

"Those first twenty-four hours are critical," Stevens agreed.

Lei kept her voice low. "I hate leaving you without any help with your mom. I want to get to know her better."

"It's okay." Stevens took a bite of perfectly spiced and steamed laulau. "Between Jared and me, we can keep Mom busy and out of trouble."

"Don't forget me," Wayne said. "I can take her on an outing or two with the baby. But shouldn't she have a medically supervised program? I mean, if she's trying to get sober…"

"I agree," Stevens said. "I haven't had time, but we'll do some research tonight. I plan to dig in a little more on what her plans are."

"Well, I'll be back late tonight. I'll just sneak in as quietly as I can." Lei's phone went off, and she frowned, checking it. "It's Omura. I have to take this."

She handed Stevens the baby spoon and stood up, then unzipped the tent and stepped out. He looked at Lei's plate as she rezipped the screen, turning to walk away into the darkness with the phone to her ear. She'd eaten maybe one of the laulau. She'd gotten thinner since she lost the baby—she'd always been fairly indifferent to food, and it was worse now. The shadows under her eyes still worried him.

Lei returned and gestured to Pono, who'd wisely shoveled in his dinner at top speed. "We gotta go into the station," she said. "So sorry to dine and dash. I'm going on TV, so I have to change my shirt."

Ellen had returned with Jared. "I hope we have a little time to visit in the next few days."

"I'm afraid it won't be right away—I have a hot case. Good thing Stevens understands my job," Lei said. "Believe me, I'd rather be enjoying family time." She bent to give Kiet's head a smacking kiss and worked her way around the table with quick hugs.

She nipped Stevens's earlobe under the guise of a quick kiss on the cheek, and he felt it all the way to the soles of his feet, his body rising to meet her.

"See you later," she breathed in his ear. In moments, she and Pono were reversing the cruiser and driving back out.

After he'd put Kiet to bed and Jared had walked his mom back to her tent, where she'd blamed jet lag for an early night, he and Wayne and Jared worked their phones and laptops for a list of treatment options for Ellen.

"Only one on the island is Aloha House," Stevens said at last. "And they've got a waiting list."

"I know a guy from my church who works there," Wayne said. "I'll give him a call, see what he can do."

"We'd appreciate it." Jared looked up at Stevens, his eyes blue flames in the candlelight. "It will be interesting to see if she really wants to get sober."

"Yeah. She said she wanted a change, coming here, but never said those words until you talked to her tonight. What happened when you left?"

"She crashed my going-away party at my LA firehouse. Threw up in the trashcan right in front of everybody. It was the worst I've ever seen her."

"That's a new low, even for her," Stevens said. "Could be her way of objecting to you leaving."

"Yeah, whatever. It sure as hell didn't make me want to stay. I didn't say goodbye or give her any contact info when I left. I was hoping to be done with her."

"Sounds kind of harsh. People make mistakes and regret them. People can change," Wayne said. Stevens knew his father-in-law was speaking from his own sketchy past as a felon who'd done time for drug dealing and manslaughter.

Jared narrowed his eyes. "You haven't been through what we have with this woman. She's a user. Used our dad, used us to take care of her. It's all about the bottle with her."

"I'm willing to be hopeful," Stevens said. "It's nice to see her with Kiet. Maybe having a grandchild, some sort of different future, will tip her into wanting to get sober and stay sober."

"We'll see." Jared's mouth thinned. "You've just forgotten, bro."

"We can deal with her together," he said, making eye contact with Jared. "We can't let anything come between us. Deal?"

"I can't guarantee we're going to agree on how to handle her," Jared said. His mouth was tight. "You really like your role as the big brother hero, and she likes you in it. I'm pretty sure I'm just the second fiddle. Always have been."

"Jared. Dammit, bro." Stevens turned to fully face his brother, leaning across the table toward the younger man as Wayne left them alone. "You saved our lives so recently. You're the hero. Never doubt it. I don't want that old shit getting in the way of what we have now, what we've built together. We're family. Let's agree on this right now—whatever happens with Mom, even if we disagree, we won't let it come between us. I'm so glad you decided to come to Maui to live, to be a part of our lives. I love you, man."

Jared ducked his head, but when he looked up, his eyes gleamed blue flame in the candlelight. "I guess I needed to hear that. We're good. Deal."

Stevens glanced over at the tent, hidden in the darkness behind the mango tree. He wished he'd searched his mom's backpack for bottles. He had a bad feeling about her desire for bed and privacy. "I haven't forgotten what Mom's capable of. I wish I could."

"GOD, IT WAS HARD TO LEAVE." Lei hadn't had time to do anything with her hair at the house, so was opting for restraint. As Pono drove, she twisted her shoulder-length frizzing curls into what her friend Marcella called the "FBI Twist," a roll at the back of her head anchored with a row of bobby pins. Looking into the drop-down mirror, she dusted her face with a little powder and whisked on mascara and lipstick.

Pono spared her a glance. "You look fine."

"You always say that. This is TV. Every time I've been on TV,

I've looked like I was dragged backward through a bush and I have tiny eyes."

"So. Your mother-in-law. She looked rough."

"I know. I feel really bad leaving them to deal with her right now."

"Be glad you're out of it. Tiare's aunty drinks. She hasn't liked my two cents on how she should handle it at all."

Lei frowned. "So you guys don't agree on what to do?"

"I'm of the tough-love school. No contact until Aunty gets her shit together. Tiare can't handle that, gives in to the whining. I think she even sneaks her money sometimes."

Lei felt her stomach hollow with stress at the thought of the complications Ellen might be bringing. "Just gonna stay positive for now. But I'm glad there are two of them to deal with her."

"So what's the emergency that we couldn't finish dinner?"

"Captain has a press conference scheduled for us at nine-thirty and wants us to have an ID developed from your fingerprints by then."

"Not gonna happen." Pono rubbed his mustache briskly. "I've got at least fifty prints to process. It's seven forty-five. We aren't going to have time to do anything but get there and change."

Lei and Pono hurried to the fingerprint lab with the samples he'd collected from the van, but there were too many to scan and log. Omura, alerted to their predicament, called every available officer in to help with the scanning, but there were only two machines anyway. Lei and Pono left the other officers at it and, after putting on clean shirts, went to the conference room Omura liked for press conferences. Its gracious koa-wood podium and big brass Maui Police Department emblem on the wall sent a solid and dignified message.

Lei, Pono, and Captain Omura sketched out their announcement, and Lei felt somewhat ready when the reporters and a cameraman from KHIN-2 News came in. Omura brought the conference to order and addressed the group, giving the sad news confirming the homicide in a carefully worded statement: Surf star Makoa Simmons had drowned, and "foul play was suspected." She introduced Lei and Pono as primaries on the case and opened up the floor for questions.

Lei felt nervous sweat prickling under her arms as she stood beside Pono under the bright camera lights. They ended up having to say, "We can't answer that at this time," way more often than Lei liked, but she finally ended the conference by looking straight into the camera and making an appeal.

"This young man was one of the best and brightest surfers to ever come out of our island. If you have any information about who might have wanted to harm Makoa, please call Maui Police Department and let us know." The hastily-set-up tip line number would run at the bottom of the clip. Once the conference was over, she and Pono went back down to the lab and relieved the officers who'd been scanning the prints.

"I'll scan, and you get the computer working, looking for matches," Pono said.

It was one a.m. when Lei called it a night. "You can send me the results if and when you get an identity off these." She yawned. "I'm going home for at least a couple hours of sleep."

"Sounds good. I'm going to stay and keep working," Pono said.

"We have another full day tomorrow. Don't stay too late."

Lei drove home on autopilot.

The tent was a dim shape in her yard as she parked, the cottage a dark bulk. Someone, probably her dad, had plugged in a night-light in the kitchen so she could find her way through the living room where her dad slept, a hunched shape on the couch. She felt her way to the little back bedroom, cluttered with a queen-sized bed and the baby's crib.

Moonlight shimmered in through the window, and there was a nightlight on in there, too. Lei could see the dark blot of Kiet's black hair as he slept on his back, one hand curled up beside his cheek, the other down alongside his body. Looking over at the bed, she could see Stevens on his back in exactly the same pose. She smiled at the sight and peeled her clothes off quickly, leaving the garments where they lay on the floor.

Because no matter the privacy challenges, time constraints, and limits of physical tiredness, she needed her husband.

Now.

The cotton sheets were silky on her nakedness as she slid in beside Stevens, and as she moved against his length, the heat of his body warmed her cool one. Stevens woke at her nearness, then woke further at her wandering hands and turned toward her.

His touch trailed liquid fire over and through her body, and in minutes they were joined in a moving, breath-held, quiet intimacy that felt like the solid rightness of a key sliding into a lock and opening a box of treasure. She'd never get tired of all there was to discover between them, from long, fragrant, noisy hours of extreme sensation to this soft, tender clenching in semidarkness, others asleep nearby.

Lei fell into a deep and dreamless sleep for the few hours given her, held close in his arms.

STEVENS SAT up and hit the Off button on the alarm. He was still in bed, since Kiet had slept later than usual. Lei had left early. The bed still smelled like her...and he wasn't eager to leave the nest of warm sheets.

As if discerning this thought, Kiet rolled over and, using the bars of his crib, pulled himself upright. He was early at that—and many other milestones, they'd discovered. Spotting his father still in bed, he smacked the top of the bar with his hand.

"Da, da, da!" he stated.

"Daddy," Stevens enunciated carefully, sitting up and realizing he was still naked. He reached over onto the floor for last night's boxers, shed during that surprise visit from Lei. "Da-da-da-ddy."

"Da-da!" Kiet yelled happily.

"Okay, close enough, little man." Stevens picked up and changed the baby on his little changing table nearby, talking to him as he did so. Kiet grinned, kicking his legs. Kiet was such a joy. He thought of their lost child with a pang. It would have been challenging but fun to have two babies. Lei would have been seven months along by now if she hadn't had the miscarriage.

Stevens thought of the Big Island case that had brought them so much heartbreak. An old enemy from Lei's past had been behind a series of vicious attacks, and the stress of dealing with them had caused Lei's traumatic miscarriage. That was his secret opinion, in spite of the doctor's "these things happen" commentary, but he'd never say so because Lei blamed herself, questioning her ability to be a mother.

It was going to take time, and the love and relationship she had with Kiet, to heal her enough to be ready to try again.

He mentally shrugged off the sorrow, setting Kiet on the bed as he got into a cotton robe. He carried the child out into the kitchen. "Let's go over and get your grandma up for some coffee."

Wayne was already up and had the fragrant Kona brew going. So, a few minutes later, Stevens, clad in robe and rubber slippers with a mug of coffee in one hand and the baby on his hip in the other, made his way across the dewy morning grass to the tent.

"Mom?" He couldn't see inside because the interior flaps were zipped shut. "Mom, I brought coffee."

No answer. He frowned and set her mug down on the grass. Awkward with one hand, he drew up the zipper and poked his head in.

Alcohol fumes met his nose, along with a musky smell he associated with old people and closed spaces. "Mom?"

Kiet wriggled to get down. He loved to play in the tent, and now Stevens had to use both hands to keep a grip on the baby. Kiet grunted and writhed, eager to crawl around, and Stevens stepped back out. Making a decision, he backtracked rapidly across the yard and up the steps, setting Kiet in the playpen in the living room.

Wayne turned away from refilling his mug. "You're back quick."

"Mom's been drinking. I need to leave Kiet here."

"No problem."

Stevens walked rapidly back to the tent. He peered inside again. "Mom?"

Still no answer. He unzipped the tent and entered. He squatted in the dim light beside the air mattress. He reached out a hand and shook her by the shoulder. "Mom."

Her head flopped, but her mouth opened, and he heard and smelled her boozy exhaled breath. His stomach tightened with repulsion and frustration. He glanced around, spotted the empty quart bottle of Scotch. She'd always been fond of that particular liquor, believing that it was the drink of "real women."

Stevens was just lucky she hadn't puked all over Lei's nice patterned rug, but there was still time for that to happen. He backed out of the tent and strode across the grass to the newly erected carport, where he found a plastic utility bucket and brought it back, setting it down next to his mother's passed-out form.

Just in case.

He backed out and rezipped the tent. His gut churned with familiar emotions: anger, disappointment, disgust, and grief, too, that she'd come all this way and this was what happened on day one.

No wonder she'd wanted to go to bed early. She'd had that bottle waiting. He left the coffee mug where he'd set it down. She could drink it cold when she woke up.

He reached in the pocket of his robe and pulled out his phone to call Jared.

"I should have searched her backpack," he said when his

brother answered. "She had a bottle, and she's passed out in the tent."

"Listen to you, bro," Jared snapped. "She got drunk, and it's your fault because you didn't take away her booze in time."

A long pause. Stevens pushed a hand through his unruly hair, struggling not to snap back at his brother even as he admitted to himself Jared was right. Fighting each other wasn't going to help them, or deal with the problem of their mother. It was frustrating to be tested this way so quickly after their pact of the night before.

"I'm sorry for biting your head off," Jared said, heaving a sigh. "I just woke up. Haven't had my morning coffee. And I admit I was a little taken in last night. Let myself get hopeful. She was so sincere. So happy to be a grandma."

"I felt the same," Stevens said. "And you're right. Searching her, trying to prevent her getting something—none of it works."

"Wayne said he thinks she's so thin because she's unhealthy. Maybe she's sicker than we know, and we need to talk to her about rehab anyway. I'm off today. How about I make an appointment for a doctor visit and come get her?"

"Sounds great." Stevens headed back to the cottage. "I have to go in to work. First day on my new detail as official trainer for new detectives. I don't think the captain would look kindly on me calling in."

"Well, after the doctor we'll know more and we can decide what to do about her."

Stevens agreed and said goodbye, the ominous sound of his brother's last sentence reverberating in his mind: "what to do about her."

What to do, indeed.

And though things had gone quiet with their enemies supposedly dead or in jail, Stevens would never be able to forget the relentless attacks of the one they'd called the shroud killer. The man they'd brought down on the Big Island had his trial in a few weeks, and Lei would have to go to the Big Island to testify.

Stevens wished he was more confident that the one in custody really was the shroud killer. He still had concerns that the remaining member of the Chang crime family, Terence Chang, had some long-term plan to move on them when their guard was down.

When there was vulnerability in their lives, like his mother the raging alcoholic.

CHAPTER SIX

LEI SIPPED her second cup of inky coffee at her workstation, giving a swizzle with the little plastic stir stick and hoping the chunks of creamer would dissolve. An email from Pono had come through before she left the house in the morning, and she'd been able to print out the IDs and mug shots of two men with minor records he'd identified last night from the prints. Pono had gone home at three a.m., according to the time stamp on his e-mail.

Lei scanned the photos she'd printed out. Unfortunately, either of them could have matched the description Shayla Cummings had given, and both of them resided on Oahu.

"Too many average-height men with black hair and brown eyes, medium build, and no visible tats or facial hair," Lei muttered to herself. That was the general description Shayla had given Kevin, the sketch artist, of the suspect's overall appearance.

She inspected the photos more closely. One of the suspects, Freddie Arenas, listed an address in Kahuku, a town near the North Shore where the pro surfers hung out this time of year. The other, August Jones, had a downtown Honolulu address.

Lei flipped through her file folder for the artist's sketch.

Holding it carefully next to the photos, she tried to see which one most matched the pictures.

It was really hard to tell. Freddie Arenas had a mustache and one of those chinstrap beards in his photo, and August Jones wore a goatee that covered the center of his chin. The man Kevin had sketched had been clean-shaven.

Stumped for the moment, Lei put the pictures and sketch away and pulled out the reference file she'd begun on the Triple Crown of Surfing and Makoa Simmons's sponsors and career. She'd hurriedly printed some references on the event.

According to the website, the Triple Crown was won by a scoring system that went across three events: the Hawaiian Pro held at Haleiwa, the World Cup of Surfing held at Sunset Beach, and the Pipeline Masters held at Ehukai Beach Park. Events were held when surf was judged good enough, between November and December of any given year. Participation in the contests was by invitation only, and those invited were considered "big wave masters" of surfing. The contests were a part of the main American Professional Surfing circuit of contests, but were also scored and managed separately from the bigger roster of worldwide events.

Reading up on it, she found Makoa's talent and drive even more extraordinary. To have achieved such a level at his age, and from Maui, where there wasn't as well developed a surf scene as some other islands, was remarkable.

Lei flipped to the bio she'd found on Makoa. He'd attended a private school, Paradise Preparatory Academy, and graduated in the top of his class. According to interviews, he'd said, "I made a deal with my parents: if I didn't make a living within my first year out of high school on the pro surfing circuit, I'd go to college."

He'd secured a host of sponsors within his first few months of turning pro, chief among them Torque, an international surf and skateboard company with subsidiaries in motocross and snow-boarding. He lived during the winter season at the Torque surfing team house on the North Shore of Oahu, famous for its regular, excellent surf during that time of year.

Lei had a business summary about the sports brand, which made clothing and "incidentals" for surfing, including wax, leashes, neoprene pads for surfboard decks, backpacks, and board bags. Torque was a division of a much larger sportswear company, NeoSport, and even Lei, who only browsed an occasional surf magazine, was aware of their successful ad campaign, "Be Amazing."

The "Be Amazing" campaign showed athletes at the peak of their sport: oiled beach volleyball bodies flying through the air, football players crashing like rams in rut, and a shot of Makoa Simmons doing a reverse off-the-lip air on a wave much too thick and intense for that kind of freestyle maneuver. According to the blurb, he'd stuck the landing and had been able to end his ride successfully—and he'd only been at the beginning of his career.

The more Lei studied Makoa Simmons, the more tragic his death seemed. Lei traced the photo of Makoa flying with her fingertips, remembering her last glimpse of him as they'd zipped up the body bag to carry him off the beach, accompanied by the sound of the girls crying. Their grief echoed in her own heart. Her losses were never far from the surface.

The phone rang, startling Lei out of her dark thoughts. "Sergeant Texeira."

"Lei, it's Doc over at the morgue. I wanted to have you and Pono over for a quick review of my autopsy findings."

"Sure." Lei's stomach tightened at the prospect of the morgue. Only Pono knew how much she hated going there. The morgue always reminded her of the first time she'd identified a body, that of a dear friend. "When do you need us?"

"I worked late and got the post done, but I wanted to be extra careful because I know this case is going to get a lot of scrutiny. Soon as you can get here is good."

"Okay, thanks." Lei hung up and phoned Pono, waking her partner. "Meet me at the morgue. The post is done."

It wasn't long before Lei and her partner were on the elevator at Maui Memorial Hospital, riding down to the lowest floor, marked with a nondescript "B."

Pono was rubbing his eyes. He hadn't shaved, and his shirt had a splotch of coffee on the front.

"Sorry to get you up so early," Lei said. "I guess I could have gone on my own."

"No. It's the first twenty-four. We have to get as much traction as we can on this." Pono glanced at her, and his mouth quirked up. "Have you seen your hair today?"

"No. And I don't plan to," Lei replied, but she tried to smooth the springing, frizzing curls off her forehead. She'd avoided looking at the newspaper the office stocked as well as her hair. She knew the Simmons case would be the headline, and reading what was being said would only distract her, intensifying the sense of pressure they were under.

The morgue was through swinging doors designed to respond to wheeled gurneys, and the inner sanctum was accessed by an automatic button on the wall or a push bar. Pono hit the push bar, and Lei took one last breath of fresh air, bracing herself, and walked in.

Dr. Gregory was behind his desk, typing. At the sight of them, he dropped his glasses to dangle around his stout neck. Today's shirt was embellished with red and green leis. The sight reminded Lei that Christmas wasn't far away. They'd been trying to get the house done by then, but it didn't seem like that was going to happen.

"Ah. I'll get our young man."

Lei wished she didn't have to see the body again. *What I do is at least a way to get justice for Makoa.* The thought brought steel back to her spine. She glanced around the large room.

The bodies were all put away at the moment in their pull-out drawers. Every other time Lei had been here, the stations had been occupied. The open space with three steel-topped tables with drains beneath them, bright lights gleaming on metal, saws, scales, and other impedimenta neatly stowed, reminded her of a restaurant kitchen.

The thought made her stomach lurch.

She and Pono followed Dr. Gregory over to a bank of square metal doors. Gregory popped the clasp on one of them with a sound like opening a soda bottle and pulled out the drawer.

Makoa Simmons's body was naked. His tan had yellowed as blood drained from his tissues. The Y incision on his broad, once-muscular chest looked cartoonish, the skin rubbery. Lei grasped her hands behind her back as Gregory put his readers back on. He pointed to shadowy marks on the young man's neck and forehead.

"See these? Consistent with a forceful grip used to hold him under. I've sent the stomach contents and blood work out, but that's probably not notable. Cause of death is drowning."

"So no surprises from your early assessment of homicide," Pono said.

"Right. But I'm still wondering how the suspect, whom I heard described as medium height and weight, was able to hold Makoa down. Must have caught him by surprise."

"I can't imagine Simmons saw it coming," Lei said. "He was at his home break, surrounded by friends. Or people he thought were friendly, at least. A guy dropped in on him—but that guy wasn't just any ordinary wave-stealing jerk. I wouldn't have seen it coming, either."

"Right."

"So do you have anything else for us?"

"Well, I was hoping to get something more specific off the marks on his neck. Hand size, maybe some trace. But I went over it with a fine-tooth comb, and there was nothing. The ocean removed anything that might have remained."

"That's a shame. We have two possible fingerprint matches

from the van the suspect rented, and they both could be the sketch we worked up with a witness yesterday." Lei drew back from the body, breathing shallowly through her mouth. "We're going out on a couple of interviews this morning, and one of them is with his parents."

"Oh. Then you can give them his clothing." Gregory pushed the body back into the refrigerated shelving and led them to a locker. "He only had on this bracelet and these shorts."

The humble items were in a plastic bag, neatly labeled. The shorts were emblazoned with TORQUE down a side seam, and the bracelet was made of heavy silver links with a tiny plaque on it with the initials "SC."

"Shayla Cummings," Lei said aloud, fingering the bracelet through the plastic. "His girlfriend. She'd probably like to get it back."

They swung by a Starbucks on their way out. "So here's the lineup today," Lei said. "We have the sketch and APB out on Oahu for our suspect, but I still want to go over and find these two van rental suspects. I have reservations going out this afternoon. We should also interview the parents again and find this Eli Tadeo, the jealous boyfriend."

Pono yawned as he doctored his coffee with sugar and cream. "I vote boyfriend first. Don't know that the parents are going to be in a whole lot better shape to talk than they were yesterday."

"Still. They may know something more about his rivals, et cetera. I also want to find out how much the dad was opposed to his surfing career."

Pono snorted. "You think that dad would stoop so low as to take out his own son? Why?"

"We have to follow every line of inquiry. I don't like to fasten on one theory too early," Lei insisted. "We need to find out what Makoa's money situation was, check if there is any financial motivation anywhere."

"I have a lead on that. He had an agent. Harvey Nebel. He's on my list to visit."

"Harvey Nebel. What kind of name is that?"

"The successful kind. Harvey is one of the best sports agents in the country. He represents every kind of athlete, from soccer players to shot-putters."

"Okay. Let's leave your truck here at Starbucks and take mine today. Eli Tadeo, here we come."

STEVENS WALKED INTO THE BIG, square, urban carbuncle of modern utility that was Kahului Station. He'd heard his new office was on the third floor, and he'd be sharing it with the island's top recruiting officer, Eric Tadeo. Third floor was dedicated to accounting and operations, away from where most of the detectives on the island had cubicles. Riding the elevator up, with his box of personal items, he wondered if this meant he was as sidelined in his career as he felt personally these days.

Maybe he'd finally be able to keep his work hours as a trainer to a straight forty a week and have more time with Kiet.

He didn't fool himself that he'd see Lei more, and that depressed him.

The door *ding*ed and slid open to reveal a warren of cubicles, much quieter than the bullpen on the floor below. Air-conditioning whispered, and the main sound was the *tappity-tap* of keyboards as the various support personnel went about their business. Stevens stepped off the elevator and walked around the cubicle perimeter, looking for 312.

He was surprised to find it was a large corner office, one wall of which was a smoked glass window offering a view of the dramatic crenellated green folds of Iao Valley behind the building. There were two desks set opposite each other, and one of them was marked with a blotter and various personal items: photographs, a baseball on a little stand.

The other desk was empty except for a new flat screen computer. Stevens set the box on what must be his desk and looked around. The large office area was apparently meant to double as a classroom, because one wall was taken up by a retractable over-head screen with a whiteboard beneath it. A projector on a handy stand was wheeled against the wall.

This didn't have the feeling of a demotion. The sight of the teaching tools lifted Stevens's spirits, and for the first time, he considered looking forward to this new challenge.

He began unpacking his meager office equipment and realized he'd somehow left behind all of his pens. His roommate wouldn't mind if he borrowed one. He glanced over at his new partner's desk, got up and went to it and pulled out the drawer. He picked up a pen and paused.

A dog-eared *Sports Illustrated* occupied the drawer, folded open to a photo of bikini model Shayla Cummings. The stunning brunette was seated like a modern mermaid on a lava rock, wearing a skimpy hibiscus-print bathing suit. His nerves on high alert, he glanced toward the door, picked up the pen he'd come for, shut the drawer, and returned to his own desk.

"Hey."

Stevens turned to the voice at the door. A handsome young mixed Hawaiian man with a short, tailored haircut and a painfully neat uniform stood in the door. "I'm Sergeant Eric Tadeo. Recruiter—and your roommate."

"Lieutenant Michael Stevens." They met in the middle of the room and clasped hands. Tadeo's grip was strong, the kind of handshake that conveyed confidence but no need to dominate. Up close, Stevens could see Tadeo's eyes were bracketed by fine sun creases. He was older than he'd first appeared, in his early thirties, but Stevens could see why he'd been tapped for recruiter—he made the uniform look good.

"How long have you been up here on the third floor?" Stevens asked.

"Just a couple of months. I was down on the first floor with the patrol officers for my first year on the job, but too many of them would come find me and complain the stuff I'd told them when they were recruited was hot air." He gave a rueful chuckle, hanging up his hat and jacket on an old-fashioned wooden rack. "I asked the captain to move me somewhere less distracting, where I could keep the illusion going."

Stevens smiled, going around to his desk and taking the lid off the box he'd carried up. "Well, this is a change for me, too. Had my own command, just a little station out in Haiku, but with the budget cuts, we were reabsorbed. I'm developing a new detectives training program."

"Yeah, I heard that was in the works." Tadeo sat down and booted up his computer. "So you've been on Maui awhile?"

"Couple of years. We bought a house on a couple of acres out in Haiku."

"I heard you're married to a cop."

"I am. Sergeant Lei Texeira. She's out chasing a hot case right now."

"She related to the upcountry Texeiras?" Now they were getting into the history and connections Stevens had learned were always a part of getting acquainted in the islands.

"No. She's related to the Big Island Texeiras, and half Japanese from Oahu. Me, just a *haole* from Los Angeles. You?"

Tadeo was part of a large upcountry family, of Portuguese, Hawaiian, and Filipino descent, and had a wife and two daughters.

"Let me know if you ever need any help with your program," Tadeo offered. "I can work the clicker switching slides while you talk, or whatever."

"Will do." Stevens finished unpacking. He was done stowing everything and had moved on to navigating his new computer when a knock came at the door. "Lieutenant Stevens?"

71

It was Brandon Mahoe from his old station. Brandon looked good, clean-shaven and his uniform crisp. Stevens grinned at the sight of him. "Brandon! What are you doing on the accounting floor?"

"Came by to tell you I'm studying for the detective exam," Brandon said. Stevens shook his hand and invited him to sit in one of the chairs at the desk, then introduced Eric Tadeo. The two men grinned at each other.

"I know Sergeant Tadeo," Brandon said. "He got me to sign up."

"Yeah, and I'm off to drag a few more recruits in today," Tadeo said, grabbing his jacket and hat. He exited, and Stevens sat down, eyeing his former protégé. He was glad to see the young man, and not surprised to hear of his ambition.

"I'd like to be your first trainee," Brandon said. "You've been a great mentor."

"Well, I hope you pass the exam the first time, then. How's your mother doing?" Stevens and the Mahoes had intersected on a case in which Brandon was injured in the line of duty. They caught up for a few minutes, and then Stevens's cell phone rang. He checked it and frowned. "I need to take this, Brandon."

"No worries. Just wanted to say hello and let you know my plans. See you around the station."

The young man exited, and Stevens answered the phone, alone at last. "Hey, Jared."

His brother's voice was clipped. "Do you want the good news on Mom first, or the bad news?"

"Gimme the good news first," Stevens said.

"Good news is we're at the doctor's here in downtown Kahului, and she's had a full physical. Blood work's already back, and liver enzymes are up, indicating liver damage. Her pancreas is inflamed, and she's anemic and malnourished."

"That's the good news?" Stevens shut his eyes, running a hand through his hair.

"Diagnosis: chronic alcoholism. She doesn't have cancer or even heart disease, amazingly. Ready for the bad news?"

"If you must."

"Mom's skipped out. She told me she was going to the bathroom, and she disappeared."

CHAPTER SEVEN

LEI AND PONO went in Pono's lifted truck this time. Lei glanced at her phone, checking the time. She had four hours until she had to get to the airport, and the day seemed to be slipping through her fingers. There were too many leads to follow. She frowned as the GPS directed them up into the *mauka* subdivision of Kuau, a section of upscale new development homes off Hana Highway on the mountain side of the road.

They turned in to a smooth poured concrete driveway trimmed with palms in front of a large, two-story home. Off to the side, Lei spotted an ohana cottage. The cottage made sense as the young man's possible abode. She and Pono didn't have anything but the main address, however, so Pono rang the main doorbell.

A young woman, dark-haired and pretty, wearing exercise clothes, answered the door with a toddler on her hip and a big-eyed little girl hiding behind her legs.

"Hi. How can I help you?" she asked. Her demeanor was calm and confident. Lei held her ID badge up.

"We're looking for Eli Tadeo," Pono said, with a smile at the kids, who smiled back. "You look familiar. Have I met you somewhere?"

"Yeah, I'm Rachel Tadeo. Sergeant Eric Tadeo's wife."

Lei glanced from one face to another as Pono and Rachel reacquainted themselves. They had to tread carefully now. Their person of interest was the brother of MPD's recruiter, the "poster boy" of law enforcement in their county.

"My partner, Lei Texeira," Pono finally said, gesturing to Lei.

"Hey. Why don't you two step inside? Girls, go clear off the table!" Rachel exclaimed. She set the toddler down, and the girls scampered into the next room. "Come in. Have a drink of something. Eli lives in the back cottage."

"I think I'll go straight there, thank you," Lei said politely, turning to retrace her steps. Rachel held up a hand.

"I need to know what this is about."

"I'm sorry. We can't say right now," Lei said, smiling to take the sting out of her words. "We just have a few questions for him, is all."

"I have a right to know what's going on right on my own property," Rachel flared. "This is about Makoa Simmons, isn't it? I can't believe you could even imagine Eli would have anything to do with that!"

Lei kept her face still and gave Pono a meaningful glance, spinning on her heel and walking down the steps, hearing Pono's mellow bass rumble trying to soothe the recruiter's wife.

She walked across a series of paving stones to the cottage's door. It was a cute place with plumeria-print curtains in the windows and a rack of surfboards on the wall beside the door. Several pairs of rubber slippers on the ALOHA-emblazoned welcome mat indicated Eli Tadeo might be home.

There was no bell, so Lei knocked.

And knocked again.

She turned, looked around. There were cars and trucks parked across the street and along the road, so Tadeo could be home and not answering the door. Perhaps he'd seen who it was, or maybe his car was parked in the big closed garage off the main house.

She took out one of her cards, jotted *call us ASAP* on it, and stuck it in the doorjamb, turning and tripping back down the steps.

Pono was just saying his goodbyes. Rachel Tadeo frowned at the sight of Lei.

"Your brother-in-law wasn't home," Lei said. "Please tell him to call us as soon as he can."

"I will," she said, and shut the door unnecessarily hard. Pono walked down the steps to join Lei.

"That was awkward."

"Yeah. Too bad he wasn't home. I would have liked to rule him out quickly," Lei said as they headed back to the truck. "Jealous boyfriend he might be, but getting someone else to do the deed for him? Doesn't fit the MO for the usual domestic violence offender."

"We're not even speculating that way yet. Right now we're just interviewing anyone and everyone who might have had an interest in Makoa Simmons's death. Shaking the trees and seeing what drops. Mrs. Tadeo's protective, but I found out her husband, Eric, and Eli are twins, so I think I understand her attitude a little better."

"Twins. That is close to home," Lei said thoughtfully, as they got on the road to Makoa's parents' house.

On the way back to the Simmonses' house, Pono's phone rang. Lei answered it for him since he was driving. It was Makoa Simmons's agent, Harvey Nebel.

"I have a little time now," the sports agent said. "Why don't you come to my office in Wailuku?"

Lei glanced at Pono. "Financials," she mouthed, raising her brows in inquiry. "Makoa's agent can fit us in."

"Let's do it," Pono said.

Fifteen minutes later, they pulled into the underground garage of one of the few high-rise office buildings on Maui. Located on Main Street in Wailuku, the Iao Office Complex was across from the city and county buildings and commanded a view of the deep waist of the figure-eight-shaped island on one side, with waving sugarcane fields and Haleakala in the distance. Stunning green, waterfall-carved Iao Valley bracketed the other side. Lei got an eyeful of both views as they got off the elevator, stepping into an elegant glass-windowed lobby with a reception desk at one end.

Emblazoned in gold script above the reception desk were the words SPORTS UNLIMITED.

"I'm surprised the Nebel brothers have such a fancy office here," Lei said in an aside to Pono. "Maui's not exactly a sports hotbed."

"Bet he has a house here and works virtually most of the time," Pono said. "Most of the work's probably by phone anyway."

Harvey Nebel was much as Lei had expected from his name: short, balding, with a paunch like a soccer ball and bright blue eyes, crinkled with good humor.

"Pleased to meetcha." Nebel came around from behind his desk to shake their hands. "Never had occasion to meet any Maui Police Department personnel before." His aloha shirt was lurid enough to give Dr. Gregory competition.

"Nice to meet you as well." Pono grinned at the little man. "It was great how you got Winston Pepper traded to the Chargers."

They went off into football-speak for a few minutes, and Lei used the time to look around the chic space, furnished in shades of slate and silver, with pops of red in a vase and in pillows on cushy-looking chairs set in a conversational grouping. Harvey gestured to these, and they sat.

"I understand from your message that you need some financial information regarding Makoa Simmons's career. I'm so sorry, but I can't provide you with that information without a warrant. I'm sure you understand." He crinkled his eyes ruefully, turning up his hands.

"I do." Pono continued to lead the conversation. "I anticipated you'd have strict confidentiality rules, and I brought one." He took a folded paper out of a folder he'd carried in. "We need to examine every possible motive for this young man's death, including financial. I'm sure you understand."

"Yes, I do." Harvey adjusted his glasses as he examined the document. "Appears to be in order. Well, I had my girl prepare a folder just in case. We're both Boy Scouts, I see—always prepared." Harvey included Lei in his smile. He got up, fetched the folder off the desk, and rejoined them.

"Let me explain it a bit to you." He sat on the low, Danish-styled backless couch between them, and Lei and Pono leaned in from either side to look on. "Makoa has sponsorships of various kinds. Some of them are contingent on completing tasks or events, some of them are monthly stipends, and some of them are what amount to gifts of swag or product."

He went through the contracts, explaining Makoa's income stream. The young man was making what amounted to several hundred thousand dollars a year. Lei blinked. "That's a lot of money. What happens now that he's dead?"

"Well, Makoa was smart for a young man of his age. He had most of his money going into a central account, which was being managed by a financial planner and invested. He lived on a monthly allowance. He was saving to buy a house."

Harvey removed his red plastic reading glasses and, to Lei's surprise, mopped his eyes with a bandanna. "I'm sorry. He was such an amazing young man. He was just getting started with his future. Anyway, most of his sponsorships will end with his death, of course, but there is still some residual income that will be coming in from licensing of his name, image, et cetera."

"What about life insurance policies and things like that?" Lei asked.

"Funny you should ask. I was just talking to Makoa about this last week. As part of his contracts, he had to carry a couple million dollars of insurance against being handicapped or killed. He'd just found out that his father had taken out a big policy on him, and he wasn't happy about it. They didn't see eye to eye, and Makoa thought it showed how much his father didn't believe in him and expected him to fail."

"So how much is a big policy?" Lei frowned. She was now glad they'd come to this interview before visiting the parents.

"Three million."

"That is a lot. Didn't Makoa have to agree to the policy?"

"Actually, no. Parents can take out a policy on children without their knowledge or consent, and children on their parents. Siblings on each other. Spouses. Et cetera."

Lei and Pono glanced at each other. "So who was Makoa's beneficiary?" Pono asked.

"His parents—but Makoa was so upset when he found out about his dad's extra policy, he changed the beneficiary of his insurance to his girlfriend, Shayla Cummings. Some of the companies he had contracts with will also get payouts."

Lei resisted looking at Pono again for fear of communicating anything.

Now, not only did the dad have motive, but so did Shayla Cummings—not to mention Eli Tadeo. He might have had a powerful motive to kill Makoa and make his ex-girlfriend rich. And what if Shayla knew? And they'd colluded together?

They shook hands with the energetic little agent and left with the folder of contracts.

In the elevator, Lei shook her head. "The plot thickens," she murmured, flipping through the papers. "I think we need a look at the dad's financials, too. I have to get on a plane in an hour. I think you should get the dad's financial information before you interview him. And if I can find the guy who actually killed Makoa on Oahu, we might have a much better idea of why."

"I'll take you to the airport and find out who does the bookkeeping for Simmons Construction. I'll visit there first before I go interview the parents again," Pono said.

"You might want to take Gerry or one of the other detectives,"

Lei said. "That dad seems like the kind to lawyer up, or deny things were said without another witness."

Pono nodded. They both worked their phones on the way to the airport: Lei called Omura to update her on their progress, and Pono got the name of the bookkeeping firm that handled Simmons Construction's books from Rory Simmons's administrative staff.

After Pono had the name, he hung up. "Now to get my next subpoena going," he said.

"You were pretty slick with that," Lei said. "You got a stack of them pre-signed?"

"I do. Won 'em from Judge Natides in a poker game," Pono said. "He made me raise my hand and swear they'd be justified, but he trusted me enough to presign five of them. Can't tell you how handy they've been."

"That's why I like having you for a partner," Lei said. "I never know what you're going to come up with, and you pretty much know everybody."

"And you keep things interesting on our cases. Never a dull moment when Lei Texeira's around." Pono grinned.

He dropped her at the airport, and Lei went through the check-in process with her weapon and small backpack. She didn't call Stevens until she was sitting in the waiting area, her eyes on the great purplish bulk of cloud-wreathed Haleakala in the distance through the giant glass viewing window, planes and ground crews in the foreground.

The phone rang and rang.

CHAPTER EIGHT

S<small>TEVENS</small> <small>MET</small> Jared in the cafeteria in the basement of the police department building. He clapped his brother's tense shoulder in a half hug. "Didn't take Mom long to disappear," Stevens said. "Let me buy you a burger for spending your morning with her."

"Okay." Jared pushed a hand through short, chocolate-brown hair. His eyes had gone gray-blue with frustration. "I thought she was going to go for the rehab thing." They got into the straggling line at the cafeteria counter. Stevens made a brief throat-cutting gesture not to talk about it. The station loved nothing better than gossip, and he hoped to get his brother alone in a corner for a bit more of a war council rather than advertising their personal business in line.

They got their burgers and a plastic basket of fries, and Stevens led his brother to a table in the far corner. He sat with his back to the room to signal he didn't want company. The station was a friendly place generally, the cafeteria ebbing and flowing with on-and-off duty officers and support staff coming and going from one another's tables.

Jared picked up on this and hunched in beside Stevens, squirting mustard onto his burger from a plastic bottle on the table.

"So anyway. The doctor met with both of us and went over her results. Mom seemed pretty shaken. Kept saying she was just a little run-down, needed some rest and vitamins. The doc said, "Yes, Mrs. Stevens, that and you need to stop drinking. And to stop drinking, you need professional help and medical support.""

"I bet she didn't like hearing that." Stevens took a bite of his burger, narrowing his eyes.

"Not one little bit. She acted all insulted, said she'd always had a weak constitution but she'd come here for the fresh air. Trying her whole delicate-flower act. The doc didn't buy it a bit. Anyway, we went back to the reception area, waiting on some urine analysis results, when she said she had to go to the bathroom. The office told me the results were in, and it had been twenty minutes by then. I got a little concerned she was feeling emotional about it all, went to the bathroom and knocked. Needless to say, she wasn't there. Or anywhere else in the building that I could find."

"What was she carrying when she left the house?" Stevens asked.

"She had that little backpack she'd arrived with. I guess that should have made me suspicious." Jared took a savage bite of his burger, scowling. Done chewing, he looked at Stevens. "Can we put out an APB on her? Have her picked up?"

Stevens shook his head. "For what? She's an adult with rights, and she's exercising them. I'm not happy she's going to be wandering around here on her own, but we can't misuse county resources having officers look for her."

"She's a danger to herself?"

"We'd have to have her declared incompetent, and I don't think that's going to fly. At least not yet."

They both ate some more, and finally Stevens sighed, picked up his drink, and took a long draft. "I don't think we're going to have to wait long to hear from her, though. She'll call when she needs something or runs out of money."

They collected their rubbish and left the cafeteria. Jared raised a hand as he headed for the front entrance. "Call me if she gets in touch."

"Will do."

On his way back up to his office, Stevens decided to stop off at the second floor, where his men had been redistributed. He found his former detective Joshua Ferreira in a cubicle with a couple of other men. "Ferreira."

Ferreira stood up, hoisting his belt higher up his paunch. "Boss! I mean, Lieutenant."

Stevens flapped a hand with a grin. "Not your boss any longer. How's it going down here?"

"Captain's got me working Vice." Ferreira introduced Stevens around. "Lieutenant Stevens is training new detectives."

"So now we know who to blame when the pups screw up," one of the men joked. Stevens spent a few minutes talking with them and then headed back to the elevator. As the doors closed on the warren of cubicles and the busy hum of police work, he again felt a jab of something way too much like loneliness.

His phone vibrated and he saw that it was Lei and that she'd called several times.

"SWEETS." Lei heard a roughness in Stevens's voice when he finally picked up.

"Michael. I wanted to tell you I'm at the airport on the way to Oahu. I told you I'd probably have to go."

"I wish I could come over, too. I could use a distraction."

"What? You don't like the new training detail?"

"No. It's not that. Mom skipped out on Jared when he took her to the doctor."

Lei sucked in a quick breath of dismay as she listened to her husband's story about Ellen's physical situation and then her disappearance. "So there's nothing you can do?"

"I don't see what. I've got no grounds to report her a missing person."

"But she is missing. You could do a BOLO at least."

"And draw attention to the situation? Have one of our teams pick her up, drunk in her own vomit on the street? How would that look for us?"

A long pause. Lei shut her eyes at the pain in his voice. She rubbed the white gold medallion at her throat. She didn't care about the embarrassment factor, but he obviously did.

"She might be in danger," Lei said mildly. "I mean, the homeless scene's nicer over here than in some big cities, but we have plenty of overdoses, attacks, rapes, and deaths."

"She's made her choice." Stevens's voice went hard. "I came all this way to get away from her, and she followed us over with her shit. Jared and I don't deserve this."

"Honey." Lei didn't call him endearments often, but this time one was called for. "I wish I could kiss you and make it better. But it is what it is, and she is who she is. I know because my mother was an addict. Their disease doesn't have anything to do with us."

Another long pause. She heard him blow out a breath. "I know. On one level, I know. But it still feels personal. I guess I need to get over that. I'm sure she'll call as soon as she needs something."

"Probably," Lei said. "And you'll help her. Because that's who you are."

"I love you," he said in a whisper. She could tell he was walking somewhere.

"I'll call you tomorrow. Kiss Dad and the little man for me."

"I'll pass on kissing your dad. Kiet can have both kisses," Stevens said, and Lei smiled as she cut the connection.

They called for boarding. She stood, slinging her pack onto her shoulder, and got into the line along the huge viewing window, glancing one last time at Haleakala's shadow.

The good thing about the flight was that it was short. The bad thing was that she had to fly at all. Lei sat in the window seat of the Hawaiian Airlines midsize jet. Oahu was the hub of most activity in Hawaii, from government to business, and having to take a plane and spend a couple hundred dollars (not to mention renting a car or paying for transportation once you got there) was one of the minuses of living on the neighbor islands.

Lei felt a painful constriction in her chest as she buckled her seat belt—and realized it was anxiety colored by grief.

It reminded her of another time she'd buckled into a plane's seat belt, on her way to another island. She'd been pregnant, and the seat belt had felt tight. She touched her waist now, feeling a familiar pang of emptiness. Sometimes she even imagined she felt the fluttering kick of the baby she'd lost.

This was the first time she'd been on a plane since the commuter flight she'd been on from the Big Island had been hijacked. After she lost the baby, she had been on that flight back from Kaua`i with Stevens. She'd been so heavily medicated, she couldn't even remember it.

Lei couldn't remember much from that dark time three months ago.

She reached up behind her neck and took off the white gold medallion she always wore. Thank God she always wore it, or it would have burned, along with everything else she owned, in the house fire that had happened around the same time.

With the medallion in her hand, Lei settled back, shut her eyes, and began doing relaxation breathing. She'd learned the technique during therapy early in her career on the Big Island. It still worked, but Lei was glad no one had taken the seat beside her. She just wanted to be alone to get through the short trip.

Once they were in the air, Lei relaxed enough to look out the window at the spectacular coast of Maui on her left. The land draped like crumpled velvet, the clouds a swan's-down edging. Maui's rugged topography ranged in color from the deepest, darkest green to the pale yellow of new growth. The edge of the coast was rimmed in black rock and yellow sand, the ocean a navy blue blanket tufted with spindrift far below.

Lei took out the sketch the artist had done, along with the photos of the two men she was pursuing. She'd taken the copies of Makoa's professional contracts and told Pono she'd fax him a copy when she got to Honolulu Police Department. Sorting through the contracts, she made a list of contact people and representatives she could interview if she had time—beginning with the personnel at Torque, Makoa's biggest sponsor. Torque had leased the beach house at Pipeline where Makoa lived during the season along with some of his competitors.

Lei looked up as the plane began its descent and realized she hadn't thought about the hijacking at all once they were in the air. The current crime she was investigating was too absorbing. She looked out the window as the plane curved down over the waters of Pearl Harbor, the wreck of the *Arizona* and its memorial clearly visible under a veil of shallow turquoise ocean. From their line of descent, the iconic profile of Diamond Head was clear in the distance, punctuated by the gleaming skyscrapers of Waikiki.

Lei's spirits rose. Since her stint in the FBI and living on the busy island nicknamed "the gathering place," she'd had a special affection for Oahu, traffic-heavy and crowded though Honolulu was. Marcus Kamuela was meeting her at the airport. He'd texted her that he'd been assigned to be her temporary partner, and she was looking forward to working alongside Marcella's fiancé.

She texted Marcus that she'd arrived after the plane landed and got back a laconic *ok.* She made her way through the airport, inhaling the warm, plumeria-and-diesel scent of the busy thorough-fare outside Hawaiian Airlines.

Lei was just setting her backpack down when Marcus Kamuela drove up in a black Ford truck with metal racks and a couple of surfboards on it. "Hop in," he said.

She grinned, opening the door. "Didn't know you surfed."

"Of course. And we're going to the North Shore, so we'd better blend." Kamuela's brown eyes crinkled at the corners, and his very white grin had a dimple. One muscled arm draped casually in the window frame, he was the picture of laid-back Hawaiian charm—but Lei knew how relentless he could be as an investigator. She was glad to have him on her side for this case.

"How long've you been surfing?"

"Since small-kid time."

"Stevens and I go out. We suck. It's hard to get better if you start when you're an adult."

"Keep tellin' yourself that. Maybe you're just uncoordinated."

Lei opened her mouth in indignation and saw Kamuela was teasing her by his grin. He pulled out into the busy traffic. "Listen, I've been monitoring your APB on the sketch and airport screen-grab photo. So far, nothing."

"I've got more now. One of the addresses is in Honolulu, so maybe we'd better go by there before we trek out to the North Shore." Lei pulled up the address on her phone. "Okay if we get right to it?"

"That's the plan."

"Well, we're going to see August Jones. His prints were found in the van the suspect rented, and he could match our ID mock-up." Lei pulled out the man's printed driver's license photo and compared it to the screen-grab photo. "Too bad the resolution and angle aren't better on this."

"Can you plug the address into the GPS?" Marcus tapped the dash-mounted device as he continued to navigate the busy morning traffic into downtown Honolulu.

Lei punched it in, and fifteen minutes later they were pulling into a long driveway with a series of duplex apartments branching off of it. Marcus braked the truck in front of 2A. "This is it."

"Gimme a minute." Lei took her weapon out of its case and reholstered it, put her light jacket on over the shoulder holster, and buckled on her ankle piece.

"Getting extra-strapped?" Kamuela quirked a brow.

"This ankle rig saved my life not long ago. I'll tell you about it later." Lei got out of the truck, and she and Kamuela mounted chipped cement steps to the apartment's beige door. Lei knocked. A few minutes later, a young man opened it. He was clean-shaven, around five foot ten with dark skin and black hair. Lei mentally compared him to the sketch and the photo—he could be the suspect, but she didn't feel a sense of recognition.

"August Jones? We're from the police department." Lei and Kamuela showed their badges. Jones didn't blink or look worried.

"What can I do for you?"

"We were wondering if you could tell us a little about your recent trip to Maui. May we come in?"

The young man invited them in, and they perched on a stained vinyl couch. He picked up a few pizza containers off the coffee table. "My roommates are a little messy," he said. "What's this about?"

"We just need to know a few details about your trip to Maui, if you don't mind."

"Okay." Jones sat down in a recliner with a built-in cup holder containing an empty beer bottle. "I went over there a few weeks ago to do some windsurfing. I had some vacation time and hooked up with some friends." He shrugged. "It was fun. Why do you want to know?"

"Where were you yesterday morning?" Kamuela leaned forward and gave the young man some intimidating eye contact.

"I was at work."

"And where is that?"

"I work at a dive shop on the North Shore."

"Can anyone verify you were there?"

"Hey!" Jones struggled to get up, but getting out of the chair with its heavy padding and reclined angle made it an undignified process. "I need to know what this is about."

"We have reason to believe that someone who rented the same van you did may have been involved with a homicide."

Jones had escaped the chair. He put his hands on his hips. "I rented that van two weeks ago! And I was at work yesterday. You can ask anybody!"

"We will," Lei said. "Name and address of your workplace, please?"

Jones gave it, and she noted it down. "Thanks for your cooperation."

Back on the road, Kamuela rubbed his chin thoughtfully. "Not our man," he said.

"I agree, but I'll check this alibi while you drive." Lei punched the next address into the GPS. Then she called the dive shop and verified that yes, August Jones had been working the retail end of the shop yesterday. "Does August surf?" she asked on a hunch.

"Sure he does. You can't work on the North Shore of Oahu and not surf!" the manager exclaimed.

Lei smiled at Kamuela as she hung up. "Scratch August Jones. On to Freddie Arenas. He lives in Kahuku."

"That little town is out past the Seven Mile Miracle, so we should probably stop at the Torque team house first."

"The Seven Mile Miracle?"

"Nickname for this stretch of North Shore coast with all the surf breaks."

"I lived on Oahu a year and a half and never heard that," Lei said, propping her feet on the dash as they finally left the outskirts of the city. Wide-open farmland, former sugarcane and pineapple fields, opened up before them as they drove through the middle of the island.

"How many times did you get out to the surf zone when you lived here?" Kamuela drove casually, arm outstretched, hand draped over the steering wheel.

"Not enough. I was a total workaholic. I think Marcella and I went out to Sunset Beach one time in the summer to lie out and work on our tans."

"No cases out that way?"

"No. And I hope I can get home tonight, but in case I can't, I better call your fiancée and see if I can spend the night."

"I'm sure you're welcome."

Lei phoned Marcella and left a message asking to spend the night at her friend's apartment. More than likely they wouldn't get through everything today. "Just left a message. So you guys are good?"

"Stressed out with the wedding stuff, but that'll settle down after we get hitched. What about you guys? How's the house coming along?"

Lei updated him as they wound down from a higher elevation toward the small town of Haleiwa, where the famous coast began. The road narrowed to two lanes, growing windy and picturesque, lush with tropical foliage and studded with coconut palms. They crested a rise, and the ocean, folding in on itself in corduroy-like lines, generated enough mist from breaking waves to give a gauzy texture to the air.

"It's firing!" Kamuela exclaimed, and Lei felt the elemental excitement of the thundering surf give her a jolt of exultation. She'd come late to surfing and still hesitated to even call herself a surfer—but she'd done it enough to know there was nothing quite like the physical excitement of paddling out, punching her board through the walls of approaching waves, finding just the right spot to take off, and then the all-out effort of takeoff followed by the breathless drop, the turn into the curve of the wave, the wall of water pure moving energy beside her, the tuck to try to make it under the falling lip...and the washing-machine ragdolling under-water when she didn't make any of the steps she tried—which was most of the time.

It didn't matter. There was simply nothing like it to take away stress and flush every pore with excitement. And this bit of coast was every surfer's fantasy—on steroids.

She bounced in her seat. "We have to look at the surf. Orient ourselves."

Kamuela grinned at her. "Want to go out for a quick session?"

"Oh my God, it's way too big for me. You know I only started a couple years ago at Waikiki."

"We can go to one of the inside bowls."

Lei's heart pounded with fright and excitement. "Is there a beginner spot here? I'm not kidding."

"I won't let anything happen to you."

"One thing I learned pretty quickly in the ocean—no one can really help you when you're surfing."

"And the biggest danger is panic," Kamuela added. They passed the turnoff to Haleiwa, the little beach town providing restaurants and amenities to the area. "Most of the contests are over already, so that's good. It's less crowded."

"Still looks full." Waimea Bay's parking lot was jam-packed with cars and trucks piled high with surfboards.

"You're used to Maui. You folks don't know the meaning of the word."

They drove on slowly, with Kamuela identifying the individual spots for her. "This is Ali`i Beach Park. Got a lot of groms surfing on the inside here. It's the mellowest spot for us to stop."

Lei took in the crowded beach park. The waves on the inside still looked big to her. "You know, Marcus, we should work. Let's come by here on the way back and check it then. I just feel bad taking that kind of fun break on the county's dime."

"Girl's gotta grow a conscience, huh? Don't you think you put in enough overtime?"

"I know I do, but I came all this way to check out these surfers, and I just won't be able to enjoy myself until we get that out of the way."

"Slave driver." Kamuela drove them on, pointing out the parks and breaks all along until they came to Ehukai Park. "This is Pipeline. Let's get a look at the scene."

They turned into the crowded beach park, and Kamuela pulled up behind one of the lifeguard vehicles, setting his police placard out on the dash. They got out and walked across the bunchy grass, past a billboard advertising the latest Triple Crown event with Torque's sponsorship emblazoned all over the giant poster trimmed in nailed-up palm fronds.

Lei sucked in a breath of awe as they approached the expanse of beach. The Pipeline break was so close to shore that Lei could see the huge, hollow wave exploding in both a right-and left-breaking expanse of gloriously bright aqua water, expending itself in surging foamy drifts across great yellow rafts of sandy beach.

Something about it called to her, as if the blood in her veins was the same consistency as that surging ocean.

The lifeguard tower was well-manned, a great sturdy yellow steel structure, and Lei spotted the many DANGER signs along the beach, marked with red flags. She wondered how any tourists could be ignorant enough of the raw power of the ocean to go out into the pounding surf.

But the surfers at the break showed no such lack of confidence, jockeying for position across the heaving, glassy surface and taking off in almost synchronized form, pulling deep and working maneuvers that she'd only dreamed of in her own efforts.

A swath of spectators, everything from tourist families in lurid aloha shirts to bikini-clad beach babes, filled the sand directly in front of the break. Photographers with huge lenses and tripods peppered the crowd, and an atmosphere of excitement lent a carnival feeling.

Lei and Kamuela drew adjacent to the tower, and Kamuela lifted a hand and went to "talk story" with one of the lifeguards as Lei took in the scene.

From all reports, Makoa Simmons had been a regular here, well respected in the lineup, and had even frequently pulled off aerial maneuvers at this heavy barrel. Lei squelched the arrow of grief she felt. *Regrets don't find killers. Police work does.*

Kamuela gestured her over to the tower. She shook hands with Eddie Nanaio, one of the lifeguards. "Yeah, I knew Makoa

Simmons. Great kid. He was out here almost every day. Got more than his share of waves, too."

"Know anyone who had it in for him? Tried to snake waves from him, like that?" Lei asked, digging her spiral notebook out of her back pocket.

Nanaio narrowed sharp brown eyes in a weather-beaten face. Mirrored Oakleys turned backward gripped his thick neck. "Makoa had rivals, that's for sure. Bryan Oulaki was the main guy who went head-to-head with him. They both rode for Torque, and Bryan, he didn't think a Maui guy should be getting so much ink and publicity. He trash-talked Makoa, and they dropped in on each other a lot, but personally, I think that was all part of the PR Torque used to get YouTube views of their shootouts and like that. I saw those guys talking story plenty times at the team house, all mellow-kine." As Nanaio talked, his pidgin thickened.

"Shootouts?" Lei wasn't sure of the term.

"Heats against each other. Torque even featured a short film with the two of them trying to outdo each other during a free-surf session—it played up the competition and bad blood, but again, when they were off camera, they seemed fine with each other."

"Thanks. That's good information," Lei said. Kamuela fist-bumped the lifeguard, and he ascended the steps again, binoculars back up to his dark warrior's face.

"Whatever lifeguards get paid, I don't think it's enough," Lei said as they walked back to Kamuela's truck.

"You got that right. They save lives and risk their own every day. Let's find that team house."

They followed the GPS prompt along the narrow, sandy frontage road winding between stands of coconut palms and wind-battered beach naupaka running parallel to the main highway. Older homes, weathered by the constant salty air, hunkered beneath wind-battered kamani and ironwood trees.

The GPS steered them down a sandy driveway, ruts worn deep and patched unevenly with gravel. They turned at the address, painted on a piece of driftwood, and Kamuela was hard-pressed to find a parking place in the narrow backyard clogged with trucks and every sort of surfmobile, all of them sporting racks and stickers of every color and style.

Kamuela finally parallel parked behind several other vehicles. "We'll just have to move it if someone needs to leave."

"Who are all these people?"

"Well, could be anybody associated with the company, really. Houses are rented for the surf season, which usually runs from November to March, by the company. They invite their top-tier riders to live in them, and they get interns or groms to come clean and do the yards or whatever, earning a place to crash. Usually there's some sort of company rep living in, too, keeping things from getting too out of hand."

"Out of hand? What do you mean?"

"Partying. Chicks. Drugs."

"Oh." Lei opened her door and straightened her jacket. "From what I've been hearing, that wasn't Makoa Simmons's lifestyle."

Kamuela shut his door and beeped the truck locked. "Yeah. A lot of the riders are serious athletes and the body is a temple, *yada, yada*. But in any late-teens, early-twenties group of young males, there are always a few who don't feel really alive unless they're pushing all the limits. Not just surfing."

They walked up the sandy walkway trimmed in coconuts to a front door with a big oval Torque logo mounted on it. Kamuela rang the bell, causing the sound of a gong to echo inside the house.

A few minutes later, he rang again.

They heard the padding of bare feet, and a blond teen in yellow Torque board shorts, no shirt, opened the door. His hair was a mass of sun-bleached, salty-looking tufts, and his body was deeply tanned, making hazel eyes look even greener under the thatch of hair.

"What's up?"

"Detective Kamuela and Sergeant Texeira. We need to speak to whoever's managing the house."

"This about Makoa?" The kid blinked.

"Yes."

"I'll get Pete. Come in." The kid gestured them in, and looking around at the copious amounts of sand on the floor, Lei decided to leave her shoes on.

They followed the kid down a tiled hall, past a staircase rising to upper floors, and into a front room. Salt spray misted the windows, but Lei could see a lanai crowded with chairs, a weedy lawn in front of the house, and between the framework of a pair of palms, the aqua of pounding surf.

"Pete, these cops are here about Makoa Simmons." The grom introduced them to a man Lei assessed as mid-thirties, Caucasian, five ten and a hundred fifty pounds, blue eyes, buzz-cut blond hair, wearing a Torque team shirt in black.

The man stood up from his deck chair, setting aside a laptop he'd been typing on. Lei noticed a row of cell phones on the deck beside him. "Hey. We've been expecting some sort of visit since we heard about the tragedy. Pete Cantor—I'm the Torque team manager on site."

Lei shook his hand and introduced herself. "I'm the investigator working the case from Maui. And I'm sorry to tell you if you haven't heard already, but Makoa's death was no accident."

Pete Cantor's face paled under his tan. "No shit?" he said faintly. "I heard that, but I didn't want to believe it. Bad enough he's dead. Unreal someone would take him out deliberately!"

"That's why we're here. A suspect rented a van on Maui and deliberately drowned him in the lineup at Ho'okipa." Lei took the artist's sketch out of her backpack and handed it to him. "Know anyone who looks like this?"

Pete frowned down at the rendering, and the paper shook in his hands. "This is kind of a generic face. Could be any of a half-dozen local guys that come and go from the house. We kind of have a revolving door here."

"Well, we need to search Makoa's room and get a list from you of anyone you think that could be. Can you point me to his room?" Lei asked, eager to see if she could get his computer and collect the hate mail Shayla had alluded to.

Pete's cheekbones flushed. "Bryan Oulaki's already moved into his room. We boxed up his stuff, though. It's in the garage."

Lei stared at the team manager a long moment. She could feel Kamuela beside her doing the same. Pete held up his hands in apology and protest.

"We thought it was an accident, okay? And the front room, the master bedroom, is a major perk for the top-ranking rider. Which, after Makoa, is Bryan."

"Shit, man. The kid's not even cold on the slab," Kamuela said from beside Lei in his dark-edged voice, and Lei was glad he did.

"Let me take you up there. It will make more sense when I do." Pete led them up sand-speckled wooden stairs to a second-story master bedroom that dominated the front of the house. A king-sized bed took up the center of the room. Stacks of boards lined a wall, and a bathroom at the back completed the decor, but the view through sliding glass doors fronting a deck looked directly into the Pipeline lineup.

A row of shirtless, tanned, chiseled-looking surfers in webbed deck chairs hooted and commented loudly on the action, beers in their hands.

Pete slid the door open. "Hey, guys. These are some cops here about Makoa."

Immediately, silence fell. Lei stuffed down the intimidation she felt at looking at the row of famous faces she recognized from ads and write-ups in the surf magazines. *Makoa should be sitting here, and one of these guys might have had something to do with why he isn't.*

"Sergeant Texeira, Detective Kamuela," Lei said, as they

flashed ID. "We're going to want to take statements from each of you, beginning with whichever of you is Bryan Oulaki."

The young man closest to Lei set his beer aside in a cup holder on the folding chair and stood.

"I'm Bryan." He was around five ten, with black buzz-cut hair. A tribal-style tattoo of interlocking triangles circled muscled shoulders, dipping down across a tanned chest and continuing around his back. Dark brown eyes and the shadow of a beginning goatee completed a description that could easily match the sketch she'd taken back from Pete Cantor.

Lei's heart rate spiked as she shook the young man's hand. "I'd appreciate your time answering a few questions. Privately."

"Sure."

Lei didn't think she was imagining the uneasy set to Bryan Oulaki's mouth. He reached down and grabbed up the black Torque team shirt hanging over the back of his chair and shrugged into it. "Right this way."

Kamuela followed her back into the bedroom and slid the glass door shut behind them, closing Pete and the other surfers out on the deck. Lei liked the way he was letting her take the lead but seemed to know when to provide a seamless backup.

"There's an office we can use to talk back here." Oulaki led them down the hall to a carpeted office. One wall was lined with computers networked with blue cables. Awards and trophies cluttered a shelf that ran the length of the room, and a back window overlooked the crowded parking lot.

Kamuela closed the office door as Oulaki pulled three rolling chairs from the length of computer desk. Lei and Kamuela took seats facing Oulaki. Lei took out her phone and set it on the edge of the round conference table against one wall.

"Mind if I record this? Saves time and hassles later." Lei smiled, trying for reassuring, but she'd been told her smile in interviews wasn't the kind that lent itself well to "good cop."

Oulaki stiffened up even more, brown face going immobile, arms crossed defensively on his muscular chest. "Whatever."

"Relax, man. We're just trying to get a feel for Makoa's life here in the house," Kamuela said. Lei knew the other surfers would have heard by now from Pete Cantor that Makoa Simmons's death was a homicide, but she hoped they'd been able to isolate Oulaki before he heard that news.

"Tell us about your relationship with Makoa," she said.

"What does this have to do with me?" Oulaki said, frowning. "He was on Maui and drowned. Why are you getting all up in my grill?"

"And why are you so defensive?" Lei rapped out. "I see you wasted no time moving into his room."

"That was Pete. Said I earned the perk," Oulaki said, voice low and eyes cast down. Lei believed him about that, at least.

"Just tell us about your relationship with Makoa Simmons. We've been hearing all kinds of rumors about it," Kamuela repeated.

"We were good, man." Oulaki looked up, made eye contact with Kamuela, who was doing well with the default "good cop" role. "All that rivalry jazz, that was just to get publicity to raise both our profiles. Pete came up with the idea last season, and we have been playing it up. It worked too. That YouTube video of our free-surf session got more than a million hits worldwide."

"So there was no actual bad feeling between you two?" Lei asked. "Come on, now. I was hearing about it over on Maui, from people close to Makoa."

"Okay, yeah, once we got into the competition thing, we worked it. I'm not gonna lie. I didn't think Makoa deserved all the buzz he was getting. I'm North Shore born and raised, been surfing Pipe since I was thirteen, and here he comes, Mr. Haole Prep School Maui, acting like he's all that." Lei could see by the young man's tense shoulders and flared nostrils that the resentment was real. "But we never had a problem anywhere but in the water. It was all just for the cameras."

"Sounds like you had motive." Lei gestured toward the front room they'd just left. "With Makoa gone, that sweet view's all yours, not to mention Torque's top billing."

"Hey, I never wished nothing on the guy." A hint of pidgin had crept into Oulaki's sullen voice. "Except that he would go back to Maui."

"Maybe you helped him stay there," Lei said, leaning forward to pin the young man with her cop stare. She slid the sketch out of the folder toward him. "This a picture of you?"

Oulaki's black brows snapped together as he took the sketch. "Why are you asking? Makoa clocked his head on his board and drowned."

"How'd you hear that?"

"I don't know—that's what I heard. What makes sense." Oulaki looked flustered, frowning and moving restlessly on his chair as he gazed at the sketch. The gold earring in his ear caught a stray sunbeam. He could have so easily changed his appearance: shaved, worn a black rash guard to cover up those distinctive tats, taken out the earring, which she remembered seeing in most publicity photos. When Oulaki got back to Oahu, he could have buzzed off the longish hair in the sketch. In another surf break on a different island, he wouldn't have been readily recognizable.

"Makoa was murdered. Someone dropped in on him and held him under." She delivered her words as smoothly as sliding a knife between Oulaki's ribs.

Oulaki looked up directly at Lei. Color ebbed from beneath his tan, leaving him jaundiced. "This isn't me."

He thrust the sketch back at Lei. She didn't take it, and it fluttered to the ground and lay on the floor, looking up at them accusingly. Things devolved from there into a mute stare down between Lei, arms folded, and Oulaki, equally closed off.

Finally Kamuela said, "We need an alibi. Where were you day before yesterday?"

"I went to visit family in Honolulu."

"So you weren't out here at the team house?" Lei said.

"No. I have family in Mililani. I saw them. Spent a couple of nights at a friend's house, too. He can verify I was there."

"We'll need that information," Kamuela said, and took down the contact names.

Lei tried not to react when she heard his friend's last name was Tadeo. Hoping her voice was neutral, she said, "We have a Maui family by that name."

"It's common enough." Oulaki eyed her sullenly. "Are we done now?"

"For the moment," Lei said. "Don't go anywhere."

After the surfer left, Lei got up and shut the door. "I like him for it."

"I kind of do, too—though if his alibi checks out, we aren't going to be able to do much unless your team can find some trace that ties him to the body. We don't have his fingerprints in the van."

"He isn't dumb. He could have found a way around that, and the van was filthy and full of trace from a dozen possible contributors. Unfortunately, we already know the body was clean. Let's just get names, contact info, and alibi statements from the rest of the guys here, and then get out to that van driver Freddie Arenas's address in Kahuku. Let's take all of Makoa's boxes, and I can go through them carefully elsewhere."

"Sounds like a plan."

CHAPTER NINE

LEI HELD the pile of threat letters and printed-out e-mails Pete Cantor had given her as Kamuela navigated out of the crowded driveway at the Torque team house. Glancing down at the pile in a manila envelope, Lei frowned.

"I don't think Cantor would have given these to me if I hadn't known to ask for them."

"Seemed like that to me, too. He didn't like us hassling Bryan Oulaki," Kamuela said. The team manager had stormed in after Bryan left, blustering and defensive. But between the two of them they soon had him groveling as he handed over the collection of threat letters and Makoa's boxes of possessions, stored in the garage.

"Well, if Oulaki's Torque's anointed successor, I can see that. But withholding the letters shows he suspects someone, someone who may be in that house. I think I should go back and reinterview Cantor later. Maybe bring him into the station, intimidate him a bit."

"Let's see about this Arenas guy in Kahuku first." Kamuela finally got the truck turned around. He pointed to a coconut tree in the team house's yard. A surfboard emblazoned with Makoa's name was propped against it, surrounded by flowers, cards, and other offerings. "It was good to hear they're doing a paddle out for Makoa."

"Yeah. That helped me not bite Cantor's head off for how he threw Makoa out of the master bedroom so fast," Lei said. The paddle out was scheduled for the next day. The informal ceremony that had sprung up among the surfing community was a way to give honor to their fallen. Surfers paddled their boards out into the ocean, made a circle, and said prayers, told stories, sang songs about the one lost. Plumeria flowers and leis were tossed into the circle at the end, and waves were surfed to honor the dead. Lei had seen flowers from these ceremonies washed up on the beaches, and they never failed to give her a bittersweet pang.

"No one else popped for me besides Oulaki. What did you think?" Lei asked.

"Agree." Kamuela gave a terse nod as he navigated the narrow frontage road and got back onto busy two-lane Kamehameha Highway.

They'd taken statements of whereabouts during the time of Makoa's murder from all the surfers in the house and had taken prints and hair samples as well in case they got lucky with some trace. Lei hadn't enjoyed the stony stares and attitudes some of the riders showed, but there hadn't been anything more definite to go on.

Now they headed out past Sunset Beach, a wide swath of yellow sand alongside the highway. Lei rubbernecked across Kamuela's broad chest to get a look at the surf at the famous beach, where the wave break was visible from the road. "We don't have anything like this on Maui."

"Yeah, but you have Jaws." Kamuela named the break famous for huge twenty-to-fifty-foot surf off the rocky coast north of Paia on Maui.

"It's not really accessible like this is. Jaws is a real project to find, out in the pineapple fields. You need a car with four-wheel drive and mud tires just to get to the overlook. No wonder North Shore Oahu's such a tourist attraction." Lei could actually feel spray from the pounding surf curling her hair into even tighter ringlets as Sunset's waves detonated off the beach.

They drove on past the end of the famous stretch of coast, through a wide area of squared-off, grassy ponds that were freshwater shrimp farms. Food trucks featuring the island delicacy dotted the side of the highway.

"Never seen so many food trucks as out here," Lei commented. "You got all kinds, too." She pointed to Thai, Vietnamese, Mexican, and, of course, Hawaiian.

"Yeah. Food trucks are a thing out here with real estate so high for restaurants," Kamuela agreed.

Kahuku was a depressed-looking bend in the road. Cinder block buildings dingy with permanent mildew held down weedy yards cluttered with rusting vehicles and decrepit boats. The school was a barracks-like cluster of buildings. "Economy seems down out here."

"Kahuku's too far out here to commute into Honolulu for work," Kamuela said. "And the beaches here get the full prevailing winds, so there's no demand for the beachfront houses you see along the Seven Mile Miracle."

"So much contrast in just a few miles."

"Isn't that always the way in Hawaii?" Kamuela slanted her a glance from sharp dark eyes. "Rich people from somewhere else and the people who take care of their vacation happiness."

"I know." Lei sometimes hated the steep division between rich and poor, the struggle of the middle class in Hawaii, a pricey place to live in so many ways. Her experience with the Smiley Bandit a few years ago had brought that situation into sharp focus, and she'd never forget how close to the surface resentments simmered. "The real price of living in paradise."

Freddie Arenas's address was a squat cube of a house made of cement block with a flat roof and the requisite dead boat and broken-down trucks in the yard. It was newly fenced in six-foot chain-link, though, with a rolling gate over the driveway, and as Lei and Kamuela got out, she saw why.

A pair of pit bulls, battle-scarred and crop-eared, barreled up to the fence, letting them know Freddie was well guarded.

They called a few times, but no one answered. Kamuela got back in the truck and leaned on the horn. Finally, a bent-over older woman opened the screen door into the garage. She called the dogs and then creaked her way to the fence. "What you want?"

"We need to speak to Freddie Arenas. He live here?" Lei held up her ID.

"He not home. He working." The woman sucked her dentures, dark eyes suspicious.

"We can go to his workplace, speak to him there. It's an urgent police matter."

"My boy a good boy. I nevah have to tell you notting."

"Aunty." Kamuela came over to the fence with that charming dimpled grin. "So sorry. No *pilikia*. He's not in trouble. Just need to ask Freddie a couple questions. "

Lei was never in favor of making false promises to potential witnesses, but Kamuela's dimpled schmoozing was definitely working better than her direct approach, as "Aunty" told him Freddie could be found cooking at one of the shrimp trucks back toward the North Shore.

"You have a way with the ladies," Lei said as they got back into the truck.

"So they tell me." Kamuela winked.

They got on the road back toward Haleiwa, and as they did, Lei flipped through her little spiral notebook. "Did you catch the name of that friend of Bryan Oulaki's? Tadeo?"

"He just said Tadeo."

"Well, the Tadeo we're looking at on Maui is the jealous ex-boyfriend of Makoa's current flame, Shayla Cummings."

"I've seen pictures of her. Bikini model, right?" Kamuela waggled his brows.

"Yeah. She's a beauty. Seems to really love Makoa. We found out he recently made her his accidental death insurance beneficiary, to the tune of a couple million. Her ex, Eli Tadeo, is kind of tricky. His twin brother is our Maui Police Department poster boy, and I mean that literally. He's our main recruiter." Lei filled Kamuela in on what she knew so far.

"So how could those two be connected? Oulaki and Tadeo?"

"No idea," Lei said as they pulled in beside a battered-looking silver Airstream sporting a big hand-painted sign reading FRESH ISLAND SHRIMP. No one was currently in the graveled parking area between two open ponds trimmed in long grass.

Lei and Kamuela got out, and Lei heard her stomach rumble. She gave Kamuela an eyeball. "Gonna get some shrimp."

"Sounds good."

"How can I help you?" The young man who leaned down into the window cut in the side of the Airstream also could match the sketch: multiethnic face, medium height, black hair, clean-shaven, and well-built. Half a dozen men they'd seen met that description. The sketch wasn't turning out to be all that helpful.

"I'd like the lunch special," she said.

"Make that two," Kamuela rumbled beside her.

"Coming right up."

"So, been working here long?" Lei asked, going for casual as Freddie Arenas turned away to a bubbling kettle on the propane stove.

"Just a year."

"So these shrimp farms. Really seem to be a good thing for the North Shore," Kamuela said, picking up her thread of making conversation.

"Sure." Arenas turned to nod. "Not much going on out here besides the surf community. It's good they figured out shrimp did well here."

"Looks like it," Lei said, surveying the shallow, square ponds. She couldn't see anything beneath the wind-ruffled brown surface of the water. "So, you surf? Everybody seems to, out here."

"Not much else to do." Arenas smiled, a good-humored grin. "But I like kiteboarding better."

"I'm from Maui. That's the thing to do over there," Lei said. "You ever get over there to sail?"

"Matter of fact, I do. Like to take my gear, go for a few days. Meet buddies over there." Arenas finished putting together Styrofoam clamshell boxes piled high with breaded shrimp and accompanied by a scoop of white rice and a pile of anemic-looking coleslaw. "Anything else I can get you?"

Lei took the boxes, handed them to Kamuela, paid, and turned back holding up her ID. "Yes. The date of your last visit to Maui."

"Oh." Arenas drew back. "What's this about?"

"Just answer the question."

"Well, I was over there a week or so ago."

"What were you doing?"

"Kiteboarding. Like I told you."

"Did you do anything else?"

"I need to know what this is about."

"What kind of vehicle did you drive?"

"I rented one of those windsurf vans. I slept in it, parked at Kanaha Beach Park. People do that all the time. That's why I rent a van." Arenas was talking fast now. "I never did nothing."

Lei also got that Arenas had an alibi from a Maui kiteboarding buddy he'd partied with while over there. "He crashed with me one night out at Kanaha."

Lei finally went back to join Kamuela, who'd finished most of his lunch already. She opened her Styrofoam container. "Not our guy."

"I knew that."

"Don't tell me. Your gut."

"A little bit. And a little bit the grandma he lives with. Guy like that isn't going out on weekends to drown surf superstars."

Lei sighed, poking at her coleslaw. "Wish we'd get a break on this case."

"Maybe that break will be in the threat letters. Or the boxes. While you were talking to Arenas, I called Kahuku PD and asked for a room to sort and process Makoa's things. We go there next."

"Thanks, Marcus." Lei's appetite returned as the smell of fried shrimp hit her nose. "I'll get a second wind after this."

CHAPTER TEN

THE AFTERNOON PASSED in relative peace in an empty conference room at the small cement block Kahuku Police Department building as Lei and Kamuela opened the boxes of Makoa's things and sorted through them.

Lei didn't know what she was looking for as she shook out stacks of neatly folded T-shirts and board shorts. It was obvious from Makoa's lack of possessions, other than his surfboards, which Cantor had said belonged to Torque, that Makoa had lived light, with an emphasis on function.

She was surprised to find a small black velvet box in the pocket of a pair of dress slacks still on their hanger. Lei opened it to find an engagement ring with sparkling, one-carat diamond lighting up a band of tiny, channel-set diamonds.

"Check this out. Looks like he was getting ready to pop the question to Shayla."

"Whoa." Marcus frowned, taking the box from her. "That's a rock. The girlfriend's going to want to have that, I'm betting."

"Yeah." Lei's mind was whirling. "What if this is motive?"

"What do you mean?"

"I mean—maybe someone knew he was getting ready to ask Shayla to marry him. What if that person didn't want him to?"

"Male or female?" Kamuela said, with one of his wolfish smiles.

"Could be either." Lei was thinking back to Shayla's pretty friend Pippa, equally distraught over Makoa's death. And the Tadeo connection. "I feel like there's something here about his love life. Something we don't know." She took the ring box back from Kamuela and turned it over, and made a note of the jewelry store on the bottom.

"Well, this needs to go into a safe." Kamuela put the velvet box into an evidence bag.

"I want to interview the salesman at the store where that was bought. And dig a little deeper into Makoa's love life."

"After we process the threat letters." Kamuela pulled over a high-powered lamp and the manila envelope with the letters in it. Kamuela had asked the station chief for processing materials for paper. Lei handed him a small pile of handwritten letters and kept a pile for herself. The e-mails she set aside for later computer IP address tracking.

She and Kamuela used gloved hands to alternate spraying the postcards, letters, and folded cards with ninhydrin and then set them under the lamp where prints fluoresced. It was slow and quiet work as they photographed the prints that bloomed on the paper.

Only when all the prints had been collected and processed to the case file did Lei look through the letters for content.

"Does this strike you as a lot of hate mail? For a guy who, according to everyone we've talked to, was a likable kid?"

"I was just thinking the same." Kamuela held up one of the letters he'd finished processing, crude letters cut from a magazine and glued onto paper spelling out, HAOLE, GO HOME. "Nice."

"I like this one." Lei held up a block-printed card with genitalia on the front and THE NORTH SHORE BELONGS TO REAL MEN. "Real men don't need to indulge in this kind of localism. Cream rises to the top, and Makoa had what it took to win the Triple Crown this year."

"A damn shame. I had no idea he was facing this kind of harassment," Kamuela said. "They sure kept it quiet in the media."

"Well, Oulaki expressed a common sentiment, that the North Shore should belong to those born and raised. But it's always been a magnet for the world, and that's part of what makes it special."

They forged on, and Lei made a pile of any that looked like they might have been authored by the same person. Most were the ones with the cut-out squares of magazine letters. "I think these were by the same harasser."

"Agree."

Lei liked how non-talkative Marcus was. "Did you get any prints off these?"

"No." Kamuela rubbed the top of his ear, an expression of frustration wrinkling his broad brow. "Of course, the ones that look like something don't go anywhere."

"Let's take a look at the e-mails. I might be able to get Sophie over at the FBI to track the computers for me." Lei handed a stack of e-mails to Kamuela, and moments later looked up at him. "I think these are all from the same source."

"Yeah." Though origin e-mail addresses had been obscured by some program, the language of the e-mails was similar, and the threats escalated from "Go home to Maui" to "Get off the contest circuit or we'll kill you and your woman."

"Why didn't he go to the police with these?" Lei wondered aloud. "Why didn't Cantor insist that he do that?"

"Bad for his image, I'm guessing," Kamuela said, sliding the e-mails back into the envelope. "I'm betting Torque didn't want anything getting out to the media. Reporting it would make it potentially public and could have damaged Makoa's reputation."

"So stupid," Lei said, feeling frustration tighten her stomach. She glanced at the window and saw the sun was slanting long across the plumeria tree outside the dusty louvers. Something was telling her to stay with the case, immerse in the North Shore scene. "You know what, Marcus? I think I'd like to spend the night out here. Do a little undercover, see what I can see."

"Marcella will be bummed to miss you, but I get it. I can come out here as early as you want me tomorrow." They gathered Makoa's belongings back into the boxes. "We can log these into Kahuku's evidence room overnight."

"I think I can take everything back to Maui when I go. Just check it onto the plane." They carried the boxes down to the locked evidence room, more of a temporary storage closet at this tiny station than anything else. After filling out the requisite forms, Lei stuck the bagged engagement ring deep into one of the boxes. "I hate just sticking this in here, but I can't keep it safe with me."

"Where are you going to spend the night?"

"I don't know. There are so many vacation rental rooms out here. Let's ask around, see if I find something. If I do, you can drop me off on the way back out."

She and Kamuela engaged the Kahuku Station staff with Lei's dilemma, and it wasn't long before she had a bedroom booked for the night in a beach house owned by the cousin of one of the officers.

On the drive back to that vacation rental's address near Pipeline, Lei called Pono to check in on the day.

"Hey, partner. How'd the interview with the parents go?"

"Not well." Pono sounded irritated. "I've been having a shitty day with this. How'd I pull the stay-back detail?"

"Sorry." Lei looked out her window as they cruised by Sunset Beach again. The sight was no less awe-inspiring the second time around, with sunset turning the spume flying off the waves to liquid gold. "Just give me the scoops, or I'll tell you mine first."

"You go. I'm eating." She heard him crunching something.

"Okay. We had an interesting time at the Torque team house. Lots of politics." She filled him in on the interviews. "And the really interesting thing, besides all the threat letters we picked up, was an engagement ring I found in Makoa's pants pocket."

"Whoa."

"Right. But other than that, nothing hard. We have a lot of fingerprints and hair samples to go through that I'm hoping we can match to something you vacuumed out of the van."

"What we need is trace on or near the body."

"And we're not going to get that. But I have a couple of interesting coincidences." She told him about Oulaki's friend named Tadeo and the attitude the team rider had. "His attitude was consistent with the hate mail Makoa was getting."

"All good but circumstantial. Well, Makoa's father, he didn't want to answer why he had taken out that big life insurance policy on his son. Threatened to call his lawyer, got all pissed off."

Lei nodded, then remembered her partner couldn't see that gesture. "Yes. He'd be insulted we'd even imagine such a thing, yada, yada. You didn't tell him that Makoa's policy benefits Shayla Cummings, did you?"

"You're kidding, right?"

Lei snorted a laugh. "I was. It wouldn't be good for him to find that out. Did you find Eli Tadeo? Because if you do, I want you to ask him if he knows a guy named Bryan Oulaki." Lei told him how unhelpful the suspect sketch Shayla and the artist had worked up was turning out to be. "It looks like half the guys on the North Shore."

"Well, I haven't found Tadeo yet, and he hasn't called me. I called the number listed for him; it's out of service. I thought I'd try one more drop-by today. I don't want to issue a BOLO or something with his brother's position in the MPD."

"Anything else?"

"Yeah. The reporters have descended. They're hassling anyone and everyone at the beach, agitating Makoa's parents, calling the station. Makoa's paddle out and memorial being planned here are getting a lot of press. We need to bring something in, and soon. Omura's getting restless."

"Working it as hard as I can." Lei frowned. "More pressure isn't going to speed this up, because it's not an easy one. Tell Omura I'm going to be staying out here by the beach, doing a little undercover work tomorrow and seeing what kind of gossip and impressions I can pick up. I have a feeling there's something we're missing. Something that provides a clear motive. So far all we have are murky possibilities."

Marcus had turned the truck off the Kamehameha Highway and back onto the frontage road. They bumped through rain-filled potholes and over a couple of steep speed bumps before pulling up to an imposing wooden gate topped by coconut finials. "Gotta go. We're at my crib for the night."

"I'll call you if I talk to Tadeo." Pono hung up.

Marcus put the truck in Park. "The cousin said to ring the bell and they'd open the gate."

"Got it." Lei hopped out of the truck and rang a bell concealed under a little plastic flap. A few minutes later, the gate retracted and they pulled inside a lushly planted compound. A large, two-story older home took up the bulk of the lot, but palms and fern trees coiled with orchids created an oasis-like feeling.

Lei and Kamuela greeted the landlord, an older mixed Hawaiian man with a buzz cut, going through the ritual of establishing who you are, where from, and who might be relatives. Lei took her backpack out of the truck and turned to Kamuela.

"I'll call you in the morning. If I'm on a roll with this undercover thing, I won't need you right away."

"That's fine. I can get started on processing and uploading the prints from the hate mail." Kamuela lifted a hand in goodbye and pulled the truck back out.

"Do you happen to have a camera I can borrow?" Lei asked the landlord. She'd spotted special license plates on his jacked-up Ford

F-150. Retired military, Lei guessed. He'd probably bought this house, worth millions now, for a song back in the sixties.

"Sure. Can't guarantee it has batteries, but I got something you can borrow."

"Thanks. I just need it as a prop." Looking around at the scene at Pipeline, Lei had decided posing as one of the many photographers would give her the best ability to move and mingle on the beach.

That, and one other thing.

Lei went into the simple above-garage apartment and dug into her backpack, pulling out the bikini Marcella had talked her into buying months ago, before she knew she was pregnant. Lean to begin with, Lei had lost weight after the miscarriage, and now the cups of the top felt loose. Her hand brushed her flat abdomen in a gesture that used to be almost habitual and now just reminded her of loss. Still, she knew she looked good in the low golden light of sunset falling through the window—honed and toned. Lean and mean. But definitely not like a cop, with her unruly mane of curls and the bronze-metallic bikini setting off her skin.

She came back outside with a beach towel over her shoulder and a long tee over the suit. The landlord handed her a decent Canon camera on a strap. "Turns out it has batteries and an empty SIM card."

"Thanks. I'll give you something extra for the rental."

"You're working on the Makoa Simmons case, right?" The older man squinted. "No charge. He was a nice kid. Didn't deserve to go so young."

"Did you know him?" Lei asked, fiddling with the settings on the camera. It was refreshing to hear something positive about Makoa from someone local.

"Not to speak to. But I watched him surf plenty times. Good manners in the water but didn't take any shit. A great surfer."

"That's what I've been hearing. Thanks for the loan."

"You need one of these. Every real photographer has one." He handed her a tripod.

Lei set off down the beach. The setting sun was going down behind the mountain that marked Kaena Point, but there was still a crowd in front of Pipeline. Getting into character, Lei tied a knot in the corner of her big MAUIBUILT T-shirt, drawing it up off one thigh.

She took long strides, loving the soft feeling of the moisture-rich air on her bare skin, the sensation of the deep coral sand massaging her toes. The camera slung around her neck and tripod under her arm, she kept heading toward Pipeline's distinctive lineup as she speed-dialed Stevens.

"Hi, Sweets." His voice sounded tired.

"Hey. Can you guess where I am?" They might not have a clear suspect in Makoa's murder, but there were a lot of possibilities, and right now she felt good in her body in this place and time. The gorgeous setting was energizing, the regular thump of the surf fizzing her blood.

"Probably somewhere more interesting than me. I'm trying to get some peas and carrots into Kiet. And you know how he feels about peas and carrots." Lei heard the baby smack the tray of his high chair, burbling. She felt a pang, missing her stepson's sturdy little body in her arms. Kiet was Stevens's son with his first wife, Anchara, whose murder had brought on the baby's birth. Though the events leading up to their adoption of him had been shocking, Lei had fallen totally in love with the happy, easy child.

"Kiss him for me."

"After the peas and carrots are off his face. And hands. And high chair, and the floor."

Lei laughed. "I miss the little man. But you're right, this is prettier than that particular scene." She described the sunset and the waves, held the phone up so he could hear the thundering surf. "The only thing that would make this better is if you and Kiet were here with me. And we were on vacation."

"I wish. Mom hasn't turned up yet."

"I'm sorry."

Lei had reached the main surf break and walked right to the edge of a cluster of photographers, setting up her tripod as she listened to Stevens describe his day. "We're going to give it a few days. See if she calls us or turns up," he finished.

"Seems reasonable. Though I still think you should put the word out. Informally."

"She's made her bed. She can lie in it," Stevens said. Lei only heard that hard tone in his voice when he was talking about suspects.

"Remember, her addiction is not about you," Lei said. "I love you. I'll be home soon."

"I love you, too. And you're not coming home soon enough for me," he said, and hung up.

Lei hit the Off button with a sigh. She screwed the camera onto the tripod, getting into character as she aimed her viewfinder toward the surf and her butt toward the watching crowd.

CHAPTER ELEVEN

STEVENS SLID the phone back into the pocket of his loose after-work jeans, feeling that negativity he'd been struggling with and not sure what to call it—depression? Loneliness. A sapping sense of futility. He longed for a slug of Scotch, and hated the thought.

He picked up the spoon and focused on the bright-eyed baby in front of him. "One more bite, buddy. Come on."

Wayne was stirring up something tasty in the kitchen, and after they'd eaten, Stevens thanked him for the meal. "If we didn't have you helping us out, I don't know what I'd be eating. Canned beans, probably."

"I enjoy it. Though I admit, I'm looking forward to your little family moving into the big house," Wayne said with a grin, touching his root beer bottle to Stevens's Longboard Lager. "How's it coming along?"

"The texture and paint crew come in a few days. So we're close."

"Lei say when she's coming home?"

"No." They cleaned up, with special attention to the circle of splattered peas and carrots around Kiet's high chair. The baby was crawling around the tiny living room, chasing Keiki who, while tolerating Kiet's climbing and ear-pulling, preferred to stay just out of reach.

"Listen. I'm worried about my mom. Can you put Kiet down for bed? I want to take a drive out to the usual homeless haunts, see if I can find her." Stevens found himself putting words to the restless urge that had been building in spite of the bluster he'd said to Lei.

"You know what we call that in the program," Wayne said. "Enabling."

His father-in-law had been a social drinker when he got out of prison, but in the last year he'd become a lay minister in his church and had given up alcohol and gotten involved with a twelve-step program.

"Keeping those demons as far away as I can," he'd explained to Stevens and Lei about his new lifestyle. "Alcohol was never my main thing, but I want to live as pure and clean as I can, and help others do the same."

Now Wayne fixed Stevens with the dark-eyed, penetrating gaze that always reminded him of Lei. "Ellen needs to hit bottom before she's ready for change."

"I know. This isn't for her. This is for me. I can't stand the thought of her on the street." A shudder swept through him. "I know too much. The street's dangerous, even on Maui."

Wayne squeezed his shoulder with a big, warm hand. "No problem. We'll be here when you get back. I hope you find her."

Stevens put on his badge and gun and picked up a light wind-breaker. Kiet, seeing this, sat up on his diapered bottom and reached both chubby arms for his father, face crumpling.

Stevens couldn't resist. He swept the boy up and buried his face in the child's neck, blowing a raspberry. "I'll be back soon, little man." He handed Kiet to his father-in-law.

Keiki, moving slower since the fire, got up out of her dog bed and trotted after him, following the truck all the way to the gate, her mournful brown eyes echoing the sentiment of the crying baby in the cottage as Stevens got on the road back to town.

Stevens picked up his radio and called in to the station, letting them know he was out in the field. "Looking for a friend I'm worried about. Radio me with any disturbance calls involving homeless or drinking."

"Will do, Lieutenant Stevens. Stay safe."

Stevens hung up the radio, glad he'd at least let the station know he was out. You never knew who was toting a gun these days.

The thought made him press down harder on the gas.

LEI SNAPPED pictures as the sunset backlit the famous heaving turquoise barrels of the Pipeline at evening. The shifting crowd on the beach around her murmured and broke into hoots and applause at a particularly good ride. Lei had never witnessed such excellent surfing concentrated in one place—but it made sense. Every surfer out there had earned their place in some way, or they simply didn't get a wave. And, once they had it, there was no better stage for deep tube rides and every sort of trick and aerial, even in the fading light.

Lei had to forcibly remind herself she wasn't there just to spectate and get pictures. Straightening up from her camera, she turned to the photographer nearest her. "You come here often?"

The guy, a grizzled-looking Caucasian wearing a battered fishing hat and Torque board shorts, grinned. "That sounds like a pickup line."

Lei laughed, tossing back her hair. "I didn't mean it that way. I'm a photographer from Maui. Lei." She extended a hand, and he shook it.

"Lee Brannan. Yeah, I'm here most days it's breaking."

"I see you're wearing Torque. Did you hear about their main team rider?"

"I did. Such a shame. Makoa was set to win the Triple Crown this year. Great kid. Photographed well, too. I sold a lot of shots of him."

"Well, the buzz on Maui is that it wasn't an accident." Lei moved closer, leaning toward Brannan as if imparting a confidence.

"No shit! That's horrible." Brannan's eyes widened. Suddenly his attention was caught by something in the surf. "You want to get this one. Oulaki's on it."

Lei applied her eye to the viewfinder and snapped off several shots of Bryan Oulaki in a yellow Torque rash guard, deep in a backlit Pipe wave. "He knows how to stand out," she commented dryly, as the young man kicked out at the end of the wave in a flashy show of spray, his bright red board catching the sunset's rays.

Brannan straightened back up. "One part talent, one part luck, one part showmanship," he said. "That's the recipe for success around here. Man. I'm having a tough time thinking about someone murdering Makoa Simmons."

Lei pointed at Oulaki, paddling back to the crowded lineup. "There's all kinds of talk about the rivalry between Oulaki and Simmons. He sure benefited from Makoa being gone from the lineup. I heard he's in the Torque house front bedroom already."

Brannan's face darkened. "That's just wrong."

Lei pretended to fiddle with her settings. "I heard another rumor—that Makoa's been getting a lot of hate mail. You know anyone who had it in for him?"

"Oulaki. Everyone knows about that. But there's a group of really local North Shore guys, always doing the 'keep the country, country' thing. Hassling guys from the Mainland and other countries who try to get into the lineup." Brannan was still frowning. "I don't like to pass anything on, because I don't want to get on their

124

bad side. Photogs they don't like get their tires slashed, equipment ends up in the surf, like that."

Lei widened her eyes and pretended to shiver. "What? Who are these guys so I can stay away from them?"

"They wouldn't hassle a pretty local girl like you," Brannan said with a reassuring smile. "They call themselves the North Shore Posse."

"Wow, and I just thought I'd take a weekend and come over here and shoot some pictures," Lei said, dimpling at him. "I write stories for the surf mags sometimes under a pen name, and I'm planning a story on the Makoa Simmons's death. Got any names for me?"

"No wonder you're asking so many questions." Brannan shook a finger at her. "You be careful stirring the shit, now."

"I write under a pen name. A *male* pen name," Lei emphasized. "What can you tell me?"

"You can't quote me no matter what your name is. But I'd like to see a spotlight on those guys, especially if they had anything to do with Makoa Simmons's death." Brannan gave her several names, which Lei punched into her phone's notes feature. "Now that I'm thinking about it, I also thought it was kind of fishy how Makoa's girlfriend's friend was always hitting on him out here, spending time with him. I met Shayla Cummings, shot her for Maui Girl bikinis, and I liked her. That friend of Shayla's, Pippa? Not really a good friend."

Lei felt her stomach lurch at this unexpected news. She'd liked the pretty blonde she'd spoken with, thought she was so supportive of Makoa's distraught girlfriend. But maybe she'd had another agenda. This was the missing piece Lei had sensed.

"When was she out here last?"

"Just last week. I saw her and Makoa arguing." Brannan's mouth tightened. "I was setting up for my shoot for the day. It was early, the sun was hardly up and no one else was on the beach yet, but the house is right there." Brannan pointed to the beach house

Lei had so recently visited. "They came out of the house and were arguing on the beach in front. It seemed like Makoa was giving her a brush-off. First he kissed her, and then he put his hands on her shoulders and talked in her face, really intense. I was feeling bad for watching, so I looked away. Then, when I looked back, he was gone and she had her hands on her hips, just staring after him. I got the feeling she was upset."

"Wow. I have a lot of leads here. Thanks so much," Lei said, batting her eyes. The light had gone, rendering the surf into shades of gray. The surfers were straggling in, silhouettes against the pearly sky. Brannan, a dim shadow beside her, shook his head.

"Like I said, you can't quote me. I hope someone finds whoever killed Makoa." He unscrewed his camera and stowed it in the heavy Pelican case on the sand beside his tripod. "See you around?"

"I'll be back out here bright and early in the morning," Lei said. "I really appreciate this."

Brannan seemed to be regretting he'd talked to her as he slammed shut his tripod and shoved the legs into it with abrupt snaps, picking up his case and departing. Lei followed suit more slowly, disassembling the tripod and looping the camera around her neck. She was conscious of gathering darkness along the edge of the beach, slanting out from the palm trees and brightly lit windows of the beach houses.

It wouldn't be a good idea to get caught asking questions out here on the long dark beach, alone and unarmed.

Lei hung the Canon around her neck and snapped the legs of her tripod in. She glanced out at the ocean and noticed that, even though the sun was gone but for a smear of gold at the horizon, she could still see surfers out in the lineup, tiny black blots against the darkening sea.

"That's how late you gotta stay out fo' beat da crowd." A rough male voice spoke from the gloom beside her. Lei spun toward the speaker but couldn't make out much besides a looming male shadow. She lifted the tripod, trying not to appear concerned or defensive.

"I'm sure they know what they're doing."

"Not everyone around here knows what they're doing." His voice was low and unfriendly.

Lei turned to fully face the man addressing her. The beach had emptied rapidly, and somehow she was alone out here with him and the ocean at her back. She didn't want to escalate whatever his beef was.

"I'm sure you've seen a few kooks," she said.

"And people who ask too many questions." He took a step toward her. Six foot, a hundred and eighty or so pounds, probably local from his pidgin—but she couldn't make out his features.

"I don't know what you overheard, but I'm a writer doing a piece on Makoa Simmons," Lei said. Her heart was hammering. She never should have left her badge and weapon at the apartment, but they'd seemed hard to conceal with her skimpy outfit. She bent her knees slightly and held the tripod in a ready position, preparing to hit him with it if she needed to.

"No talk smack about the North Shore Posse," the man continued. "If we don't speak up, this whole coast going be filled with *haoles,* Brazilians, and Euros."

"Hey, I just heard Makoa was getting hate mail and thought it was interesting. Did the North Shore Posse send that mail?" Might as well try to get some information.

The graphic sound of the man hawking a loogie was her answer. "Get gone, bitch, or you'll find out how we treat outsiders who stir the shit around here."

Lei backed up until she was on the hard-packed sand at the water's edge. The man didn't move as she turned and speed-walked away toward her unit.

She glanced back several times, but he didn't follow her. She powered back to the vacation rental and didn't draw a full breath until she was safe inside the unit with the door locked.

She called Marcus Kamuela, her de facto partner here on Oahu. "I met someone from the North Shore Posse," she said when he picked up. She described the encounter. "It seems like they might be behind the hate mail, at least, though the guy didn't confirm or deny, just launched a world-class spitball next to my foot."

"I've heard of the Posse. Now I'm going to worry about you, and God forbid you call Stevens and tell him. He'll get on the next plane over and really 'stir the shit' for you," Kamuela scolded.

"I know." She paced back and forth, burning off the last of the adrenaline. "It was just a hassle to find somewhere to stash my weapon when I wasn't wearing much."

"Carry a purse like every other woman, for God's sake. You know Marcella carries the kitchen sink in hers."

"Okay, well. I will from here on out." Lei eyed her backpack. It was going to have to continue to do everything.

"And I'll see if I can find any North Shore Posse connections to interview tomorrow."

"More will be revealed. I just wanted to keep you up to speed. I'll see you tomorrow." Lei hung up and put a chair under the locked door handle of the apartment before she took her Glock into the bathroom with her for a before-bed shower.

CHAPTER TWELVE

BREAKING A FEW SPEED LIMITS, Stevens reached Kahului, Maui's main town, a utilitarian urban sprawl built up around the airport and shipping complex at the harbor. He started his search at the harbor, pulling the Bronco up to a cluster of tents illegally pitched behind boulders at the waterfront.

He flicked on a flashlight as he got out of the truck, but almost didn't need the light because the moon was so high. Wind off the water tossed Stevens's hair and snagged at his clothes like reaching hands as he approached the tents.

Dark figures looked up at his approach. They were clustered around a smoking lantern and hibachi with hot dogs cooking on it, judging by the smell. Stevens kept the light down, off their faces, and pitched his voice low.

"I'm looking for someone, a woman. About five seven in height, a hundred and ten pounds. Blonde hair, in her late fifties."

"No, sorry, man," finally came from the fire area. Stevens was saddened to see several children clustered in the doorway of the tent. "No *haole* women here."

"Thanks. I'm looking for her and will give a cash reward for any tips." He handed the shadowy figure who had spoken his card.

"Fifty bucks, no questions asked, if you call with where you've seen her."

The man took the card. "Fifty bucks. We'll keep an eye out."

Stevens went on, working his way down the beach, giving out cards.

He'd come to know the locations of the nests and knots of homeless through his officers at the Haiku Station, many of whom had occasion to go out and answer calls at the locations for anything from first aid to assault. Like any expensive vacation area, funds were short for providing housing and services to the indigent. With real estate at a premium, the community dealt with the problem by selectively ignoring little encampments that popped up until they became a problem. One too many assaults or burglaries usually triggered a sweep, and the homeless were disbanded temporarily until they formed some new out-of-the-way cluster.

There seemed to be no long-term solution, but Stevens hated it when there were children involved. Kids should have a bed to sleep in, clean clothes, showers, good food. He'd had those things; his wife had not.

But this is America, and people are free to be poor however they like. Dark thoughts fluttered around Stevens's mind as he worked his way across town. He was getting into the truck from where he'd been talking to people in a makeshift cardboard box village when the radio crackled into life.

He heard his call sign and picked up. "Lieutenant Stevens. Go ahead, Dispatch."

"Disturbance call in the parking lot of the Ale House, Kahului."

"Ten four," Stevens said. "Requesting additional units." He'd asked to be notified of any disturbances that could involve his mother, but he didn't want to end up handling a bar brawl by himself off the clock.

Another unit chimed in. Stevens put his cop light on the dash and whipped the Bronco out of the cardboard village clustered in the graveled lot behind a decrepit shopping center where he'd been looking for Ellen.

Stevens pulled into the parking lot of the Ale House, a popular pickup bar and restaurant in the center of Kahului. He was relieved to hear the wail of the backup units approaching as he jumped out of the Bronco, heading for a knot of people around a screaming couple. His heart lurched as he spotted a whirl of blonde hair, silvery in the yellow glow of street lamps. Onlookers from the restaurant and parking lot obscured his view.

He held up his badge as he shoved through the crowd, yelling, "Police! Let me through!

The couple was down on the ground, hitting and hair pulling by the time he reached them. He grabbed the woman by the shoulders and hauled her off the man she was beating with an unbroken beer bottle.

Her shoulders felt frail in his hands, but her mouth was a snarling void, her eyes bloodshot pits as she swung the bottle at him. Dodging the blow, the only feeling Stevens had was relief as he saw she was a skinny young tweeker in a too-tight top. Not his mother. That second of distraction gave the woman an opportunity to crack him in the ribs with the bottle before he was able to subdue her.

He had the combatants separated and zip-tied by the time the other officers arrived. Getting up, he cupped his throbbing ribs.

He'd seen Ellen as crazed as the tweeker, and it wasn't pretty. The relief that this hadn't been her was tempered by renewed worry and dull anger that beat through his tired, bruised body. Getting back in his Bronco, he rested his forehead on the steering wheel, overcome by the memory.

He'd just graduated high school, and it had been bittersweet without his father, who'd died two years before. His mother had come and had managed to keep herself together through the ceremony, but he hadn't dared go to any of the many graduation parties he'd been invited to without going home to check on her—and he was glad he had.

She was totally blitzed and angry, cursing their father for dying on her and chasing sixteen-year-old Jared around the house and beating him with a bottle. He'd had to restrain her and lock her in her room until she slept it off. That was when he'd decided to go to the military instead of college—he'd just wanted to be totally gone from the house.

Stevens still felt bad about leaving Jared there to deal with her back then. He'd done his best for his brother by setting up friends and relatives to take him in whenever she was on a bender. And now, this was no way for him to spend his off-duty hours.

He had a son who needed him.

Stevens rolled down his window and got an officer's attention. "Take them in for a night in the drunk tank. I'm going home."

ONCE YOU'D BEEN GRABBED *for any reason, you just aren't the same.* Lei reflected on how the many attacks she'd endured as a police officer over the years had changed her as she showered. She wasn't going anywhere without a weapon from here on out.

She got out of the shower and noticed that her phone's battery was low. She plugged it in and opened the fridge, hoping for something left over from the tenant before.

A Styrofoam lunch container sat on the shelf of the mostly empty refrigerator, along with a couple of Longboard Lagers.

Thanks for coming to look for Makoa's killer. Least we could do! Aloha from Aunty Connie and Uncle Fred, read a Post-it note on top of the box. Her vacation rental hosts, now an aunty and uncle.

"I love Hawaii." Lei took out the meal, a typical artery-hardening selection of local food: two scoops of white rice, a mountain of teriyaki beef strips, and a mound of macaroni salad. A wilting orchid added a tropical touch. Her stomach rumbled as she trans-ferred the rice and beef to a china plate and into the microwave while she made short work of the mac salad.

Finally, dinner eaten, sipping a Longboard, she called Pono.

She heard a football game on in the background as she put her feet up against the little Formica table in the unit. "Hey, partner. Picked up something very interesting during my stint as a photog-rapher tonight."

"What?" Pono muted the TV. "Make it quick, woman. I'm going to bed early tonight, trying to catch up on some z's from the last couple of days."

"Yeah. Remember the cute blonde friend of Shayla's?" Lei told him about Pippa's apparent attempt to steal Makoa from her best friend. "Maybe she found out he was going to ask Shayla to marry him and it pushed her over the edge."

"Wouldn't she go after Shayla, not Simmons? And isn't our suspect male?"

"Yeah, but I'm wondering if she hooked up with someone who has an ax to grind with Makoa. And she helped in some way."

"What way?"

Lei took a pull off her Longboard Lager. The beer was light, cool, and delicious. She'd missed beer while she was pregnant. *Thought of a good thing about losing Baby—I get to drink beer.*

The thought made her throat close on a wave of revulsion. She coughed.

"You okay?"

"Yeah. Just a little beer down the wrong pipe," she said. Grief still ambushed her way too often, with its familiar twin, guilt. She'd lost Baby through her own recklessness. She'd always believe it, no matter what the doctor said.

"Anyway. I have this feeling about the engagement ring. That it's telling us something important," she continued.

"What if the ring wasn't for Shayla? What if Simmons was getting ready to ditch Shayla for her friend Pippa?"

The beer bottle froze in Lei's hand as she considered this. "I don't know, Pono. The photog who saw them said he saw Makoa and Pippa arguing pretty seriously outside the team house. He left her. Doesn't seem like he was getting ready to ditch Shayla. And if Shayla was acting about how grief-stricken she was over his death, she'd earn an Academy Award."

"True. I was there. Both girls were both really broken up, if I recall correctly. But they always say, follow the money. Money, love, revenge, hiding something. Those are the main motives for murder. Stopping to consider the money motive, there are several people who benefit from Makoa's death. Torque has a big payout on his life insurance, his father is going to get three million in badly needed cash, and his girlfriend is cleaning up, too. It's beginning to look like Makoa was worth more dead than alive."

"Just for the sake of argument, I'm going with the love and revenge motives. Say Makoa had something going on with Pippa, as you suggested. Or, he was going to ask Shayla to marry him but now has feelings for Pippa, so popping the question is on hold. He tells Pippa not to say anything; that he's going to break up with Shayla on Maui this weekend. Shayla gets wind of it somehow; she enlists her ex, Tadeo, who ropes Oulaki into doing the deed. So we have three of four major motives covered: money, love, revenge."

They sat for a long moment.

"I'm thinking we need to reinterview these girls pretty closely," Lei said. "Show them both the ring. See what pops. And I need to dig a little deeper here. See if I can find anyone else to say anything about Pippa and Makoa's relationship."

Pono sighed. "I don't like this new direction."

"Me neither." Lei took a long swig of beer. It burned going down as she thought of the two girls, crying in each other's arms. One of them might have betrayed the other in the worst possible way. "And that's not the only motive I've found here. There's the North Shore Posse." She described the hate mail and her encounter at the beach that evening.

"I don't like you stirring the shit without backup," Pono said brusquely. "Make sure Kamuela's with you next time you go fishing for information, or I'll sic Stevens on you."

"Funny." Lei rolled down the blinds. "But what do you think of the Posse having motive?"

"Pretty thin. If it was them, more likely it would be some beachfront beat down in front of their home break and posted on YouTube. I can't see something like what happened to Makoa at his home break being their style."

"Agree." She found herself using Kamuela's terse comment. "Well, with any luck at all, I'll be home tomorrow. Talk soon."

She hung up, still thinking about Shayla and Pippa, crying in each other's arms over the same man.

CHAPTER THIRTEEN

LEI WAS DOWN at the surf break at the crack of dawn, looking around and unobtrusively taking photos of the team house, the surfers on the deck, and the crowd that began to gather as the sun broke over the heaving ocean on another day of pristine surf.

The sand was damp and cool, its golden color muted in the early light. Silvery mist rose above the glassy ocean, the exhaled breath of spent waves condensing above the breaks. Lei wished she had a board and more time; it was smaller today, and she was pretty sure she could handle one of the smaller peaks at Pupukea. But this was work, and she didn't have much longer on the island.

Lei didn't set her tripod up this time. Instead, while she waited for the lifeguards to arrive at the big yellow shuttered tower, she shot the faces of the gathering observers and the denizens of the team house as they rose. When the lifeguards arrived, she approached them, quickly identifying Eddie Nanaio, whom Kamuela had introduced her to the previous day.

Nanaio's eyes lit up, giving her an approving once-over as she approached the tower, gesturing for him to come down to speak with her.

"Looking fine, Detective," he said with a grin, coming down the stairs.

"Thank you." Lei grinned back. "I'm just trying to pick up gossip about Makoa. I was wondering if you know or heard of anything about his love life."

"I knew he was having a thing with two girls."

Lei's pulse raced at this confirmation. "Really? Tell me more."

Eddie, rolling up a rope attached to a float device, sat on the step with an air of settling in to a story. "Both beautiful Maui girls who would follow him over. Friends. It seemed like he was with Shayla, the darker one. But then we started seeing him with Pippa, the blonde, and we didn't see Shayla come to Oahu anymore. He'd go back to Maui, and the story was, he'd see Shayla there. But the blonde, she came to Oahu all the time for work and he saw her here."

"What does she do for work?"

"Heard it was modeling. Catalogs, bathing suits. Like that."

"Shayla, too. So do you know which one he was really with?" Lei frowned.

"Both of them. Pippa here, Shayla on Maui." The older lifeguard tipped back his head to laugh. "Oh, that boy was in a world of trouble."

"Well, when we interviewed them at the scene, Shayla was very clearly presented as his girlfriend and Pippa as her BFF," Lei said. "So it seems like one of them is in the dark about this arrangement."

Nanaio shook his head. "No. They all knew about it. I saw the three of them together plenty of times. I think they had a story they all agreed to for the public. But he was with both girls, if you know what I mean. Sometimes together." He waggled eyebrows fuzzy as caterpillars suggestively.

Lei snorted. "Fo' reals?"

"Fo' reals." The lifeguard finished wrapping the rope around the float and hung it from the steep metal stairs. "Andy! Come tell her about Makoa's ladies."

"Oh, he had it going on with those two bikini models," Andy, the younger lifeguard, confirmed. "We'd give him shit about it once in a while after we saw him hanging out with one or the other, sometimes both of them. He just said we were jealous. And we were."

"So if you had to pick which girl he'd pop the question to, which would it be?" Lei asked.

They both shook their heads. "Depends if you like blondes or brunettes more." Nanaio grinned.

"Oh God," Lei said, and flapped a hand in disgust. "This is no joking matter."

"Well, then, my money's on Pippa," the younger lifeguard said, with unexpected gravity. "They laughed a lot. Seemed like friends as well as lovers. I think he liked her more."

"My money's on the brunette, Shayla," Nanaio said. "She was the alpha of the three." He went on to describe several anecdotes where Shayla had called for sunscreen on her back, or to move to a different spot on the beach, and the others had gone along. "If anyone was getting a ring, it was her. She called the shots."

Lei frowned thoughtfully. "Thanks, both of you. I may need to talk with you again." She walked away, heading down the beach toward the team house. It was time to bring Kamuela in on this information. She took out her cell and called him with her interesting news.

"Pick me up at the team house. I want to check out what Cantor and Oulaki have to say about Makoa's girlfriends."

LEI AND KAMUELA sat with Pete Cantor in the back office where they'd done yesterday's interviews. Lei tugged her cover-up shirt lower on her thighs, wishing she'd taken the time to go back to the house and change into more appropriate clothes, but time was wasting. Now that she had this lead, she was eager to get back to Maui and follow up with the girls.

Lei started off open-ended. "Tell us more about Makoa's life here in the team house."

"Makoa was disciplined. Not a partier. Some of the guys, once their heat is over for an event, they're cracking out the beer and calling up chicks. Not Makoa. He trained for his events," Cantor said. He looked stressed—bloodshot eyes, his hair in disarray. "He never cut loose."

"What about when his girlfriends visited?" Lei asked as if she knew all about both Shayla and Pippa's involvement with the surf star.

"They were supportive. They both understood his career demands."

"Which one did you see more of, here at the house?"

"Pippa. I got that was the arrangement. He was dating both of them, but they'd worked it out that Shayla was his public main squeeze, and Pippa was company for him on Oahu."

Lei felt the hairs on the back of her neck rise. "So how did he pull off such an unusual arrangement?"

Pete shrugged. "It's not that unusual for a pro athlete to get plenty of attention and have multiple partners. At least these girls were friends. We never had any drama."

"Do other guys on the team have this kind of 'arrangement'?" Lei made air quotes around the phrase.

"Not a steady situation like Makoa had, no. Most are dating multiple chicks or have a steady girl." Pete tipped his head forward, rubbing the back of his neck in embarrassment. "You don't know the kind of attention these guys get. They're the Hawaii version of football players. We get women showing up at the house in nothing but a beach towel. I do my best to keep everything safe and sane around here, because I want the guys performing their best. So I was happy Makoa had those girls and they'd worked something out between them. No jealous scenes or catfights throwing off his concentration." Lei didn't like the picture he painted, or his tone. Time to provoke him a bit.

"I see why you're single with that kind of attitude toward women," Lei said. Her potshot hit the target, because Pete's face darkened.

"Who says I'm single? Sluts and hos are a dime a dozen," he growled. "They just interfere with the guys' focus."

"Alrighty, then," Kamuela chimed in, smacking his thighs. "We get the picture. But now that Makoa's dead, we're interested in motive for his murder. What kinds of reasons occur to you?"

"I don't know." Cantor looked down, his throat working. "We have the paddle out in a few hours. I'm doing the best I can just to deal with all the fallout from his death. Frankly, I can't stand to think of it for long."

"I'd like to come to the paddle out," Lei said. "I need to observe."

Cantor handed her a half sheet of printed paper. "It's too rough here at Pipeline, so we're going out at Waimea Bay. The surf is down, so it will be mellow."

Lei took the flyer. "We may need to talk with you again. Please send Bryan Oulaki in."

"He's not here." Cantor stood up and pushed his chair back in. "He had to go in to Honolulu for a photo shoot."

"So he's not at the paddle out," Lei said. "How convenient."

Cantor didn't reply, just went out of the office and shut the door a little harder than necessary.

"That was interesting," Kamuela said. "Got anyone else you want to speak to?"

"No. I'm going to that paddle out, and then I'll go back to Maui. I'm eager to get those girls in a room and see what they have to say."

※

THE AQUA WATER of Waimea Bay, sparkling with sunshine, gave lie to the sad occasion of Makoa's paddle out as Lei, with Kamuela beside her, launched her rented longboard over the looming shore break. She churned her arms to get over the mountain of white-water and far enough out not to take the next wave on her head. Adrenaline pumped through her system, energizing her as she joined the straggling host of surfers heading out to the middle of the bay.

Glancing ahead, she recognized two gorgeous women in bikinis paddling toward the circle of surfers that was forming—Shayla and Pippa, neck-deep in leis.

Of course they are here. She wasn't going to have to go back to Maui to talk to them after all.

Lei and Kamuela pulled up and sat on their boards in the floating circle. Talking was going on between friends and acquaintances; Lei kept her gaze moving around the circle, taking note of many famous surfers and influencers in that tight-knit community.

Kamuela had brought her a small waterproof camera; she held it unobtrusively near her waist and shot photos of the people gathering in the circle.

It felt great to be in the water, even for this somber occasion. Lei sat on her board, only partly submerged, the warm sea lapping at her thighs. The deep green valley felt like welcoming arms surrounding them, and Lei could see the other half of the ceremony, onlookers, supporters, and friends, gathering on the beach.

She wished she wasn't here at the memorial on the job, but it was necessary. She glanced over at Kamuela.

He sat upright on his board, floating with the supple grace of a surfer waiting for a wave, his body gleaming with beads of water. But when he met her eyes, his were all cop. He scanned the circle with a hard, alert stare that took everything in and gave nothing away.

When the circle was several hundred strong, everyone occa-

sionally adjusting their position by paddling, the *kahu* priest offici-
ating from a nearby canoe blew a conch three times.

Silence fell over the circle as the blaring yet haunting notes
echoed across land and sea, and spontaneously the surfers reached
for one another's hands. The circle drew tighter and closer, a
changing mandala on the surface of the water. As Lei held
Kamuela's hand on one side and a stranger's hand on the other
beside her, she felt a ripple of powerful connection between the
people here and the ocean that nurtured them.

The *kahu* blew the conch one more time, and then the group
closest to the canoe, whom Lei identified as other Torque team
riders, Oulaki obviously missing, raised their clasped hands in
the air.

"Makoa! Makoa! Makoa!" they cried. The chant of the young
man's name was taken up by everyone, hands clasped and raised in
the air.

Lei felt the tears she'd been holding back since the moment
she'd seen the magnificent young body on the beach at Ho`okipa
spill to join the salty moisture of the ocean on her cheeks. She let
the tears come, and tilted her face back toward the sun.

Finally, the cries of his name died down, and the *kahu* began to
chant, the vibrating tones of Hawaii's rich native language joined
by the percussion of an *ipu* on the canoe. The mesmerizing sound
was magnified across the water and reflected back by the crowds
on the shore.

Lei kept her eyes on the team riders and Makoa's girlfriends.
They held hands even when everyone else let go, leaning in to each
other and weeping quietly in the lee of the canoe.

After the chant, spontaneous stories broke out around the
circle. Stories of Makoa's best rides at Pipe, of his grom days on
Maui, and of his generosity to others. Lei's skin shivered with the
breeze on the water and an overdose of emotion, with grief that
reminded her of all her own losses: her baby, her beloved aunt, her

grandmother and mother, her home, burned to the ground with all she owned.

But here she was, still alive.

Finally, the ceremony wrapped up with a beautiful rendering of "Over the Rainbow" played on ukulele and sung by a Hawaiian musician seated in the canoe with the *kahu*. One final cheer and chant of Makoa's name, and the lei and flowers worn by everyone were tossed in the center of the circle. They floated on the water, a fragrant offering.

Lei photographed that moment as best she could, looking for anything unusual, but there was nothing to see but heartfelt, bitter-sweet grief and love on the faces of those around her. The circle broke up as everyone turned and paddled back in, laughter and talk resuming with the release of emotion.

"I have to grab those girls," Lei muttered in an aside to Kamuela, spotting Makoa's girlfriends still floating by the canoe. "Let's wait for them on the beach."

"Mean," he said, teasing.

"It's the job. Get 'em while they're down and emotional. We'll get more out of them. They should have told us about their 'arrangement' with Makoa when we interviewed them on Maui."

The relentless drive to nail the one responsible for this heart-break rose up in Lei. She would grieve by getting justice for one taken too soon.

CHAPTER FOURTEEN

THAT MORNING PONO had e-mailed Lei the press release MPD had issued, citing "suspicious circumstances" in Makoa Simmons's death. Knowing exactly what the public knew was helpful as Lei waited for Shayla and Pippa on the beach. She listened to the swirl of conversation among the knots of people, and much of the conversation centered on who the punk was that had dropped in on Makoa and caused his death.

"I like pound that punk wen' stuff Makoa in the barrel on Maui," one burly local growled.

Lei frowned, watching the girls slowly paddle in, talking to each other and to the people surrounding them. Maybe it was a stretch that one of these clearly grief-stricken girls was involved in Makoa's death, but her gut was telling her otherwise.

Shayla and Pippa spotted Lei and Kamuela before they got to shore, but they had to pay attention to the surf to make it in past the shore break without getting ragdolled up the beach.

They both handled themselves well in the water, and Lei smiled warmly as they came up from the surf, carrying their boards. "Shayla! Pippa! Just the women we need to see. Can you spare a few minutes to talk with Detective Kamuela and me? Some new information has come to light in Makoa's case."

They glanced at each other. "Does it have to be right now? There's a party in Makoa's honor happening at the Torque team house," Shayla said. Her eyes were red-rimmed, but otherwise there was no sign she'd been crying. Her sleek dark hair clung to her perfect figure like skeins of wet silk. Pippa, on the other hand, was red-nosed and puffy-eyed, wearing no makeup. Her body was stunning even in the plain black tank suit she wore.

"I'm sorry for the timing. We'll try to be as quick as possible. Can you come with us?"

The girls made a few quick phone calls, wrapped up in towels, and the four of them climbed into Kamuela's extended cab truck.

"Where are we going?" Shayla asked. Lei remembered Nanaio had described her as the "alpha" of the two.

"We have some items to show you that we found among Makoa's personal things," Lei said. "They're stored at the Kahuku Police Station." She didn't want to give them any idea that they were anything but witnesses.

The girls put their heads together, and Lei pretended not to hear them whispering as Kamuela drove along the winding, picturesque road, ending at the barracks-like police station.

Lei waited with them as Kamuela, with his Oahu connections, went into the station to request use of two interview rooms. Once he came to the door and nodded, Lei gestured to the girls. "I'll need to speak with each of you privately," she said gently. "I hope you don't mind." Shayla frowned as she went into the battered-looking interview room with its bolted-down metal table and dirty plastic chairs.

"I have to wait in here?" She put her hands on her hips.

"Just for a few minutes," Lei said, and closed the door behind her firmly.

She led Pippa to the other room while Kamuela retrieved the box of Makoa's clothing with the ring in it.

Following her gut, she decided to interview Pippa first, as she looked the most vulnerable. She sat down with Pippa in the second interview room, no nicer than the first. The young woman had put on a caftan-like cover-up in lurid tie-dye colors, and once again Lei had the impression she was downplaying her looks.

"How are you holding up?" Lei asked.

"Okay." Pippa plucked at a fraying braided cord around her wrist, rubbing it back and forth. Following a hunch, Lei asked, "Is that a friendship bracelet?"

"Yes." Pippa glanced up, her blue eyes filling. "Makoa gave it to me."

As if on cue, Kamuela came into the room carrying a box. "We have some things that were packed up from Makoa's room at the Torque house. We were wondering if you could help us identify who they go to," Lei said. She and Kamuela had decided on this tack ahead of time. She opened the flaps of the box and withdrew a stack of neatly folded shirts.

"His mom can have those back," Pippa said. "But I'd like this one." She set her hand on a white T-shirt with a MᴀᴜɪBᴜɪʟᴛ logo on it. "I gave it to him." Her eyes filled again.

"So it seems like you two were close," Lei said.

"Yes. Um—we didn't tell you the whole situation the first time when you talked to us. I was in shock. I couldn't think how to explain it to you." Pippa picked up the T-shirt and crossed her arms over her chest, hugging it to her. "Makoa and I were seeing each other."

"But I thought Shayla was his girlfriend," Lei said, frowning as if this were news.

"We were both his girlfriends." Pippa's cheeks reddened as she looked at Lei defiantly. "We both loved him. And he loved us."

"Wow. That's unusual. Did everyone agree to this?"

"Yes."

"Tell me how it got started."

Pippa looked down. "He was going out with Shayla. But as

time went on, I realized I was falling in love with him, and he had feelings for me, too. He was going to break up with Shayla, but when we sat down and talked, Shayla said it was okay. She loves us both, and why couldn't we all stay together?" Pippa sniffed and rubbed her eye with the heel of a hand. "So we did."

Lei reached into the box and took out the little paper evidence bag, shook the black velvet box out onto the table. "I found this in the pocket of Makoa's dress slacks." She popped the ring box open and the diamond sparkled, large and fiery, in the overhead lights. "I only see one ring here. Who was he going to ask to marry him?"

Pippa turned white, her eyes rolled back, and she tilted to the side, slumping off the chair in a dead faint. Kamuela managed to catch her before she hit the floor. "Get a pillow or something! We have to elevate her feet!"

Lei opened the door and hollered into the hall for assistance. Pippa came around a few minutes later. They'd covered her with the beach towel and elevated her feet on a thick phone book.

"Oh my God. This is so embarrassing," she murmured. The tan of her skin lay like yellow paint over her pale cheeks.

"Are you pregnant?" Lei whispered, prompted by intuition.

Pippa shut her eyes. "Yes." Fat tears leaked out from beneath her lids. "I haven't told anyone but Makoa."

"Did he ask you to marry him?"

The girl shook her head. "No."

"So you don't know if that ring was meant for you."

The tears flowed faster. "He said the situation had to change, after I told him. He said he'd known for a while it had to change. But he didn't say he was going home this weekend to break up with Shayla. She'd be devastated if he broke up with her because I got pregnant."

"So you don't think…" Lei let her voice trail off, hoping the girl would say something more definitive.

"I think he wanted us all to talk about it, decide what to do. I told him no matter what, I was going to have this baby." She crossed her hands over her flat abdomen in a protective gesture Lei recognized with a pulse of remembered pain.

"How long ago was this conversation?"

"Last week. Thursday. He was going home to Maui Friday. I was going back to Maui Saturday. I had a shoot. I knew I had to get in as much work as I could before I started showing." She stared at the ceiling. "I really don't know what I'm going to do without him." The tears brimming in her eyes spilled.

"Did he say he was going to tell Shayla? Had you told her?" Lei asked

"He said not to tell her, that he would do it. That it was his responsibility. She's going to hate it." Lei saw Pippa's throat muscles move as the girl swallowed.

"Was he happy about the baby?"

More tears trickled down Pippa's cheeks. "He was surprised at first, but then really seemed to get happy about it. He was so sweet to me."

"A witness saw you two talking outside the team house in the early morning before he left for Maui. What day would that have been?"

"That was Friday morning. I told him the night before. We had an incredible night together; then he said he had to go to Maui and tell Shayla. We were arguing because I wanted to tell her. I knew she was going to feel betrayed if he was the one who told her and not me."

Lei frowned. "That doesn't make sense to me. He was the father of the baby. He was sleeping with both of you."

"Yes, but Shayla's my best friend." Pippa turned her blue eyes to Lei. "We tell each other everything."

Lei suspected this was not at all true. "Still. The witness said it seemed like you were arguing."

"Yes, a little. Because I wanted to tell her and he insisted he would. He said he needed to deal with her."

"Deal with her. An interesting phrase. Is that exactly what he said?"

"Yes." Pippa looked at Lei again. "Do you think he told her? She hasn't said a word to me, or acted any different. I can't bear to tell her now that he's gone. She's going to hate me."

"I don't know if he told her. But I'm going to ask her. Now, one last time. I need to know who that ring was for. Dig deep, Pippa, and tell me. I promise it won't get back to Shayla, whatever you say."

Pippa gazed at Lei for a long moment, and her eyes were perfectly dry when she finally said, "Me. He loved me more. And with the baby coming, I think he would have asked me to marry him."

And then she shut her eyes, opened her mouth, and wailed, a terrible cry of grief and loss that shuddered through and around Lei and filled the room with the agony of a broken heart.

Lei froze, unable to move, feeling the sound batter at her own fragile reserves. Marcus Kamuela was the one to draw the young woman up against his shoulder and pat her back soothingly, shushing her like a child as Lei withdrew out into the hall.

Lei walked into the women's room and splashed water on her face. She took some relaxation breaths: in through her nose, out through her mouth. Tried to imagine finding out she was pregnant and dealing with it alone, with Stevens murdered.

Her mind shied away from a horror too great to bear.

She bought a little more time by changing out of her still-damp suit and cover-up into clothing from the backpack she'd made sure was packed from the vacation rental. Back in jeans and a button-down shirt, her badge and gun in place, she felt better able to face Shayla.

Lei pushed rioting curls back from her face and bundled them into a rubber band. With her hair pulled back and the weight she'd lost since her miscarriage, the face that looked back at her from the mirror seemed all eyes and mouth, the cheekbones high and stark, freckles standing out across her nose.

She put a little lipstick and mascara on, hoping that would help balance things.

It didn't.

Finally, done stalling, she tightened her shoulder holster, washed her hands, and strode out.

LEI BROUGHT a glass of water in to Shayla, who was sitting at the table, playing with her phone. "Sorry for the wait."

"Who was that screaming?" Shayla's golden tan looked jaundiced under the harsh lighting. "It sounded serious."

"Nothing to worry about." Lei sat herself across from Shayla. "Detective Kamuela will be along in a moment with some items we'd like you to identify from Makoa's things at the Torque team house."

"Okay."

"Did you come over here often? Spend much time at the house?"

"Not really. I'd come over for big contests, to give support. But no. Usually he visited me at my house, when he came home." Shayla clearly considered Maui not just her home, but Makoa's.

"Would you consider yourself and Makoa close?"

"Definitely." Shayla folded her arms across her shapely bosom.

"What kind of relationship would you say you had?" Lei kept her voice neutral, but Shayla drew her brows together.

"What's this about?"

"We've heard rumors that you weren't Makoa's only girlfriend."

"You've heard about Pippa, then," Shayla stated. "I guess I should have told you when you came to the house with the sketch artist, but we were so upset, I didn't think of it. Besides, how is it relevant to the investigation?"

A long beat went by as they eyed each other, and finally Lei asked gently, "Do you want me to spell it out?"

Shayla dropped her eyes and covered her face with her hands. Lei had the feeling she was seeing a deliberate shift in behavior, and sure enough, the shoulders that had been thrown defiantly back hunched inward, and she trembled as if with a sob.

"It's all been too much," she said, her voice muffled by her hands. "I know the situation we had going was weird to people, but it worked for us."

"Shayla, I'd really like to understand it from your perspective. Just tell me how it came about. Help me understand how it worked for you." Feeding back the witnesses' own words to them helped create a connection, a sense of being understood, and sure enough, Shayla lowered her hands. Her big brown eyes were glossy with tears, and her full lips trembled.

"I had Makoa first. He was my boyfriend. But then Pippa, who works on Oahu a lot more than me, began hanging around with him. Just friends, I thought—but it had become something more. I love Pippa and I love Makoa. I didn't want to lose them both, especially to each other. So I said, why don't we just share?" She blinked, and fat tears rolled out of her eyes. "So we did. It worked for us." The phrase had begun to sound like a mantra.

As if on cue, Kamuela came in with the same cardboard box of Makoa's things that they'd shown Pippa. He set the box on the table. "Here are some of Makoa's things that Pete at the Torque house packed up," Lei said, taking out the stack of T-shirts.

Shayla scooped up a blue one, pressed it to her face. "Can I keep this?" she asked.

"Sure. We were taking the rest back to Maui, to his parents. But there was one more thing we found." Lei reached into the box and took out the small, black velvet box.

Shayla's mouth opened, and she reached over and took the ring box, flipping it open. She covered her mouth with her hand, and tears filled her eyes as she looked at the sparkling diamond. "Oh my God. He was going to ask me to marry him."

Lei blinked, glanced at Kamuela. The scene with Pippa was so fresh it was hard to process Shayla's confident statement. "So...he hadn't talked to you about this?"

"No. But I'm sure he was just waiting for the right time to ask me. He told me the morning he was killed that he had something important to talk to me about." Shayla took the ring out, slid it onto her finger as her eyes welled, and Lei couldn't help contrasting Pippa's raw grief to Shayla's pretty tears. Which display of emotion could be hiding a murderer?

"What about Pippa?" Lei couldn't help asking.

Shayla wiped her eyes with the back of her hand, still gazing at the ring. "We'd have worked something out."

"Come on." Lei snorted. "I would sooner gut another woman than share my husband. You're telling me you'd let him keep Pippa? Because from the reports we heard, you were the one getting edged out and that ring was for her."

Shayla's dark eyes flared wide, and Lei glimpsed the steely will that gave the girl her dominating personality.

"No way," she said confidently. "Okay, you're right. I wouldn't be willing to share Makoa once we were married. "

"Did Makoa ask you to marry him? Tell you anything important this weekend, before he was killed?"

"No, but he told me we had something important to discuss. He was taking me to dinner the night he was killed." She swiveled her hand back and forth, watching the light play on the diamonds. "Can I keep this?"

"Take it off. It's evidence," Kamuela growled from his side of the table. Lei could tell he didn't like Shayla's cavalier attitude.

Shayla removed the ring and put it back in the box. Lei could tell it was hard for her to part with it, as the young woman slowly shut the lid. Lei leaned forward, her eyes hard on the other woman's face, feeling like a matador baiting a bull as she said, "Makoa *was* going to tell you something important before he was killed. Pippa is pregnant."

Shayla recoiled as if slapped. "Pippa wouldn't try to steal him from me with the oldest trick in the book! Where is that bitch?" Shayla shot to her feet, knocking the chair over behind her.

"Sit down!" Kamuela grabbed her arm and bent it, and Shayla sat, glaring, but now Lei drilled into her.

"That bitch, huh? For all we know, you're lying and Makoa told you Pippa was pregnant, that he was breaking up with you. So you called your ex Eli Tadeo to help you out with a problem."

"No!" Shayla exclaimed, jumping up again. "Pippa was just a convenience. Someone for him to bang on Oahu. I figured it was better the friend you know than the enemy you don't, so I went along with it. But he didn't love her, not like he loved me." Lei and Kamuela glanced at each other, but there was no stopping Shayla now that she'd gotten started. "Pippa had it bad for him, though. She would do anything to be with him, including this ploy to try to nab a ring, now that he's gone. I bet she said he was going to ask her to marry him because she was pregnant."

"That was one possibility we were exploring, yes," Lei said. "But it's easy enough to check out her story. We'll just ask her to take a pregnancy test."

"Even if she is pregnant, it's because she trapped him," Shayla said. "That ring is mine. He was mine."

"So much for an arrangement that works for everyone," Lei said dryly. "It's amazing you were able to keep this going for as long as you did. And now I don't believe either of you." Lei took the ring box, put it back in the box of clothing. "We'll talk again. Do you and Pippa need a ride back to the party at the team house?"

"We had one until you brought us out here," Shayla said sullenly, following Lei to the door and out in the hall. She spotted Pippa sitting in a waiting area near the front door and darted past Lei, launching herself at the other woman.

"You bitch!" The sound of Shayla slapping Pippa's face rang through the small station. Lei got ahold of Shayla by the shoulders and hauled her back, twisting an arm up behind the girl in a restraint hold. Pippa jumped up off the bench and went for Shayla.

"You're the bitch and always were! I should never have gone along with your sick ideas!"

Kamuela, who had been stowing the box in the evidence room, reached Pippa just as she slugged Shayla, knocking the other girl back into Lei's arms.

They got handcuffs on both women and escorted them to Kamuela's truck, where he put Shayla in the back of the pickup and Pippa inside. Leaden silence filled the vehicle as they drove back to the Torque team house.

"Are you two calmed down enough to go to the memorial party?" Lei asked after they arrived at the crowded beach house. "Or do we need to book you both into jail for a cooling-off period?"

Shayla straightened up in the bed of the truck. Even with wind-whipped hair and handcuffs on, she managed to look like she was ready to appear on the cover of *Sports Illustrated*. "I'm done. Done speaking to that lying whore." She narrowed her eyes at Pippa.

In reply, Pippa, who had been looking green as Lei helped her out of the back of the truck, bent over and vomited in front of Shayla. Some of the warm, acrid-smelling vomit splashed on Shayla's feet, and the other woman squealed, leaping back in repulsion.

Kamuela hauled Shayla farther up the driveway before uncuffing her, while Lei helped Pippa sit down on the grass. She took off the handcuffs. "Are you okay?"

"I don't ever want to see her again," Pippa said. "I just want to go home. But I live with her."

"Well, we have another stop to make, but I'm going back to Maui. You could get a ride with us to the airport, or find another way there," Lei found herself offering.

"I'd like that. If I get home before Shayla, I can get my stuff out of the house."

"Okay. Let me ask Detective Kamuela." Lei left Pippa rubbing her wrists by the truck and rejoined Kamuela, walking back from the house. "So much for no catfights or drama," she said. "Can we give Pippa a ride back to the airport? I don't want to leave them both here, and she wants to get her stuff out of the apartment they share."

"Sure. Thought you had another stop."

"Yeah. I want to go by the store where the ring was purchased and find out when Makoa bought it."

They walked back to the truck to see Pippa talking to Bryan Oulaki. The young man had a hand against the truck beside the girl and their heads were close together. Lei went on high alert and felt Kamuela stiffen beside her as well. Pippa looked up at their approach, and her eyes were streaming.

"Bryan said he would take me to the airport."

"Okay," Lei said, keeping her voice soft and sympathetic, though this evidence that Pippa knew Bryan, their strongest suspect, bore close attention. "Have you known each other long?"

Bryan straightened up defensively. "Since Makoa introduced us. I just want to help out. Pippa's been through a lot."

"Okay. You sure, Pippa? It would be easy for us to take you." Lei didn't know why exactly she was reluctant to leave Pippa with the young man. Maybe it didn't mean anything that they knew each other, that he wanted to take her to the airport.

But maybe it was important.

Pippa wiped her eyes. "I don't want to get in your way. I appreciate Bryan offering."

Lei and Kamuela left the couple and got into Kamuela's truck.

"Interesting," said Kamuela.

"Yeah. Want to hear my favorite theory?"

"I do."

Lei clicked her seat belt into place as they backed out of the crowded driveway. "Here's what I think happened. Makoa got to Maui and told Shayla right away. She pretended to be okay with it, the way she's pretended to be okay with it all along. But she called her ex, Tadeo, and he came out to the break where Makoa was surfing and did the deed. Tadeo matches the description of the guy the surfers who rescued Makoa said they saw. I no longer believe anything Shayla says. She denies that it was Tadeo; but she's the one who provided the description and claims to have seen the guy when the whole story about the van could have been to throw us off, a red herring. That sketch turned out to be so generic it could be half the guys on the North Shore."

"Or," Kamuela said, navigating the turn back onto crowded Kamehameha Highway. "It could have been Oulaki. Pippa finds out Makoa's going to ask Shayla to marry him no matter that she's pregnant, if she even is. She calls Oulaki and tells him. Oulaki also matches the description Shayla gave. He goes over, rents the van, does the deed, and comes back to Oahu. Now he gets the girl he's wanted and his rival out of the way, and with this theory, Pippa may or may not be involved at all."

"I like Shayla more for it. She's cold under those pretty tears. Cold, and sure she's superior. Those are some of the necessary ingredients for murder."

"Let's not forget that neither of these girls actually killed him."

"No, but that ring is motive. Just like I thought it might be, and Shayla has a stronger motive," Lei argued. "She has money on the line in the form of that life insurance policy. She has both money and revenge to kill Makoa. Pippa might have been first in his heart, but Shayla was first on paper."

"So what do you want to do next?"

"Let's go to the store and find out what we can about that ring, then go get both girls' phone records and run down their phone calls on the day Makoa was killed."

CHAPTER FIFTEEN

LEI SAT on the plane back to Maui, sorting through the cell phone records that Kamuela had been able to get printed up at his station before he dropped her off at the airport. In the end, she was glad she hadn't had Pippa along for the ride when they went to the jewelry store, where she found out the ring had been purchased two months before Makoa's murder, pushing the timeline of his intentions toward either of the girls back into the unknown zone. Whatever he'd been planning to do with the ring had preceded Pippa's announcement, which still needed to be verified—but Lei didn't think the girl was acting, with all her emotions and symptoms.

Lei focused on the day Makoa had been killed. His fateful drowning had happened on Saturday morning, so she looked for numbers called by both girls on Friday evening and Saturday morning, and cross-checked them with Eli Tadeo's and Bryan Oulaki's phone records. She spotted Bryan Oulaki's number on Pippa's records as an incoming call on Friday night.

So Oulaki called Pippa, not the other way around. Now she had something to follow up on.

Shayla's records were less revealing. No calls Friday night or

Saturday until after Makoa's drowning. Lei felt a twinge of disappointment and looked out the round oval window at the rapidly approaching, corrugated green coastline of Maui. She liked Shayla as the force behind this murder: for the way she'd revealed her real attitude toward Pippa, for her confident grab at the ring, for the steely will she'd shown when looking into Lei's eyes.

But none of that made the woman a murderer, and with virtually no trace on or around the body, this case was going to be made on a confession or a strong enough circumstantial argument. And whatever had sparked the murder, neither girl had actually held Makoa under.

That was someone else. Someone with a deep enough rage, spite, greed, or jealousy to take another man's life in broad daylight, in front of witnesses.

The plane bounced around as it often did coming in on Maui in the glow of sunset, the gusty wind generated by the deep valley of the central area of the island lifting the plane with some stomach-dropping bumps that made the passengers around her gasp. Lei leaned her forehead on the window, watching the sugarcane fields rising to meet them, and remembered the hijacking of months before.

But surprisingly, it didn't bother her. Not nearly as much as the looseness at the waistline of her jeans, the emptiness under the hand that rested there.

Pono met her at the curb after she collected her weapon and the boxes of Makoa's belongings. The ring she'd kept close, in her backpack.

"Hey, partner." Pono took a box from her, put it in the extended cab. They piled the rest in the back. "How was Oahu?"

"Busy. Got some good leads. You?"

"Finally tracked Eli Tadeo. He has an alibi for the time in question."

"Shit," Lei said, hopping up onto the chrome step that led into the cab of the truck. "I have a new theory and I want it to be him."

She told Pono her theory about Shayla as they wound through the busy traffic of downtown toward Kahului Station.

"Motive she might have, but without any record of her contacting Tadeo, and with Tadeo at community baseball practice with his brother, Eric, our MPD poster boy, that theory's not going anywhere." Pono pushed his ever-present Oakleys up with a thick finger, and there was a deep dent between his black brows. "I did my best to smooth over the questioning with Eli, but Eric and his wife are pretty pissed."

"Screw them. It's a murder investigation of a high-profile guy," Lei said. "If Eric Tadeo can't get the stick out of his ass enough to understand that, he doesn't deserve the job he's got."

"You're cranky," Pono said with a quick glance at her as they pulled into the parking lot of the utilitarian downtown station.

"I've been away from my family for two days working a case with virtually no hard evidence popping and way too many people with motive. We still have a lot of leads to track, and I really just want to get home, have a shower, and see my baby and husband." Lei opened the door and jumped out of the truck. "But that's not happening anytime soon."

She took a moment to call Stevens as they walked into the station, where Pono said they had a meeting to debrief with Captain Omura, and was surprised when the phone went to voice mail—he'd usually pick up for her, especially after not talking this long. She paused before the big automatic doors to formulate her message.

"Hey, honey. I miss you like crazy, but we've had some interesting developments on the Simmons case. I'm on Maui, meeting with the captain to bring her up to speed, and we have some stuff to process and set up for tomorrow, so I won't be home until later —but at least I'll be home tonight. Hope you found your mom. I love you."

Lei ended the call and walked through the doors to her meeting.

STEVENS FELT the phone vibrate against his side and it semi-woke him, but he couldn't gather the motor skills to actually deal with it. Lying facedown on the air mattress in the tent, he felt a dark wave of shame roll over him.

Along with the need to puke.

He crawled to the flap of the tent and barely unzipped it in time to get his head outside. He vomited violently, a little of the Scotch he hadn't absorbed coming back up and burning his throat and nostrils even more unpleasantly than it had going down.

He heaved some more, but nothing came up. He fell backward to sit clutching his head, which felt like it was being stabbed through the temples. He crawled back to the mattress and along the way encountered a gallon jug of water and a bottle of aspirin, along with knocking his knee against the empty Scotch bottle.

When he was able to sit up, very slowly and carefully, he took several aspirin and washed them down with water. He drank as much as he could hold and lay back carefully.

Wayne must have put the water and aspirin out for him.

Shame returned, doubled as he thought of his father-in-law finding him that way, probably carrying baby Kiet and worried. He imagined Wayne looking at him lying facedown in the tent, fully clothed, with the empty bottle.

Shit-faced drunk like his worthless mother.

When the memories of all he'd seen, done, and touched in his life overtook him as they had last night, there was nothing he could think to do to shut them up other than drink them into oblivion. Because he was a branch off the same tree as his mother. All his activities were just an attempt to deflect his destiny for another day and mask the rottenness that hid behind his efforts to make the world a better place.

At least he'd remembered in those wee hours to call his station and tell them he was sick.

Sometime later, he cracked his eyelids again and looked through the screen across the lawn. The stand of citrus trees on the property shielded the tent from the cottage, but he could tell by the slant of the light that most of the day was gone.

He dug the phone out of his pocket, scrolled through missed calls and messages, and listened to the recent one from Lei.

She is coming home tonight. She can't see me like this.

Stevens had a few hours to get himself together. He listened to a message from Jared, asking if he'd found out anything about Ellen's whereabouts.

Mom. *God.* She was what had set him off.

How he wished she'd never come and ignited the tiny hope that something could be different, that she would act like a mother for once, like the grandmother of his child. Do the right thing.

And here he was, falling into the same pit as she had.

He wasn't ready to face Wayne yet. He got up carefully, unzipped the tent, and staggered to the far corner of the yard, where he let fly with a massive pee that seemed to drain everything out of him. Relieved, he went back to the tent, drank more water and took more aspirin, and went to his work shed, where his tools were stored.

It was time for him, Kiet, and Lei to move into the big house. Finished or not, Wayne didn't deserve one more day of having to carry the load and have them all in his meager space. Stevens could finish the master bedroom at least enough to move into, and they could sleep there. The bathroom was at least operational, even if there was no hot water.

Tightening his tool belt around his waist, then zipping a box cutter through the massive cardboard box holding all the unhung interior doors, he felt a tiny bit better.

As always, work would be his absolution.

CHAPTER SIXTEEN

Lᴇɪ ʜᴀᴅ ɴᴇᴠᴇʀ ᴋɴᴏᴡɴ Captain CJ Omura to have a bad hair day. Her sleek bob swung in a curtain of silky black strands that didn't quite touch the immaculate shoulders of her navy uniform jacket as she picked up the ring in its velvet box, turning it back and forth. The one-carat white diamond glared in a sunbeam from the window as Lei and Pono sat on the hard plastic supplicant chairs in front of her shiny black desk.

Lei felt tired and gritty and knew her hair looked like it had been stirred with salad tongs.

"So, you think this is motive?" Captain Omura's dark brown eyes swept over Lei, taking in her travel-worn appearance as she held up the ring box.

"I do. While neither girl was the one to hold him under, they both have people in their lives with reason to want Makoa dead." Lei reviewed the theories she and Kamuela had discussed. "I hear from Pono that Eli Tadeo has an alibi, though, so at this point our favorite suspect is Bryan Oulaki."

"So you think Shayla wasn't telling the truth about the suspect she saw and the van?"

"None of our physical suspects from the van have checked out, and Shayla's an unreliable witness. It could have been Tom Cruise driving a Ferrari for all we know."

"Not quite," Pono chimed in. "We have a corroborating description of a medium-height mixed-race male with black hair from the surfers who tried to save Makoa."

"That's right." Lei turned to Pono with a resurgence of energy. "I think we kind of went down a rabbit hole relying on the sketch from Shayla, but we could go back to those surfers with photos of the four possibilities and see if they can identify him."

"That, and talk to Oulaki again," Omura said. "See why he's been calling Pippa. And get that girl to take a pregnancy test. Report back when something breaks from all of that." She pushed the ring across the desk to Lei.

"Yes, sir." Lei used the moniker Omura had chosen to avoid gender bias and scooped up the ring.

"Whatever happened with those threat letters? That North Shore Posse connection?" Omura asked.

"We don't think they have a connection to the murder at this point," Lei said, after a glance at her partner. "Intimidation and localism—couple of the hazards of surfing."

They dropped the ring off at the evidence locker, and Lei called Pippa on her cell phone as they headed for the door. "Pippa? Did you get out of Shayla's place?"

"Yes. I'm at my parents' house." The girl's voice sounded sluggish, as if Lei had woken her up from a nap.

"Can we come by for a couple of questions?"

"Okay." She gave the address.

"We'll be by in an hour or so." Pono was driving them to the addresses of the two young surfers who had tried to rescue Makoa, and on her lap Lei held license photos of Oulaki and Tadeo mixed in with a variety of other photos of roughly the same description.

Pono glanced over at her as she mixed the photos around and pointed. "Why do you have Eli Tadeo still in there?"

"You said Eric was the one to alibi him at that baseball game.

His twin brother. If it wasn't Eric Tadeo with all his connections and commendations providing the alibi, wouldn't we be poking at it? I want to keep the photo in there. Just in case."

Pono frowned and rubbed his top lip under the bristling mustache, but said no more as he navigated a run-down area of Kahului, Maui's main town. At last they pulled into the driveway of a sprawling family home with a small ohana nearby under a mango tree heavy with sweet-smelling fruit. A pile of surfboards leaning against the sliding glass door marked this as Barrett Sharkey's residence, and the rusting Subaru with racks near the house and the rubber slippers on the mat indicated the young man was home.

Lei tapped on the glass door and involuntarily took a step back as a wide-chested male Rottweiler galloped to the door and barked at them, the deep-voiced Intruder Alert sound Lei was so familiar with.

"Don't see too many Rottweilers around here besides Keiki," Pono said.

"Yeah. He's a beauty." Keiki was large for her breed, but this one was even bigger, at least a hundred and fifty pounds. He had a wide chest and deep brown, intelligent eyes that gleamed with health and vigor. As they continued to stand there, not backing off, the stump of his tail began wagging even as he continued to bark.

Lei was smitten.

Barrett Sharkey came out of a back bedroom, pulling on a T-shirt and yanking the dog back by the collar. His eyes widened in recognition of them. "Let me just put this boy back in the bedroom," he said. "He's not too good with visitors."

Lei watched the young man wrestle the big dog into the bedroom and shut the door. The Rottweiler was still barking when Sharkey slid the glass door open to greet them.

"Hi. I remember you from the beach when Makoa died. What can I do for you?"

"That's a fine dog you have," Lei said. "I have a Rottweiler, too."

"He's a handful. I got him from a friend who was moving off-island, and truth is, I need to find another home for him. Too much dog for me."

Lei's mind raced. Keiki hadn't been herself since the fire three months ago; she'd taken a long time to recover from her burns, but Lei wasn't sure that was the reason her dog seemed so listless and out of sorts. Her Rottweiler almost seemed depressed, and another dog might be just the thing to perk her up.

"Let me talk to my husband. I might be interested," Lei said.

Pono gave her a look and rolled his eyes. "You need another dog like a hole in the head," her partner said.

"Does he have any bad habits?" Lei forged on, intrigued by the handsome dog.

"You've just seen it. He's overprotective. Scares off the girls," Sharkey said, with a charming grin. "But he's all bluster and blow. Never bit anyone that I've heard of. He just needs more work and exercise than I can give him. He's chewing a hole near the door trying to get out." Sharkey pointed to a hole in the drywall.

"What's his name?" Lei asked.

"Conan."

"Conan. And what a barbarian of a dog he is. Come on, Lei." Pono rolled his eyes again, holding up the folder and waving it in front of Sharkey. "Believe it or not, we came here for a reason. We have some suspects we're looking at for the guy in the lineup, and wanted to see if you could help us with an identification."

"Sure." Sharkey moved a couple of empty beer cans off the coffee table and sat beside Pono with the folder. Lei sat on the other side of Sharkey as the young man opened the folder.

Lei had hastily assembled photos she'd printed off of driver's license onto a grid with other random photos. As usual with these things, she felt the gaze of her suspects seeming to glare up at her from the lineup.

"I think I know this guy," Sharkey said, pointing to the photo of Oulaki. "He feels familiar to me."

"Think back to that day," Lei prompted. "Close your eyes. Think of the surfer you saw. Are there any details coming back to you?"

"He had dark hair. A black rash guard and shorts. Brown skin, like a local." Sharkey frowned in concentration, but a loud whine and the sound of scratching made his eyes pop open. "Mind if I let Conan out?" He jumped up from the couch and let the dog out of the bedroom, and now that they'd been identified as friendly, the big Rottweiler trotted over to Lei, his hind end waggling, and thrust his head into her chest, snorting as he inhaled her scent.

"Well, aren't you a friendly boy," she said, scratching his chest and behind his ears. "What a lover you are." The big Rottie swiped her chin with his tongue

"No," Pono said. "You're not taking that dog home."

Lei continued to pet Conan as Sharkey resumed his seat on the couch and his shuffling through the photos. "This guy looks familiar, too," the young man said, and Lei was dismayed to see he was pointing to Tadeo.

"Familiar like you've seen him around town, or familiar like you saw him that day?" Pono asked.

"I'm not sure. He was far away. I only got an impression, you know?" Sharkey looked up, frowning. "But I feel like I recognize both of these guys."

"Okay. Thanks," Lei said, giving one more pat on the Rottweiler's head as she stood. "I'll give you a call about Conan. He might be good company for my old girl. She's been in a funk lately. How's he with kids?" She thought of Kiet's relentless pursuit of Keiki around the little cottage.

"No problem. The people in the big house have a toddler. I've actually let the kid ride Conan and he was fine with it. He's a great dog, but I'm gone most of the day and this house is too small for him and there's no fenced yard here. I should have thought of all that when my friend dropped him off, but I didn't want to see him go to the Humane Society."

Lei left Sharkey her card and they got back on the road. "Need to stop by a drugstore and pick up a pregnancy test," Lei said.

Pono widened his eyes. "Already?"

She snorted, even as she felt her belly hollow with loss. "Not me. What, you *lolo*? No, we need Pippa to take it."

"You just gonna bring it to her and ask her to go pee on the stick? Not sure that's legal."

"Well, it's worth a try," Lei said. "You got a better idea? That pregnancy, or lack of it, speaks to motive, too, and Shayla says Pippa's lying."

Pono shook his head but pulled into Long's Drugs, and Lei jumped out. "Sure you don't want to buy it instead?" she teased Pono.

"No, thanks. Got a cousin who works there. That's how rumors get started," her partner said.

A few minutes later, they were back on the road, this time for Ipo Gomez's house. This turned out to be an apartment in a run-down building on the outskirts of Paia. It was late evening by then, the sunlight slanting long across the weedy, dandelion-choked lawn near the building. Ipo's apartment on the second floor had a peeling rubber welcome mat in front of the door, piled with pairs of cheap rubber slippers.

Lei knocked, and it wasn't long before the young man was shooing his roommates out so he could study the photos. "Who did Sharkey identify?" he asked.

"We can't discuss that. I'm sure you understand," Lei said.

"Yeah. I get it." Ipo, who himself could have passed for that all-too-generic sketch, rubbed a round dark soul patch of beard on his chin. "Well, I recognize this guy. Bryan Oulaki. He's a pro. But I couldn't say for sure if I recognize him because he was the guy in the water or from the pro circuit." He paused again, this time over Tadeo's picture. "He looks familiar, too."

"Tell us more about that day." Lei tried to get Ipo to narrow it down by taking him through the story again.

This time the young man said, "I think it could be that I recognize Oulaki because he's a pro and I watch all the pro surfers. But I'm pretty sure I don't know this guy, and I think I know him." He tapped Tadeo's photo. "And, come to think of it, this guy, too." He tapped the photo of another man of roughly the same height and weight, with dark skin and eyes, a man Lei knew was locked up at Halawa for armed robbery.

"Well, thanks. We may be back," Lei said.

Pono frowned as he pulled them onto the highway. "I don't like it that they both put Tadeo back in the lineup."

"Yeah. It's not good, but it opens interesting possibilities," Lei said. "Let's hope Pippa is in a mood to cooperate."

The man who opened the door of a large, well-maintained house on the Pukalani Golf Course halfway up Haleakala had a hint of blond hair on his shiny, reddened pate and the vivid blue eyes his daughter shared. "What can I do for you?"

"Sergeant Texeira and Detective Kaihale. We're here to speak to Pippa?" Lei held up her ID. "She's expecting us."

"Okay." The man opened the door reluctantly. "I'm Kellogg Thomas. I hope you're getting closer to nailing whoever that bastard is who killed Makoa Simmons. Fine young man."

"We're running down every lead, which is why we need your daughter's help," Lei said. She could feel Pono, a looming presence at her elbow. "Did you know of anyone who had negative intentions toward him?"

"No. He was a great guy."

Pippa appeared at the door. "Oh, Daddy. I hope you weren't bending their ears with your theories."

"She asked me fair and square. And I didn't have a chance to tell them anything."

"What were you going to tell us?"

"That I think that kid's sponsor had him killed. For the insurance money. Torque was doing badly the last few years. I have stock in them, and I've been watching it carefully. It's not doing well."

"Anyone specific at Torque you have in mind?" Lei cocked her head and dimpled a little to show she liked him and was ready to listen to his theory and take it seriously. "We were aware of the life insurance policy on him, but were given to understand it wasn't unusual for a professional athlete to have something like that as part of his contract. Especially in a dangerous sport like surfing."

"Well," Kellogg huffed. "No. But it bears looking into."

"Thanks for the tip. Now can we speak to Pippa privately?"

He left with a harder-than-necessary slam of the door.

Lei reached into her purse and took out the pregnancy test in a small, brown paper-wrapped bag. "Will you please go to the restroom and take this test?"

Pippa recoiled, looking around wildly. "My parents don't know!"

"And we don't need to tell them. But we do need to know if you really are pregnant. It's important," Lei said gently. "There are those saying you are faking this. For sympathy. Or some other reason."

Pippa straightened her spine. "Shayla. That bitch. Well, I took one of these last week and it was positive. So no skin off my nose to do it again. It would be a relief if it wasn't accurate, but I've been having other symptoms, too."

Pono rubbed his nose, uncomfortable. "I'll be out in the truck."

Lei followed Pippa to the bathroom, and the girl frowned at her. "Aren't you going to wait outside?"

"I'm sorry, but this test may be evidence. We have a care, custody, and control protocol. I have to verify that it's really your urine that goes on that stick," Lei said as gently as she could. "And while we're talking, I'm so sorry about how things went with Shayla. It was necessary that we saw her reaction to the news."

"Whatever. There was no way she was going to react any way

but badly when she heard the news," Pippa said, stepping inside and leaving the door ajar for Lei to follow. Lei shut the bathroom door, and Pippa unwrapped the pregnancy test. Lei's stomach clenched as she remembered finding out her own results with Baby, how joyful and excited she and Stevens had been.

She turned her back to give Pippa privacy as the young woman did her business on the stick. Pippa set the pregnancy test wand on the brown paper sacking, wiped, and washed her hands. She flushed the toilet.

"Satisfied?" Pippa's puffy eyes were narrowed angrily.

"I'm sorry. This makes me as uncomfortable as you are," Lei said softly. "Ready to find out?"

"I guess." Pippa pulled apart the two sides of the wand. The little while chemical strip was blue.

"You're pregnant," Lei whispered. "Congratulations." She stood stoically as Pippa turned to embrace her, bursting into tears.

Lei took the test and slid it into an evidence bag. She sealed and labeled it and exited the bathroom, followed by the weeping girl.

Kellogg and his wife came out of their bedroom.

"What's the matter, Pippa?" her father demanded. Pippa just cried harder.

"Do you want me to stay? Talk to your parents?" Lei asked the distraught young woman.

Pippa shook her head. "No."

Pippa's mother embraced her. "Come, sit, honey. Talk to us. Tell us what's wrong."

"I'll let you be alone with your family," Lei said, and left the sobbing girl with her parents. Out at the truck, she gave a single nod, holding the evidence bag. "Take me back to my truck. I need to get home. I've had enough for the day."

They drove in silence.

"Do you think those two sets of parents are going to be able to work out being grandparents of that baby?" Pono asked.

"Funny you should ask that. I was just thinking of Pippa's father and Makoa's father in a shouting match over who gets to babysit," Lei said. "They're both such bulldog types. It would be funny if it weren't so sad."

Lei had fallen into something of an exhausted trance, staring out the window as Pono drove, when the radio crackled into life. "Units respond. Ten fifty-six found in Kanaha Canal."

Lei lifted her head to look at Pono. "A body in Kanaha Canal? Where's that?"

"It's a slimy rain runoff channel out by the Cash and Carry," Pono said. "We're only a few blocks away. Up for a floater?"

"No," Lei said, but Pono turned on his cop light, placed it on the dash, and put his foot down on the gas.

A few minutes later they pulled up in the grocery store's parking lot, where a waving spectator drew their attention. Lei braced herself mentally as she approached the lip of the canal.

A blonde-haired woman was floating facedown in the shallow canal with its steep cement sides. She was wearing a familiar blue tunic top, beginning to swell with gases trapped in the floating body. Lei gasped as she took in the long body in narrow jeans, all of the clothing swollen tight. The sweetish smell of decomp, not too strong now but bound to become overpowering soon, wafted in Lei's direction.

"Oh my God. I think this is Stevens's mother," she said. "She's been missing."

"I'll radio Stevens. You shouldn't have to tell him," Pono said, and hooked his radio off his belt.

A few minutes later Pono came back. "He called in to work today. Not answering his radio."

Lei thought of his trip to find his mother last night. He'd been unable to find her, and now this. She took out her cell and speed-dialed him.

CHAPTER SEVENTEEN

LEI WAS WATCHING for her husband and saw Stevens's Bronco arrive right behind the medical examiner and his van. Fujimoto, a good detective who'd been hastily assigned now that she and Pono couldn't investigate the case due to possible conflict of interest, was working with the responding patrol officers and firefighters to hook the body and drag it closer to the cement embankment for retrieval. It was a clumsy business, and she'd hoped it would be completed before he arrived.

She hurried to the Bronco and he opened the door, almost falling into her arms.

"Lei," he breathed into her hair, holding on too tightly. Fine trembling, as from a fever, shook his tall frame, and she could smell alcohol on his skin and hair. "It's her?" He hadn't yet looked toward the figure in the shallow, filthy water with its gasoline sheen.

"I don't know. But I recognized the shirt and the hair. I had to call you."

Stevens raised his head, let go of her, and walked deliberately forward to the edge of the cement lip. Lei followed and took hold of one of his cold hands.

The body had reached the nearest side-sloping cement embankment, but it was too far down to drag up with the big boat hook they'd used to bring it to the edge. Fujimoto, leaning down to try to haul the body higher, slid down the cement with a cry and landed in the water with a splash.

The retrieval effort took on a darkly comic aspect as the firefighters that were part of the first response threw Fujimoto a line. Standing waist-deep in the greenish water, he tied the line around the body's waist and the firefighters hauled it up the side. Lei glanced at her husband. Stevens's face was white, with pinched marks beside his nose.

"I hope Jared doesn't hear the fire department call," he hissed between his teeth as the soggy, bloated body was hauled by main force up the steep cement wall.

Dr. Gregory, the ME, fussed around the sodden corpse as the firefighters threw Fujimoto a second line and the detective walked his way back to the top.

"Turn her over," Stevens said. "I need to see if it's my mother."

"Oh dear," Dr. Gregory murmured. "I'm so sorry. Let me get her hands covered." He finished bagging the body's hands, and then he and his assistant, Tanaka, rolled the body.

The woman landed with a wet *thunk* on her back. Her mouth was ajar, filled with water that ran out the sides of peeling lips. The eyes were open and milky. The face was bloated and pale, damaged by something that had left pockmarks of decay, probably nibbling fish or crustaceans. But it was still a distinctive face, and it wasn't Ellen Rockford Stevens.

Lei felt Stevens stagger beside her. She caught his arm. They leaned against each other in support as Stevens's breath whooshed out in relief.

"Not her," he said.

"But she's wearing Ellen's clothes," Lei said slowly. "Dr. Gregory, this is not my mother-in-law. But she's wearing her clothes. I think we should proceed as if this is a homicide."

Fujimoto brushed his hands off against each other.

"Tell me everything you know," he said. "Let me record you for time's sake."

"I'll go over the clothing carefully," Dr. Gregory told Stevens. "If there's anything on the body that can help you locate your mother, I'll find it."

"Thanks, Doc," Lei said. Stevens just nodded. Even though a little color had come back into his face, he still looked terrible. Beard roughened his cheeks, and his vivid blue eyes were sunk in caves of shadow. As she leaned in to him, she smelled the sharp reek of alcohol making its way out of his pores in acrid sweat.

He'd been drinking. That was why he'd called in to work. He'd been drinking daily since the house fire, which had begun to worry her, but he hadn't had a big binge since Kiet had come into their lives, after the murder of Steven's ex-wife.

Lei stuffed down her worry and anger and focused on Fujimoto.

"Can we talk in your car or something? Just not out here." Darkness was falling now, the gloom lit by amber pools of streetlight, but the firefighters were still nearby, stowing their equipment, and so were the patrol officers who had found the body.

"Come to my car."

They followed Fujimoto to the jacked-up SUV he drove and got inside. Fujimoto turned on a small digital recorder and stated the date, time, and those present.

"This is the on-scene statement of Lieutenant Michael Stevens and Sergeant Lei Texeira regarding the recovered body of an unknown woman from the north end of Kanaha Canal. Now, Sergeant Texeira. You asked that your husband be notified. Tell me why you made this request."

Lei described how she thought she recognized Ellen from the clothing and the blonde hair, and then the questions shifted to Stevens—who was his mother, where she'd gone, why he was looking for her but hadn't put out a BOLO on her as a missing person.

"She's an adult making adult decisions," Stevens said heavily. His voice was as raspy as a lifetime smoker's as he described driving around looking for Ellen the previous night, the bar fight he'd broken up. "I couldn't do any more at that point."

"So you think your mother has joined the homeless community and is somewhere drinking," Fujimoto stated.

"Yes, I do."

Lei spotted a yellow Maui Fire Department pickup truck pull up with a screeching of brakes. Her brother-in-law, Jared, got out, his tall, whipcord body all tight lines as he hurried to Dr. Gregory, who was just zipping the black body bag up over the waterlogged discovery in the canal.

Lei hurried to intercept Jared, putting a hand on his arm. "It's not her," she said.

Piercing blue eyes, so much like those she loved, blazed down at her. "I need to see anyway."

Mutely, Dr. Gregory unzipped the bag. The woman's ruined face stared at the sky with milky eyes.

Jared turned away, retching. Lei could tell, by the abrupt release of tension, that his reaction was not horror, but relief.

"She's still out there, Jared. We'll find her."

Stevens got out of the SUV, walking over to sling an arm around his brother's shoulders. "Fujimoto's putting out an island-wide BOLO on her. I'm not gonna lie—I'm worried the shroud killer is still at work. I'm not willing to bet it's a coincidence that this woman looks like Mom, is wearing her clothes, and is a dead floater now."

Jared flung off his brother's arm, turning to Stevens angrily. "Mom's an alcoholic. She probably traded her clothes for a drink from this woman. Anyone can see how hard it would be to get out of this cement canal once you were in, and if the woman was impaired at all, she would've drowned. There doesn't have to be any foul play—you're paranoid!"

"Maybe we are," Lei said, trying to calm Jared's agitation. "But there is a chance Chang or Ray Solomon is doing something. Solomon is out on bail."

"I think it's time we made some calls," Stevens said.

"It's just bad luck," Jared said stubbornly. "You don't know Mom like I do. You didn't live through her shit in LA as long as I did. It was nothing for her to trade the clothes on her back, which were nice at one time, by the way, for another bottle."

Lei and Stevens stared at him as he strode back and forth, pushing his hands through his short brown hair in agitation.

"Maybe you dealt with your mother for longer, but you haven't been through what we have," Lei said. "Too many people close to us have died for us to think this is a coincidence."

Stevens gestured with his head toward Fujimoto, who was directing the surrounding officers to spread out with lights. "They're searching for anything that looks like a shroud or trace that goes back to Mom. I'm going to join them."

Forty-five minutes later, the area thoroughly searched, Stevens hugged his brother goodbye briefly and then met Lei's eyes. "See you at home?"

"Pono left, so you have to take me to the station to pick up my truck," Lei said.

They got into his old Bronco. In the enclosed space, the smell coming off him was even stronger, a potent combination of alcohol, sweat, and the sweetish tang of vomit.

"You were drinking," she said.

"That obvious?" His voice was low and harsh. "What a detective you are."

"Let's just get home. Get showers. Get something to eat. Then we can talk."

He kept his eyes on the road until he got to the station. She got out of the truck and into her own vehicle, and followed him for the dark drive home along the winding coast. She used the time to think through what to say, what to do.

Keiki bellowed a greeting as the automatic gate rolled back. Lei remembered Conan, with his wide chest and sparkling, intelligent eyes. Conan would wake her beloved old girl up from her lethargy. Lei had a good feeling about that dog, and the thought of him felt like something to look forward to.

All the lights were on in the new house. The harsh cement block was softened by golden light from the bulbs. Getting out, pulling her backpack behind her, Lei could see most of the interior doors were hung.

"Michael, you were working on the house," she exclaimed, feeling her anger recede.

"Yeah. We sleep in it tonight," he said, slamming his door. "It's time your dad had his space back."

Wayne was standing behind the screen door of the cottage, Kiet on his hip.

"Mama and Daddy are home," he told the baby, who reached, squawking with excitement, for Lei. She hurried up the wooden steps to take him in her arms.

Lei buried her face in the baby's fragrant neck, inhaling his unique perfume of milk, powder, and the sweetness of baby skin. He laughed and grabbed her hair, filling his hands with the curly mass. She sank into the Adirondack chair on the deck and wallowed in the child in her arms, lifting his shirt to blow on his tummy, her whole being lighting up with joy at the feel of him in her arms.

Dimly she heard Stevens and Wayne talking, and Keiki crowded against her legs, thrusting her massive head into Lei's armpit and snorting happily.

God, it is good to be home. She never wanted to leave her baby again. *Ever.*

She might not be over losing the little life that had been with her so briefly, but Kiet was more than enough to fill her arms and her heart for now.

Wayne had dinner, a rich homemade mac and cheese casserole, still warm for them in the oven. They ate, filling her father in on the situation with the dead woman found in the canal.

Wayne's brows drew together as Stevens concluded the story. His rugged face, deeply seamed, was worried. He pushed his salt-and-pepper curls back, his dark eyes troubled. "Please tell me it's not the shroud killer again."

"We don't know." Stevens's voice had a rough, muffled quality to it, and Lei realized that he was avoiding looking at her. He must still be feeling bad for his drinking binge. "I hope it is just a weird random thing, but I don't think we should proceed as if it is. Mom traded clothes with some blonde woman and then she happened to fall into the canal? It's hard to imagine that, when we've had this many deaths around us."

"I am going to make some calls after I shower," Lei said. She ate rapidly, leaving Kiet to be fed by Stevens, and they were still at the table when she got up and went to the shower.

It felt heavenly to rinse away the nervous sweat of the exhausting day, let it flow down her body to swirl around her feet and disappear into the drain.

We are going to sleep in the new house tonight.

A sense of anticipation lifted her. "We need some alone time," she muttered, soaping briskly. Shortly after, wrapped in a terry cloth robe, she busied herself cleaning up Kiet and taking him out of his high chair, sitting with him for his bedtime bottle and putting him down in his crib while Stevens took his shower.

Underneath all that, she simmered with desire to be with Stevens. Alone. In their new home, joined together. So he'd had a drinking binge—she loved him anyway and wanted to show it, support him in the situation with his mom.

He needed her. And truth be known, she needed him just as much.

Wayne washed up, murmuring in a low voice to one of the addicts he sponsored on the phone, and Lei changed into her familiar old boxers and tank top and wrapped herself in her robe. She picked up her pillow as Stevens came to the door, a towel wrapped around his narrow hips. She took a moment to enjoy the sight of him, a smile tugging up one side of her mouth as her gaze roamed.

He finally met her eyes, and she saw a hunger that matched hers—and relief, too, that she wasn't going to berate him.

"Let's go get set up in the new house, Michael. Do we need bedding?" Lei asked.

"No. I moved the air mattress and washed the bedding from the tent in there. It's ready to go."

Lei went out with her pillow and hugged her father. "Okay to leave Kiet in here with you tonight?"

"Sure. He's a good sleeper. I'll yell if I need you." Wayne turned to her, ruffling her curls. "Glad you're home, Sweets."

"Not as glad as I am to be home," she said.

Wearing their robes, she and Stevens walked down the steps and across the lawn to the new house. Keiki followed, her ears swiveling and dark eyes worried at this new development.

"She doesn't know who to keep an eye on now," Stevens said. "She liked having all of us in one spot."

"On the plus side, the house is as fireproof as they come," Lei said. "And I think we'll all sleep better at night for that."

"Could sure use a break from all the psychos in our lives," Stevens said, pushing a hand through his hair.

"This is already a break, for me," Lei said softly. Stevens had brought in the carpet and air mattress from the tent, even strung the tiny battery-operated Christmas lights Lei'd originally decorated the tent with around the harsh, unfinished walls of the room. Lei walked around the large, square space, trailing her fingers along the unfinished cement.

"It feels good to me," she whispered. "Like a fortress. Like a castle. Our castle."

"And you're my queen." Stevens drew her into his arms. He so seldom said crazy romantic things like that. Lei felt herself instantly melt, reaching up to pull his head down to hers. Wrapped close in his arms, Lei let go of the relentless tension of the investigation, the horror of the body discovery this afternoon, even the powerful and sometimes conflicting feelings she still carried about being a mother.

All of it rolled away and disappeared, leaving her in this intensely sensual moment, held in the arms of the man she loved.

He slid his hands into the opening of the bathrobe, removing it from her body, gently but confidently undressing her even as their hungry mouths never left each other. The slow-burning flame that never left them heated up and consumed every thought and feeling, distilling it to pure, exquisite sensation that fed more than their bodily hunger.

STEVENS ADJUSTED Lei's head on his shoulder, pushing the thickets of her curling hair away from his face even as he felt the urge to bury his face in those nut-brown curls, inhaling the smell of her almond shampoo.

She was naked against him, every inch of her slender frame touching him, warming him deeper than mere flesh. The longer they were married, the more he realized he was never going to slake his thirst for her. He wondered if he'd ever be able to resist a look from her smoldering brown eyes, a look that told him she'd be climbing him later like a vine up a tree.

He didn't think so. They'd be old and crabbed and he'd still be hers for the taking.

He smoothed the chaotic hair back off her brow, looking down at the fans of her closed eyelashes, his gaze traveling down her smooth, cool body wrapped around his, lying alongside him in that space where she fit so well.

He was glad to have this time. Alone together, in the stark shell of their new house, before the demands of the day began—beginning with their son waking up, which would happen in the next hour or so.

Dawn's glow pushed the night back and washed out the stars as he made her his again. He needed every moment they had together, because they lived in the long shadow of death, and walked in it every day so others didn't have to.

They showered in the rough enclosure in the bathroom, which at least had running water, even if it was cold. She laughed, teasing him with the slippery bar of soap he'd remembered to bring over.

"Could this water be any colder?"

"Only if it wasn't Hawaii," he said. "Do you like the new bedroom?"

"I like being with you, alone. Wherever we are," she said, and put her mouth on that place she'd just soaped and rinsed.

They were getting dressed when they heard Kiet fussing over at Wayne's house.

"Hang up those towels, will you? Let's bring his crib over tonight. I want us all together," Lei said. She hurried over to the cottage.

Stevens followed more slowly, making a mental list of all the work that still needed doing on the house. It seemed like such a never-ending project, but really they only needed the plasterers, the painting, and finish work done. It wasn't worth setting anything more up inside. The plasterers were due in a couple of days and the end was in sight.

Stevens thought of all Lei hadn't confronted him with last night. She'd only mentioned his drinking once, though she'd smelled it on him at the scene with the body. He knew and he'd recognized by the way she wrinkled her nose how she hated it.

He loved her for letting it go without further comment.

By the time he finished the tidying and hanging the bathroom door for their coming night in the new house, Lei was already dressed with her weapon and badge on, feeding Kiet in his high chair.

She looked up, a frown above her eyes. "I have to get going early. We're close to breaking something on the Makoa Simmons case, I hope."

"Anything I should know?" He poured himself some coffee and angled a glance at her.

"Yeah. Don't engage with Eric Tadeo about this case. I know you're sharing an office with him."

"Don't tell me anything, then," Stevens said.

Wayne had slept in and he joined them. "What are you going to do about that dead woman wearing your mother's clothes?" he asked Stevens.

"I'm not sure yet. I plan to offer support to Fujimoto, but he's the main man on the case. I need to let him take the lead. I thought, though, if he was agreeable, I'd go do some pavement pounding and see who might have seen the woman, seen where those clothes came from."

"Sounds like a plan." Wayne tossed Keiki a piece of toast from his plate. "I know a lot of people from the program who lived on the street, and I have a meeting today. I'll see if anyone knows a blonde, blue-eyed street woman."

"I'll see if I get time to go by and talk to the doc," Lei said. "Now, bye to all my favorite men." She started with a kiss on Kiet's head, then Stevens, then her father. "I may not be home for dinner. Depends on what's happening with the case."

She skipped down the steps and got in her truck, Keiki watching sadly from the top step.

Stevens dressed in the bedroom, realizing his night with Lei had shucked off the last of his hangover and angst. In spite of his mom's disappearance, he felt better than he had in days. As long as he and Lei had each other, they could survive anything.

Now he had to go and find his mother. *Dead or alive.* She was his weakness, and the best way to deal with weaknesses was to keep them close.

"Wayne." He approached his father-in-law in the kitchen. "I'm sorry about the drinking the other day. Thanks for the water and aspirin. It won't happen again."

Wayne gave him a long look from uncompromising eyes. "See that it doesn't." His father-in-law took the baby down from his high chair. "You have people who need you."

CHAPTER EIGHTEEN

LEI DROVE DOWN THE MORNING-SHADOWED, winding road. She turned on the radio and called Dispatch. After identifying herself, she asked, "Did you get any calls about that blonde woman Ellen Stevens?"

"Sorry, Sergeant. Nothing tonight," Dispatch said. "We have the BOLO and will alert you if she's found."

"Roger that." Lei hung up the radio and pressed down on the gas. She wanted today to be the day she brought in Makoa's murderer, and to do that she needed to stir the pot, see what came to a boil.

Getting a sudden idea, she phoned Pippa. The phone rang and rang, finally going to voice mail. Lei thought of the scene she'd left the girl with the night before: holding a positive pregnancy test, alone to tell her parents she was pregnant with a murdered man's baby.

She wouldn't have wanted to talk to Lei, either.

"Hi, Pippa. I hope it went okay talking to your parents last night. Listen, I have a huge favor to ask. I wouldn't ask it if I didn't think it might help flush out Makoa's killer. Please call me back so I can talk with you about it."

In her cubicle at Kahului Station, Lei scrolled through her departmental e-mail while stirring a mug of inky coffee and trying to dissolve the chunks of creamer. She'd finally made some progress when Pono slid into his squeaky office chair beside her.

"Glad that floater wasn't your mother-in-law," he said.

"Me too. I think that would have pushed Jared and Michael right over the edge. They've already had so much heartbreak from her. I hope she turns up today. Anyway, I want to bust this case open. I think we should bring Oulaki and Tadeo in. Along with the girls. Mix it up, see what we can get to pop."

"I think heads are what's going to pop if you throw those four in a room," Pono said.

"Or we could stir up something interesting. You know as well as I do that this case needs a confession since there's so little forensic evidence. Let's start with Eli Tadeo, since he's here. His phone records show short calls to Shayla's number; from the length of the calls, it looks like she wasn't taking them, and unfortunately I don't see anything on his cell or hers on the day Makoa was killed. But then eventually there's a number appearing on his bill that could be a burner. What if Shayla got smart and was communicating with him, but with a burner?"

"I'm not seeing Eli as the doer. When you meet him, you'll understand. He might not be as squeaky-clean as Eric Tadeo, our recruiter, but it's a stretch to imagine him having the sack to do Makoa the way it was done."

"Indulge me," Lei said. "I still like him as the jealous boyfriend with a revenge-profit-love motive."

"It's your hassle," Pono replied. "Here's his number. I'm getting more coffee." He pushed the case file over to Lei.

Lei used the station phone to call Eli's cell, knowing Maui Police Department would show up in his caller ID. Sure enough, no one answered.

"Mr. Tadeo, this is Sergeant Lei Texeira. Please call me back about an interview regarding a police matter. This is not a request.

If you do not comply, we will issue a bench warrant for your arrest." A bluff, but one she didn't think he'd be willing to risk.

She hung up, pushed back her chair, did a few spins to discharge energy, and picked up the phone as it rang. "Sergeant Texeira."

"This is Pippa, calling you back." The young woman's voice was hesitant. "You wanted to ask a favor?"

"Oh, Pippa. How did it go with your parents?"

"They didn't know I was with Makoa at all. That's been a tricky thing. So I had to tell them that and that I was pregnant. They're pretty upset."

"I'm sorry to have left you there, but it seemed like a private family matter."

"It wouldn't have helped to have you there, that's for sure."

"Well, I'm sorry you had to go through that, but hopefully they'll come around. That kind of brings me to what I have to ask you. How do you feel about Bryan Oulaki?"

A long pause. Finally, "I like him. He's been a good friend to me."

"Do you think he might like you...more than a friend?"

"I don't know. I don't want to think about that."

Lei could feel Pippa withdrawing, so she pushed ahead. "Never mind. But could you ask him to come over here? To Maui? Tell him you need his support right now."

Another pause. "Do you suspect him?" Pippa's voice shook.

"I can't talk about that right now," Lei temporized. "But I need to know if he would come if you asked him to, and when he's here, I need to talk to him."

Another long pause. "Okay. I'll do it. If he had anything to do with Makoa's death, I want him dealt with, no matter what," Pippa said, an unfamiliar hardness in her tone. "I'll let you know."

The young woman hung up.

Lei lifted the phone away from her ear thoughtfully, then set it down. It would indeed be interesting to see if Oulaki got on a plane and came all the way to another island when Pippa called for him. Pono reappeared with another mug of coffee for her.

"Thanks, partner," she said, clinking her mug to his. "Operation pot-stirring has commenced."

He rolled his eyes with an exaggerated grimace. The phone rang, and Lei picked up.

"This is Eli Tadeo. I'm responding to a threatening phone message from Maui Police Department."

"This is Sergeant Texeira." Lei put the call on speakerphone so Pono could hear the conversation. "I simply informed you that returning my call was not optional. Thank you for complying. Please come into the station. We'd like to ask you a few questions regarding an important matter."

"I talked to that big *moke* cop yesterday." Eli's voice was sullen. Pono frowned at the derogatory word.

"I know, and I thank you for the alibi you provided. However, we have some additional questions." Lei set up a time for the young man to come in. She continued to arrange the rest of the day, including a meeting to brief the captain at the end.

"We have just enough time to run over to the morgue for a look at that floater Jane Doe from the canal," she said. "Coming?"

"Wouldn't miss it." Pono took his jacket from the back of his chair.

They drove the few blocks between the station and the hospital, and Lei did some relaxation breathing as they got on the elevator for the short trip to the basement, where the morgue was located. She kept hoping it would get easier for her to visit the morgue, but it still took a lot of effort to manage the anxiety triggered by the smells alone.

"Hey now." Dr. Gregory was wearing one of his bright yellow, smiley-face rubber aprons today. It was already smeared with dark stains. "Come on in. I guess you're here about the blonde floater?"

"You guessed right. Did you find anything on her?"

"She had a state-issued ID card stuck with her food stamp card way down in her bra. Her name's Adele Lassiter." He popped the refrigerator door and pulled the shelf out. Adele was uncovered, and Lei winced internally at the sight of her body, empty as a waterlogged, crumpled sack. She had a farmer's tan coloring the skin of her face, neck, and arms, and brown roots an inch or so long. The state of her exposed face and skin had not improved since Lei had seen it last. Her breasts hung like empty leather pouches on either side of her ribs.

"Cause of death is drowning. I sent a blood sample to the lab, but I anticipate that her blood alcohol was very high because her stomach contents consisted of mostly alcohol, mixed with a few Pringles." He held up a glass vial and gave it a swirl.

"Did you find any trace on her body? Anything that ties her to Ellen besides the clothes?"

"That was probably the connection. Yesterday was food stamp day; I'm guessing Adele used up her food stamps, trading them for alcohol, because when I checked her card, it was empty. Then she must have traded some of the booze for Ellen's clothes." He held out a plastic bag holding the sodden garments. "For you. You can take them to your lab for some more processing, but I went over them looking for blood, hair, food stains, anything. I couldn't find anything, but CSI this lab is not." He handed the bag to Lei.

"Thanks." Lei took the bag. "That's too bad. We'll have to coordinate with Fujimoto on this. It's his case, really. But I'm guessing canvassing the homeless is on the agenda. Do you have one of those doctored-up photos?"

"Sure do." Gregory picked up a remote and hit a button. The printer whirred, and a photo of their victim appeared. "I didn't have a lot of time to do the Photoshop necessary to restore her appearance, but this should help with showing it around."

"Thanks. You're the best." Lei smiled at Gregory.

"I try."

"I don't know about your apron, Doc," Pono said. "I get that you're being ironic, though."

Gregory blinked his eyes owlishly behind his magnifiers. "Who's being ironic? I'm just trying to cheer myself up around here."

Lei called Fujimoto as they left the morgue. "I'll have the clothes down at our lab for further processing," she said.

"Whose case is this?" the other detective said, but his tone wasn't as irritated as she knew she'd be if some other cop with a personal connection to a case got to the morgue ahead of her.

"I'm sorry. I had a few minutes and thought I'd swing by and check in with the doc," Lei said. "I'll submit the clothing to the lab under evidence seal."

"Okay. Wait for me to call you next time," Fujimoto said, and hung up.

"Guess I better let him work his case," Lei said. "Anyway, we have to get back to the station because Tadeo's coming in."

"So what's your plan with this?"

Lei grinned a toothy smile. "I plan to wing it and see what happens."

ELI TADEO WAS GOOD-LOOKING, of medium height and weight, with clean-cut mixed Hawaiian/Portuguese features that included dark hair and eyes. Lei hadn't met Eric, his twin, but she'd seen pictures, and they wore their hair the same way, in a neat razor-cut, slightly longer on top. Eli had a small badge of a beard beneath his lower lip.

"Hi, Eli. Thanks so much for coming in." Lei stepped forward to shake the young man's hand, introduced Pono. "I need to apprise you of your rights and that this interview is being record-ed." She recited the Miranda warning.

Eli frowned. "I need a lawyer?"

"That's your right," Lei said, with a contemptuous twist to her mouth that conveyed only sissies called for lawyers.

The door of the interview room opened suddenly, and a handsome dark-haired man who looked exactly like Eli stepped into the room.

"Sergeant Eric Tadeo," he said. He shook Lei's hand, squeezing it too hard. "I work with your husband. We share an office." He wore an immaculate uniform and was clean-shaven, the only difference in looks to his brother.

"I heard. That's very nice." Lei kept her voice cool and neutral. "What can I do for you?"

"Nothing. Just here as informal support for my brother."

"Well, that's not necessary, Sergeant." She didn't have to call him "sir." They shared the same rank. "Eli's just being interviewed. Routine."

"There's nothing routine about it," Tadeo growled, sitting beside his brother. Lei glanced between them. Their resemblance was remarkable when seated side-by-side. Lei didn't think she'd be able to tell them apart if they were dressed the same and Eli didn't have that soul patch.

"Sergeant, you may observe the interview through the window." Lei indicated the mirrored glass portal nearby.

Eric turned to his brother. "Let me call a lawyer."

"No need. I've got nothing to hide." Eli folded his arms and stared defiantly at his twin.

Eric scowled but pushed back out through the door. Lei shifted in her chair, trying to reestablish a connection with the sullen man before her.

"Okay, then." Pono, next to her, turned on the recording equipment and sat down beside her.

"Eli, tell us about your relationship with Shayla," Lei said.

"What does that have to do with Makoa Simmons?" Eli asked angrily.

Lei just looked at him. He tapped his fingers, finally said, "I don't know what you want me to say. Did I like Makoa Simmons stealing my girl? No. Did I want to get her back from that trumped-up prep-school poseur? You bet I did. Did I have anything to do with his death? Absolutely not."

"Well, that's nice, and now that we have your official statement out of the way, I'd like to ask you why you were calling Shayla when she'd already clearly told you she didn't want to hear from you."

"I thought she might change her mind. I knew he was seeing that blonde friend of hers, too. I figured she'd get sick of playing second fiddle. Shayla was never the type to do second fiddle very well."

Lei held up a highlighted phone bill. "Phone calls to Shayla that she doesn't pick up. Daily, sometimes three or four times a day. Then suddenly the calls stop, and this incoming number appears." Lei pointed to the circled unknown number. "Who is this?"

"I don't know." Eli folded his arms. "I have an alibi for the time of the murder."

"An alibi your brother gave you. Pono's been following up with that. Pono, how's the alibi holding up?"

"Actually, you two look so similar, especially when wearing your baseball league outfits, no one has been able to totally, positively identify if Eli or Eric was there," Pono said. Eli's color paled, but he lifted his chin defiantly.

"Well, I have an idea who this mysterious number is," Lei said. "I think it's Shayla. She got a burner phone and began to call you again. Look at the length of these calls." Lei pointed out the highlighted minutes. "I think she was warming up to you again, Eli, and she asked you for a favor."

Suddenly a tap came at the door and Torufu, the big Tongan Lei had worked with on the bomb squad, stuck his head in. "Excuse me. There's a couple out in the foyer asking for you."

"We'll be right back." Lei and Pono exited the room, closing the door carefully. Lei made sure it was locked behind them.

"Who is it?" Lei asked Torufu.

"Pretty blonde girl and a local guy," he said, waggling the toothpick he liked to chew between his Chiclet-sized teeth.

"Wow," Lei breathed to Pono. "The gang's all here but Shayla. That sounds like Pippa and Oulaki."

Sure enough, Pippa stood to greet them, beautiful as a beach Barbie in a pink sundress. Oulaki stood a little too close to her, glowering around the lobby of the station.

"Thanks so much for coming in," Lei said with a huge smile. "What a hassle, Bryan. I'm sorry. Follow me. This is very exciting. I think we're about to find out who killed Makoa." Lei glanced back at them as if sure they'd be thrilled about this, but neither of them so much as nodded.

"I'm here because Pippa asked me to come," Oulaki said.

"And we appreciate that," Lei said. She slowed as they walked past the interview room where Eli Tadeo was stashed, and she saw Tadeo look up and make eye contact with Oulaki.

Good.

She escorted the couple into another interview room. "We're just waiting on one more person."

"That had better be Shayla," Pippa said.

"I just hope she shows," Lei said, with a tiny doubting head-shake. "Make yourselves comfortable."

They sat. Pono turned on the recording equipment and stated names, time, purpose of interview, and the Miranda warning. Lei folded her hands and leaned forward. "Now, Bryan. We've got some interesting phone records to ask you about." She took out the folder with the phone bills and removed his and Pippa's. "See this? You called Pippa the night before Makoa was killed. Why?"

"We talk sometimes," Oulaki said, eyes down as he addressed the table.

"You see, I have a theory. My theory is this. You called Pippa. She told you Makoa was going to break up with Shayla, maybe ask her to marry him. She may even have told you some important personal news. Did you tell him your news, Pippa?"

The girl's skin had paled alarmingly. "No," she breathed. "But I did tell him Makoa was finally breaking up with Shayla."

"Well, you should tell him the rest," Lei said. "He really needs to know."

Pippa turned to Oulaki, and her eyes filled as she said, "I'm pregnant. With Makoa's baby."

Oulaki tensed. He seemed to withdraw into himself, becoming hunched and tight, his arms crossed over his chest.

"I'm sad for you, Pippa. That's a lot to deal with alone," he said, each word pressed out flat through lips that looked stiff. But when Lei glimpsed his eyes, they were alive with mortal pain.

"You thought you'd fly over to Maui and get rid of your rival," Lei said. "Get the front room of the Torque house and the girl you'd fallen in love with, all in one stroke."

"No," Oulaki said, but he didn't say it to Lei. He said it to Pippa. "I would never hurt the man you loved."

"Is what she's saying true?" Pippa asked, ignoring Lei and Pono. "Did you kill Makoa? Did you ever imagine that would make me love you?"

Oulaki stood, pushing back the chair behind him. To Lei's astonishment, he dropped to his knees before Pippa.

"No. Never. You loved him, and I would never hurt someone you loved, even if I thought you deserved more. Deserved better. Deserved someone who loves only you."

"Holy crap," Lei breathed, as Oulaki put his arms around Pippa's waist and pressed his head into her lap.

"I will do all I can to make you happy," he said, his voice muffled. "I know I'm not him, but I'll be there for you in whatever way I can."

Pippa seemed frozen, and then slowly her hands came down to stroke Oulaki's head, his shoulders. They might as well have been completely alone, for all the attention they paid to Lei and her partner.

Lei cleared her throat. "Excuse me. That's all very well, but I think I'm looking at motive here."

"I didn't do it," Oulaki said, without raising his head. "And I will take care of you, if you will let me."

He was still embracing Pippa's midsection in a way that communicated, more than any words, that he didn't care she was pregnant with another man's baby; that he'd care for that child as if it were his own.

Lei found herself clearing her throat again, because of a lump that had gathered there.

"We'll give you a moment of privacy." Lei said.

Pippa was crying, tears rolling down her face, but she was still stroking Oulaki's hair, his shoulders, as he knelt before her. Lei and Pono exited, and the two never looked up.

"I didn't see that coming," Pono said out in the hall.

"I suspected he might have feelings for her, but I had no idea of the depth," Lei said. "I can't believe I'm saying this, but I don't know anymore if he's the guy."

"Me neither."

They were gathering their resolve outside the door containing Eli Tadeo, when Shayla Cummings came striding down the hall, trailing a uniformed officer from the front desk. She looked amazing: flags of color on her high cheekbones, long brown hair bouncing in fat, flowing curls, a sprigged sundress grazing her knees, and kitten-heeled sandals on her feet.

"Shayla, you look great," Lei said, infusing her voice with a warmth she didn't feel.

"I have to keep going somehow," Shayla said. "And find a way to deal with all this stress." Her big brown eyes filled with tears.

"Well, we're sorry to keep having to check in with you about things, but we have one more interview we need to do."

Pono opened the interview door and held it ajar, and Shayla stepped inside, immediately pulling up short as she locked eyes with Eli Tadeo, seated at the table.

"Eli! What are you doing here?"

"Same as you. Came when MPD called," Eli said, with that sulky edge to his voice.

Lei grabbed another chair from the hall and then made sure the door was locked once they were all seated. "I need to review your rights and remind you that this is a voluntary interview." She recited the Miranda warning.

Shayla turned accusing eyes to Lei. "I don't know why I'm in this room with him. I'm sure you know this is my ex-boyfriend, who's been harassing me and Makoa for months."

Eli remained seated, his dark eyes locked with Shayla's. "I can't believe you're saying that."

Shayla's eyes widened in panic, skittering away from Eli's, as Lei opened the folder of phone bills.

"I brought you in, Shayla, to check if the two of you were in contact. Were you?"

"No!" Shayla cried.

"Yes," Eli said.

"Well, I think these phone records tell the tale." Lei ran her finger down the list of phone numbers. "I was showing Eli and Eric these records earlier, Shayla. The calls Eli kept making to you, which you didn't take. And then, suddenly, this unidentified burner number appears."

Lei took her own phone out of her pocket and, very deliberately, punched in the burner number. The door of the room burst open, and Eric Tadeo, face flushed, stomped across the room. He grabbed his brother's arm and gave a hard tug. "Eli, we're out of here."

He tugged his brother by force toward the door as Shayla jumped to her feet, clutching her purse and looking around wildly. Lei pressed Send.

"Let us the hell out!" Eric Tadeo yelled at Lei, his face congested with blood, cords standing out in his neck. Pono rose to his full height, facing down the other man protectively as a tinny beep began in Shayla's purse.

Beep. Beep. Beep.

"You going to get that?" Lei asked. "And everyone can just sit their asses right back down. We're not going anywhere."

Shayla sagged back down into the plastic chair. *Beep. Beep. Beep,* went the phone in her purse, but she made no move to take it out.

Lei punched the Off button. "Take out that phone and give it to me."

"I don't have to."

"Yes, you do. It's evidence in a murder investigation," Pono growled, and held out his meaty brown hand.

Her own hand trembling, Shayla pulled out a cheap Nokia burner phone and set it in his hand. Lei's phone number showed clearly in the little identification window.

"We aren't talking to you for another minute without counsel present." Eric's hand was still clamped around his twin's arm, just above the elbow.

"Screw that," Eli said, yanking his arm out of his brother's hand. "You always think you know best. You think you can tell me what to do. I'm sick of it. Sick of covering for you."

Lei's heart leaped to trip-hammer speed as the twins confronted each other before Shayla. Shayla's head was lowered, glorious hair hiding her face as she played with the edge of her dress. Turned toward each other, the twins' faces were as similar as two sides of a coin.

"Don't do this," Eric snarled. "Shut your mouth. Now."

"No. You thought you could have it all. Your pretty wifey, the kids, and Shayla, too."

Now Shayla's head flew up, and she leaped to her feet, pushing her chair back. "What? What are you saying?"

"What do you think I'm saying?" Eli screamed. "Half the time you thought you were screwing me, you were screwing my brother."

Lei watched this revelation settle in on the haughty young woman.

She screamed. "No! No, you didn't!" and launched herself at Eli.

The room erupted into the violence that Lei had sensed simmering under the surface between the brothers and the beautiful woman they'd shared. Lei wrestled Shayla back and cuffed her hands in front while Pono tried to separate the brothers.

While this situation created a scenario where murder might have occurred between the combatants at the table, this particular drama didn't constitute any sort of confession. Lei had to push them further.

"Lawyer, dammit!" Eric bellowed. "I want a lawyer!"

Lei caught Pono's eye, and her partner clapped cuffs on the other officer's arms and dragged him out of the room.

Technically, neither Shayla nor Eli had asked for representation. As Lei clipped Shayla's handcuffs to the ring on the steel table, she knew now was the time to strike.

Eli was still unrestrained, pacing like a caged animal, darting hateful glances at Shayla, who was resting her forehead on the table and sobbing.

"It's great that you are finally breaking away from your brother." Lei hoped she wasn't laying it on too thick. She edged toward Eli in case she had to restrain him. "You don't need him telling you what to do. Look at how that turned out."

"Damn straight. Eric's sick. He has a dark side," Eli said. "I'm sick of being his screw-up, always taking the fall for what he comes up with."

"So whose idea was it to kill Makoa?" Lei said matter-of-factly.

"Eric's. He knew about Shayla inheriting Makoa's money, and when she called me and began talking about getting back together, we both realized Makoa must be getting ready to break up with her. Shayla's not someone who can be by herself." Even as Eli said this, his eyes softened, looking at her bent head. "She didn't know. She needs us."

"She didn't know what?" Lei probed gently.

"She didn't know that we both loved her. And we both wanted to keep loving her. But only one of us could marry her, and that was going to be me."

"You're sick." Shayla flung her hair back as she confronted Eli, her eyes flashing. "I would never have married you when I could have had Makoa."

"You and Makoa were over. You told me yourself," Eli said. "When you called me crying and asked that I do something. About how he was dumping you now that he'd gotten Pippa pregnant."

Lei restrained herself from leaping in the air and doing a fist pump. She still needed to know who'd actually held Makoa under.

"Hmm, what a tough situation. You must have felt trapped," she said.

"Yeah. I didn't want Shayla to be left broke and brokenhearted. She told me where he was going to be surfing in the morning. It doesn't matter anymore," Eli said, gazing into Shayla's eyes. "You didn't ask me, but I knew what you were really asking me—and Eric and I took care of it."

"Shut up, you sick, cheating pig!" Shayla screamed, jumping up. "I hate you! I hate you!" She thrashed against the restraints.

Eli stood frozen for a moment, and then Lei saw the pain in his eyes turn to something else. He lunged across the table and seized Shayla's throat in his hands, squeezing.

Lei leaped around the table to restrain him. He let go long enough to elbow her viciously in the solar plexus, and Lei flew backward to hit the wall, the breath knocked out of her so that she couldn't even cry for help as Eli refastened his hands around Shayla's throat.

Shayla gurgled helplessly, unable to even lift her hands, her eyes bulging as he ruthlessly squeezed.

Lei drew her weapon and pushed forward, trying to get enough air to yell at Eli to stop, but Pono flung the door open, lunged into the room, and launched himself across the table, knocking Eli back so that he lost his grip. Eli's face was unrecognizable with a mask of violence that distorted his features.

"Don't move." Lei got enough air to speak. "Don't even breathe."

Pono came around the table and cuffed Eli, heaving him into the corner and holding him tightly.

Shayla had collapsed over the table, her hair over her face. The second Eli was no longer a threat, Lei rushed to her, uncuffing her and turning her over. She was breathing in ragged gasps. Her bloodshot eyes opened.

"I didn't tell him to kill Makoa," Shayla whispered brokenly. "I didn't."

"I believe you didn't use those words," Lei said. "But I think you knew exactly what you were doing when you called Eli to complain about your imminent breakup. You're under arrest, Shayla Cummings, for accessory to murder. And Eli Tadeo, you're under arrest for the murder of Makoa Simmons."

STEVENS ARRIVED AT WORK. Sipping coffee, he sat down and tried to concentrate on the training curriculum he was putting together, but found he couldn't focus. He kept glancing over at Eric's empty desk and wondering how Lei's investigation was going.

And his mother was still missing. Maybe this was a hands-on training opportunity in the offing. He picked up the phone.

An hour later, Stevens drove out of the police station, his new detective trainee, Brandon Mahoe, seated beside him in the Bronco. Brandon turned toward Stevens. He was dressed in a clean, muted aloha shirt and jeans, his longish, wiry black hair pulled back into a neat ponytail, a shark tooth on a leather thong showing at the neck of his shirt.

"I can't believe I'm not wearing my uniform right now," he said, grinning.

"Definitely a perk of being detective," Stevens agreed, navigating out of the parking lot. He'd gotten permission from Captain Omura and Detective Fujimoto to go out to the homeless enclaves and canvass for the dead woman they'd found yesterday, as well as for his mother. This would still the restless voice clawing at his insides, urging him into action. He knew that feeling, that voice... and it had seldom been wrong.

They pulled up to the encampment he'd left to break up the bar fight the other night. Rickety lean-tos clustered around a big green Dumpster like chicks around a hen.

Stevens got out. After Brandon slammed the Bronco's door and joined him, he handed a folder to the junior detective. "Here are the photos. I want you to take the lead asking questions. Don't be afraid to use pidgin. Emphasize any connection you can make with these folks. Put them at ease. Emphasize that we're concerned for their safety and just want to make sure Ellen Stevens is alive and safe."

"Stevens. Is this woman a relative?" Brandon's curious brown eyes looked concerned.

"My mother."

"Oh, damn. I'm sorry, boss."

"I am, too. And I'm not your boss." Stevens put his hands on his hips. "You're the lead here. I'll just step in if I need to."

"Yes, sir." Brandon took the folder from Stevens and walked into the village with a spring to his step. He dropped to his haunches beside an older man sipping from a bagged bottle inside one of the shelters.

They spent hours looking, working their way from one end of the encampments to the other. Many knew Adele; a few had spotted Ellen. The pattern of Adele's food stamp fraud was well established by the time they hit a more solid tip.

"Hey there. We're looking for a woman we're concerned about." Brandon showed the photo of Ellen Stevens. Stevens, watching, felt his stomach clench. The photo he'd given them to use was an older one, in which Ellen was smiling, her face fuller, her hair a glossy fall to her shoulders. It was a fifteen-year-old photo, but the only one he had.

"Yeah, I've seen her. Doesn't look like that anymore, though," the homeless man said, sucking his lips where his front teeth should be.

"Where was she?" Brandon asked, lifting his head to look around.

"I think she's still here. Made herself a little squat." The man pointed toward the edge of the cluster of dwellings.

Stevens's heart rate picked up as the informant haggled with Mahoe for payment. He turned toward where the man pointed and strode rapidly in that direction.

He found his mother lying in the lee of a pile of flattened card-board boxes. He recognized her instantly—the long shape of her skull, the flutter of her blonde hair protruding from the mouth of a filthy nylon sleeping bag. An empty bottle of Scotch lay on the ground next to her.

Looking down at her, Stevens felt that familiar dark shame rising to swamp him. This had been him just a day ago.

Stevens squatted down beside Ellen, smoothed the greasy hair back off her brow. She was either deeply asleep or passed out, because she didn't move. Her eyelids fluttered, though, and her thin chest rose and fell. She was alive.

"Mom?" he called softly. "It's Michael. I'm here to take you home."

CHAPTER NINETEEN

Seated in the conference room with Captain Omura and several other higher-ups, Lei finished with her account of what had happened in the interview room.

"Let's watch the video." Captain Omura hit a remote to play the recorded footage on a flatscreen across from the table. Lei winced as she watched the mistakes she'd made play out across the grainy feed.

She hadn't cuffed Eli Tadeo and he'd attacked Shayla.

He'd been able to fight Lei off, and he'd almost killed the woman.

"What's missing from this video? Besides proper procedure, which is going to give Shayla Cummings a huge hole to appeal her charges?" Omura said, her crimson nails tapping each other.

"A confession," Pono said. "He never directly says he killed Makoa. It's only implied. And then he attacks Shayla when she says she hates him."

"Right."

They replayed the video. Lei stood up and paced, her fists balled. "He did it, though. He practically admits it. And his behavior shows how unbalanced he is."

"This case has to be made on a confession because we already know there's no trace that we can use connecting to any of the players. Let's watch this again."

They watched the video again. This time Omura paused it at the frame where Eric Tadeo, his face congested, yelled for his lawyer.

"Sergeant Tadeo is going to be a problem."

"I know," Lei said. "But did you hear the part where Eli talks about how Eric slept with Shayla, too?"

"How was your interview with Eric Tadeo?"

"Not good. After he talked to his lawyer, he barely answered any questions. One word-answers. Admitted nothing. At this point I'm happy to be able to charge Eli and Shayla."

Omura tapped her nails again. Lei realized she hated the sound.

"I don't think this whole thing, compelling as it is in terms of drama, is going to hold up in court. We need something harder. We need one of them to admit to killing Makoa."

"They'd be crazy to do that," Lei said.

Omura smiled. It wasn't a nice smile. "I see a whole lot of crazy people in this video. You can make this happen, Texeira. I think you should reach out to Tadeo's wife. You talked with her early on. I don't think she's going to take this kind of betrayal lying down."

"At least we've cleared Pippa and Oulaki," Lei said. "I feel a little better about this case after that interview."

"Talk to Rachel Tadeo. See what she says about her husband's affair. I bet she comes up with something that helps us put one of them in the surf with Makoa." Omura flicked those nails in dismissal.

LEI AND PONO knocked on the pretty door of the neat house in Kuau where Eric Tadeo and his family lived. Lei looked over at

Eli's tidy little cottage, feeling a twinge at the sight of the welcome mat empty of his shoes and the surfboard by the door.

"What do you want?" Rachel Tadeo didn't pretend to be polite as she opened the door, the toddler on her hip.

"We want to speak to you," Lei said, feeling her stomach tighten a bit. She was about to ruin this woman's world. "About the murder of Makoa Simmons."

"I have no idea what I could say about that," she said, but she stood aside and they entered.

Rachel ignored them as she took her two young children into a playroom filled with toys and a television and got them settled in front of a video with sippy cups and a snack. Finally, she gestured for them to follow her into the living room.

Rachel's face was a stoic mask as she seated herself on a chair across from the couch Lei and Pono perched on. "I'm sick of this witch hunt," she said. "You're going to be facing charges yourselves, for harassing our family."

"A man has died. A man who deserved to live. A man who had a bright future ahead of him and was going to be a father." Lei leaned forward, making sincere eye contact. "Your brother-in-law practically admitted he did it, and then he tried to kill Shayla Cummings right in front of me. I don't know why you're protecting him."

Rachel dropped her eyes, plucking at a loose thread on her shorts. "I don't know what you need to talk to me about."

"We need to know everything we can about Eli and Eric's relationship with Shayla Cummings."

Rachel looked up, frowned. "Eric? He didn't have a relationship with that bitch."

"Oh, but I'm afraid he did." Lei told Rachel the gist of what had come out in the interview room. "Your husband was, at least sometimes, sleeping with Shayla. Impersonating his brother. They shared her."

The color drained out of Rachel's face, and her eyes flew to the door of the playroom, where the children watched television. She got up and walked silently across the room, shutting the playroom door and going quickly upstairs. Lei looked at Pono, and they jumped up and hurried after her.

They found her in an upstairs office furnished with a desk. A shelf filled with trophies and commendations took up one wall, a lounger and flat screen TV the other. Rachel was behind the desk, unlocking it, pulling out a drawer. As they watched, she reached inside and took out a small metal box.

She set it on the desk and looked up at them. "He keeps something in here. Something he didn't want me to see."

"Do we have your permission to open the box?"

"Please." She gestured.

Lei came around the desk, took a paper clip out of the drawer, and opened it. She inserted the paper clip into the lock, excitement surging up at the same time as regret for the pain she was causing. Rachel covered her face, beginning to cry.

"I knew something was going on. I knew something wasn't right," she muttered.

Lei got the lid unlocked. Inside was a box filled with authentic-looking soul patch beard sections on clear plastic.

Rachel leaped to her feet. "Oh, God!"

She grabbed handfuls of hair, pulling it, her face contorted with anguish. Lei reached over to both hug and restrain her.

"Don't hurt yourself. He was the one who did wrong," she soothed.

"No, no, no!" Rachel sobbed. "I had a feeling. He would be gone nights on training exercises. Something in me knew!" Her hysteria was increasing as she wailed. Just then they heard the rumble of the big truck Eric drove pulling into the driveway. Lei wrapped her arms around the other woman, pinioning her, as they heard the front door crash open.

"Rachel!" Eric bellowed. "Don't listen to them! Rachel!"

The woman in Lei's arms thrust a hard elbow back into Lei's

stomach, winding her, then stomped on Lei's foot with her athletic shoe so hard Lei felt the crack of bone.

Lei staggered back with a cry. Rachel scrabbled in the drawer of the desk and pulled out a black gun case.

Pono, who'd been watching in bemusement, leaped forward to stop her, but Rachel already had the Glock out. Pono fell back, his hands in the air.

Lei leaned on the wall, shame that she'd been disabled by this cop's wife with her weekend self-defense training combined with horror as the scene went from bad to worse. Eric Tadeo appeared in the doorway of the office. His wild-eyed wife pointed the gun at him.

"You scum!" she screamed. "You cheated on me with that bitch!"

"Put the gun down." Eric spoke in a quiet voice, his hands in the air. "Please, honey. Please, Rachel. Let me explain. We can work this out."

"There's no explanation you can give that would make this right," Rachel screamed, throwing the metal box at Eric. It caught him in the midsection. The fake soul patches scattered across the carpet.

"I'm sorry, Rachel," Eric said. "I'm so, so sorry. I didn't think anyone would get hurt."

"You're getting hurt!" Rachel pulled the trigger. The report was deafening in the enclosed space.

The round caught Eric in the shoulder, and he crumpled in the doorway. Rachel stared at his fallen body, the gun wobbling, and Pono wrestled it out of her hands. He slammed her onto the floor and cuffed her.

Lei heard the piping sound of the older daughter's voice approaching up the steps. "Mommy? Daddy?"

Rachel twisted her head on the carpet and yelled, "Go back downstairs! Everything is fine!"

Lei hobbled to Eric, tugged him inside the room by his feet, and shut the door so that the children wouldn't see what was happening inside the room as Pono called for an ambulance.

Eric's mouth opened and closed as he struggled to breathe. Lei grabbed a magazine off the desk and set it over the wound, pressing down hard. She leaned over Eric, alarmed by the blood pool spreading beneath him.

"Did you kill Makoa?" she asked.

Eric's chest heaved in a valiant effort to bring in oxygen. His face was turning blue. Frantic eyes, filled with terror and determination, fastened on her face, and he nodded.

"I did it for my brother," he gasped.

Blood filled Eric's mouth. He heaved upward, splattering Lei with the viscous fluid. Then he fell back into the sodden carpet, and his eyes rolled back, his mouth slack.

So much blood. It seemed to be everywhere. Lei stood, momentarily forgetting about her broken foot, then staggered to sit on the office chair.

"Holy crap," Pono said. Rachel keened beside his feet, her sobs a monotonous backdrop as the emergency response personnel arrived and went to work on Eric.

The children were still downstairs, with no one watching them.

Lei got up and hobbled to the couple's bathroom. She stripped off her shirt, noticing a red patch on her sternum. Rachel's elbow, layered on top of the blow she'd received earlier in the interview room. Worse than that was Eric's blood, splashed in a vomit pattern down the front of her shirt. On her face. On her arms.

Lei hastily splashed her face and arms, wiped with a towel, and pulled on a shirt from the nearby laundry hamper. It must have been Eric's, because it came to mid-thigh.

Good, that would cover Eric's blood on the front of her pants.

She hobbled past the emergency techs intubating Eric, Rachel's prostrate, desolate form, and Pono on the phone updating the captain. Holding on to the railing, she hopped downstairs and into the playroom.

"Hey, girls." The older daughter had turned the TV up and was close beside the toddler, who was seated in a wheeled chair. Both children had their attention fixed on *Sesame Street*. "What's Cookie Monster up to now?"

"He's trying to steal Big Bird's cookie," the little girl said. She glanced at Lei, her dark eyes wary. "Where's Mommy?"

"She has a meeting upstairs. Do you have a *tutu* or an auntie I can call? Mommy needs to go out for a while."

"What's your name?" the girl asked. "I'm not supposed to talk to strangers."

"Lei. I'm a police officer."

"My daddy is a police officer. My name is Anuhea." Anuhea got up and went to the sideboard, where a cordless phone sat on a charger. "Our grandma is number three. I can call her if you want."

"No, thanks. I'll do it. Do you need any more snacks?" Lei hobbled to take the phone from the little girl.

"No, thank you," Anuhea said, with careful good manners.

Looking down into the child's dark eyes, Lei saw the knowledge that something was deeply wrong, but the child gave no other sign. She went to sit close beside the walker, where the toddler was playing with beads and watching the television.

Lei limped out into the hall. Turning these children over to Social Services would be even more traumatic than what they were bound to go through in the days to come. She pressed and held down the number "three," formulating words that would shatter a parent's world forever.

CHAPTER TWENTY

STEVENS PICKED Lei up at the emergency room after her foot was examined and casted. "Greenstick fracture," the doctor pronounced. "Stay off it."

"Easier said than done," she'd replied. Now she crutched her way across the lobby toward the entrance.

Stevens strode through the pneumatic doors, his tall form radiating tension as he looked for her, spotted her, homed in on her. "Sweets. How many times have I had to pick you up here?"

"Dunno, but this isn't likely to be the last time," she said. "I need a kiss. A hug, too." Right there in public, she reached for him and let go of the crutches. He tightened his arms around her and lowered his head, his mouth meeting hers.

His eyes were a little hazy, hands sliding over her lightly when he raised his head.

"Any other damage besides the foot?"

"Took some blows to the midsection. And my pride," Lei said.

He picked up the crutches, handed them to her, and they made their way out the doors. Once in his Bronco, the crutches settled in back, he turned to her. "What happened?"

"I wanted to stir things up. And I did." Lei felt her eyes fill, thinking of the little Tadeo girls, meekly leaving the house with their distraught grandmother. Follow-up interviews with other responding officers, the debrief with the captain, and all that time her foot was swelling bigger and bigger until Pono almost had to carry her to his truck to get to the hospital. "I wish I'd gone slower. Been safer. I should have restrained Eli Tadeo, interviewed Rachel Tadeo at the station. I had no idea the situation was as complicated and explosive as it was."

"You get all the crazy ones these days," Stevens said. "I spent my day training Brandon Mahoe and looking for Mom. The good thing is, I found her. And she's in the Aloha House acute unit now."

"Really? That's great news!"

"I got to her in time. She was passed out in a cardboard box next to a Dumpster. Totally dehydrated. Looks like she might have some kidney damage, not to mention liver damage from this latest binge. They took her in an ambulance and stabilized her at the ER. When Jared showed up at the hospital, we pulled out all the stops to get her to agree to go to treatment. Emphasized how it could have been her in the canal. She agreed, but it remains to be seen if she'll stay."

"But that's a start. What did she say about that blonde woman wearing her clothes?"

Stevens shrugged, his mouth tight. "Like we supposed. She traded her clothes for the bottle."

"So what was she wearing?"

"Underwear. A filthy shirt. But she was in a sleeping bag, so she wasn't lying around naked, at least."

"God, Michael. I'm so sorry." Lei stroked the corded muscles of his arm, and he took her hand.

"It will be okay if she stays in recovery. But I'm not holding my breath."

"So…what do you think about the Changs, the shroud killer? Think they had anything to do with Adele's drowning?"

"I don't know. There doesn't seem to be a connection."

"Thank God for that. I'll check in with Terence Chang when I go to the Big Island for Solomon's trial," Lei said. They navigated the two-lane Hana Highway out of town. Lei glanced at the glitter of sunset glow on the ocean off Ho`okipa Beach, where this case had first begun. She thought of Pippa and Bryan Oulaki. Maybe something would happen there, maybe not. At least he'd shown a prerequisite for real love—willingness to sacrifice for another. None of the other people in the tangled relationships they'd uncovered in this case had known that secret.

"I can't wait to get home," she said. "We're sleeping with Kiet in the new house, right?"

"Right." Stevens smiled at her, his dark hair lit by golden sunset rays through the truck's window. "Can't wait to get into that cold shower again."

CHAPTER TWENTY-ONE

L<small>EI STOOD</small> in front of Terence Chang's immaculate house on the Big Island several weeks later. As on her other visits, his two brindled pit bulls roared down off the lanai to hurl themselves at the chain-link fence. Terence eventually appeared at the door. He lifted a hand to her, called the dogs. They subsided as he came down the steps wearing a black T-shirt and jeans, his demeanor casual.

"Lei Texeira. You keep turning up like a bad penny. Here for Ray Solomon's trial?"

"Exactly." Lei wore her dress uniform for the trial, the brass winking with polish, the commendation she'd earned on Kaua'i so long ago a splash of bright ribbon on her left breast. She wore a little makeup, and her hair had been wrestled and sprayed into a bun. It was fragile armor in which to face the enemy. She'd have preferred Kevlar.

"What's the problem this time?"

"No problem. Just checking in." She slid her hands into the pockets of her uniform slacks, close to her weapon. Her badge caught the light as the material moved. "I want to make sure we're still on the same page."

"What page is that?" Humor lurked in the crinkled skin beneath Terence's intelligent dark eyes. "The final chapter?"

"The chapter where you and I agreed to bury the hatchet. And you told me you were going straight."

"Ah. That chapter. I seem to remember some threats, a gun being waved around. Getting handcuffed inside your car, turning on my own flesh and blood to help you and getting little thanks. But hey, no problem—the ol' hatchet is buried."

"Hey now," Lei said mildly. In spite of everything, she liked Terence Chang. She dared to hope it was mutual. "I came here because—I just want to make sure we're good. You know, keep your friends close and your enemies closer."

"And which am I?"

"I'm never quite sure. Hence my visit. Again."

Terence grinned, and she noticed how young, how handsome he was. "We're good. I'm glad to have put all that shit behind me."

"Terence? Everything okay?" a light female voice called from the doorway of the house.

"Nani. Come meet Lei Texeira."

"Whoa." Nani, a pretty, dark-haired local girl wearing a skimpy T-shirt dress, slid her feet into high-heeled rubber thong sandals and came down the steps. "That Lei Texeira?"

"The very one," Lei said. "I'd shake, but then your dogs would likely rip my hand off."

"You can come in," Terence said, hooking an arm around the girl's waist and making as if to open the gate. "Lei, this is my girlfriend, Nani."

"No, thanks. I don't have time. But here's my personal cell. I want you to call me if ever—I can help you. Or if there's a problem." Lei tried to pass Terence her card through the chain link. Sure enough, the dogs went nuts barking.

"I appreciate the gesture, but you forget I live most of my life online. I know exactly where you are and how to get ahold of you." Terence smiled and backed away from the gate with his arm around Nani. "Good luck at the trial. Hope Ray doesn't ever get out of prison, for both our sakes."

The couple went up the stairs. Lei turned to clump back to her rental car in the walking cast she wore now that she was off crutches.

LEI STOOD behind the podium beside the judge's seat in the closed courtroom in Hilo a couple of hours later. "Do you swear to tell the truth, the whole truth, and nothing but the truth, so help you God?"

"I do," Lei said, loud and unwavering.

"You are sworn in," the clerk said. Lei sat down. She gazed out over the packed courtroom and looked into the defendant's eyes. They were still beautiful. Large and a changeable golden hazel, they stared at her unblinking, radiating hatred.

Ray Solomon had let himself go in his paralysis. If it were possible, he was even bigger than he'd been when she'd taken him down. Fat surrounded him in rolling layers, overflowing his wheelchair, as protective as a turtle's shell.

How she wished she hadn't taken that last shot at his fleeing vehicle in Volcano Park all those years ago—or at least, having taken the shot, that she'd killed him. This was the worst possible outcome for both of them. He sat there, trapped in his body, with nothing to do but plot revenge, and she still felt guilty about it.

Hours later, wringing with nervous sweat, Lei clumped in her cast down the steps of the courthouse to be met by Dr. Wilson, her colleague and former therapist.

"How'd it go?"

"Good as can be expected. Doesn't look like he'll be getting out in this lifetime."

"Excellent. My car's over here. Hop in." The petite blonde psychologist drove a cream-colored Mini Cooper. "I'll bring you back to get your rental later."

"Please tell me you have somewhere good to eat on the agenda," Lei begged.

"I do. The Banyan Tree."

They drove to the well-known seaside restaurant, with its view of wind-ruffled Hilo Bay and the song of coqui frogs in the background.

As they dug into salads, Dr. Wilson smiled at Lei. "You're looking good. I was worried about you after you lost the baby."

"I was worried about me, too." Lei took a sip of white wine. "It was the toughest thing I've ever been through. And I've been through some shit."

"Seems like you and Michael are doing well."

"Very well." Lei pushed away the worry about Stevens's drinking and tore off a piece of bread, took a bite. "We're finally all the way moved into the new house. Having my dad live with us has been great, but it was too cozy all together in Wayne's cottage. He's glad to have his space back. We couldn't do what we do without him taking care of Kiet, and he seems to love it."

"When did you finish the house?"

"We moved into it a month ago. I'm planning a housewarming. You're invited, of course."

"I'd be delighted to come." The psychologist's blue eyes reflected the flames of the candle at her elbow. "What's happening with Ellen Stevens?"

"She stuck with Aloha House. She's a week or two from completing their initial program. I guess the drowned woman we fished out of the canal wearing her clothes was bottom for Ellen. She started to waver in the program, and Michael took her to the morgue and made her look at the body. She finally realized it would be her in the canal next if she didn't sober up."

"So I was following your last big case in the news. Makoa Simmons."

"Yeah. What a tangled web that was, and we kept most of the juicy stuff out of the news. It ended so tragically." Lei told the psychologist about the dynamics of two beautiful bikini models in love with the same man and twins in love with the same woman. "I had to make the case by getting a confession, and things went badly at the end, especially for the Tadeos' two little girls."

"What's happened to them?"

"They're living with family. Rachel pled out to assault with a deadly weapon and is doing some time. Eric is being charged with Makoa's murder, Eli Tadeo's charged with conspiracy to commit murder, and Shayla Cummings is an accessory. They're awaiting trial and proving anything against either of them would be tough if I didn't have recorded interviews. Still, I wouldn't be surprised if Shayla gets off with a slap on the wrist. At least the insurance company has denied her claim and is awarding it to Makoa's immediate next of kin, which I am hoping ends up being his baby. Pippa is healthy and the pregnancy is going well, and with any luck, she'll fall a little in love with Bryan Oulaki, who adores her."

"So what's next for you and your family?"

A small interruption came as the server removed their salad plates and set down platters of juicy steak before each of them.

Lei grinned. "It's funny to see you with such a big slab of meat in front of you. Somehow I thought you'd be the shrimp-over-pasta type."

Dr. Wilson stabbed her T-bone and sawed. "I could say the same of you. Now you know I love nothing more than a slab of local Big Island beef. But you're dodging answering my question."

Lei took a bite, chewed, and swallowed. "I don't know that I'm dodging the question so much as not sure of the answer. We finished the house, we've moved in, which has been our focus ever since the fire. Michael's hard at work on his training program, and I think he's finally seen what a good fit that job is for him. Kiet's getting bigger, going to be walking soon. We adopted another dog, a male Rottie named Conan. He's keeping Keiki on her toes, really has given her a second wind, just like I was hoping. I keep getting cases. Every one of them interesting."

She took another bite.

"Sounds like a full life."

"It is."

"Do you ever think of trying to have a child again?"

"Every day," Lei whispered, feeling her eyes fill as she looked at the woman who'd been such a part of her healing from the past. "Every day I think of it. And I'm too afraid."

Dr. Wilson lifted her water glass. "A toast."

Lei lifted hers, waiting.

"To being afraid. And choosing to live fully anyway."

They clinked glasses.

Lei swallowed a burning sip of wine. She knew she didn't want to be so afraid of the pain of a possible tragedy that she missed out on another child. Not when she had Kiet filling every day with love and surprises, his dark green eyes sparkling with delight, his big grin lighting up their lives.

Not when she knew what joy, as well as heartbreak, a child could bring. She still dreamed of Baby. She guessed she always would.

"Good toast. I should write that one down."

"I'm known for quotes," Dr. Wilson said. "A big part of my therapy technique."

"I'm aware," Lei said. And they both laughed.

Turn the page for a sneak peek of book ten of the Paradise Crime Mysteries, *Bone Hook!*

SNEAK PEEK

BONE HOOK, PARADISE CRIME MYSTERIES BOOK 10

THE DLNR AGENT for the area, Mark Nunes, was on his way to meet with them, so Lei took the time to call the University of Hawaii. She was connected with Dr. Rebecca Farnsworth.

"How can I help you, Sergeant?" The woman's voice sounded older, deep and confident.

"I'm calling regarding one of your staff. Dr. Danielle Phillips." Lei had the case file open. She felt a twinge of sorrow seeing the bright, fresh smile on Danielle's face in the driver's license photo.

"Lani? What's going on?" Dr. Farnsworth's voice quickened with alarm.

"We're calling to inform you she's deceased and that there was foul play involved."

"Oh no!" A gasp. "What happened?"

"We can't discuss an open homicide investigation, but anything you could tell us regarding her responsibilities for you would help. And if you could assemble a list of people for us to interview, that would be great. Also, keep this confidential for now. MPD is working on a statement for the press."

Pono looked up from the notes he was jotting with a nod. Pono was in charge of their PR, never Lei's strong suit.

"Okay. Wow, I'm in shock. But I guess, on second thought, I'm not that shocked. I knew what Lani was doing was dangerous." Lei could tell the woman was working hard to regroup. "She answered to me and she was the senior marine biology staffer here on Maui. As you know, we're a smaller satellite college in the University of Hawaii system. She was our only full-time marine biologist."

"What can you tell me about her?"

"She was working on several research projects, most notably a longitudinal fish-populations study for Maui, which was going to be coordinated with projects on the other islands. Oh, dear, what's going to happen to her research?" The woman was still trying to assimilate the news.

"Did Danielle have a private office? We're going to need to search that."

"Yes, she does."

"I'll send an officer over to seal it. Please don't allow anyone in or out until we've had a chance to go through it."

"All right. It's kept locked anyway, but I'll make sure."

Lei turned aside to tell Pono about the office. "Seal the home, too," Lei said. "And get us the search warrants." Pono got on the phone to Dispatch.

Dr. Farnsworth went on. "Anyway, Danielle was such a hard worker. She was never too busy to help a student or another staffer. She loved what she did and she will be greatly missed."

"I'm sure. What can you tell me about her use of the University's Zodiac?"

"Was that involved?"

"Yes, it was. It's still anchored out at Molokini. I might as well tell you, she died scuba diving off Molokini." Lei made a note on a paper and passed it over to Pono. *Call Coast Guard about retrieving the Zodiac and impounding it for our search for trace.* He was still on the phone about the warrants, but he nodded.

"Oh no! I bet this was something to do with her illegal-fishing documentation. When she was out doing her fish counts, she kept seeing fishing violations. So she started documenting it for the DLNR, to get it stopped."

That had to be Danielle's GoPro footage they'd retrieved. Pono had been right in his guess about the fishing documentation, and it looked like it might have gotten her killed.

"Thanks for this information. After we search the vessel, we'll return it to the University of Hawaii. In the meantime, if you could work on a list of other useful interviewees for us, that would be great."

"She had a stalker, you know," Dr. Farnsworth said.

"She did?" Lei's pen was poised over the notes she was making. "Tell me more."

"He was a grad student whose work she was supervising. She complained to me about it. I had the kid in for a lecture. We were actually processing paperwork to get him expelled from the campus and dropped from the PhD program because he hadn't stopped his activity toward her."

"What did he do?"

"He would follow her around on campus. Take pictures of her all the time. Texted and called her constantly. She asked him to stop, then told security. After that he would wait by the parking lot for her. I advised her to take out a temporary restraining order on him. Did she do it?"

Lei had already punched up Danielle's police record, which was clean. "Nothing on file."

"I think she thought it was getting better."

"What's this man's name?"

"Ben. Ben Miller. He lives somewhere in Kahului. She told me she was going to cut him from the program if he didn't stop bugging her."

"Do you think he would be angry about that?"

"Oh, yes. He was several years into his PhD. To continue, he would have to move and start all over, if he could even get a university to accept him. She told me she was documenting his behavior in his student file."

"Hmm. I will probably want to re-interview you, Dr. Farnsworth, later down the line." Lei got the contact information for Ben Miller and Dr. Farnsworth's personal cell and hung up.

She turned to Pono with a tight grin. "Got a hot suspect here."

"I'd say let's go get him, but here's Mark Nunes now, here from the DLNR to answer our inquiries." Pono gestured to a man standing in the doorway of their cubicle.

Nunes was dark-haired, around five foot ten, deeply tanned, with the tilted eyes and lean but muscular build of a local. He was dressed in the DLNR uniform of navy pants and shirt with identification patches, boots, and a duty belt much like a police officer's. Lei stood and shook his hand.

"Sergeant Texeira. Did you know the victim, Danielle Phillips?"

"I did." The man nodded, his eyes on the floor.

"Yeah, I talked with him while you were on the phone," Pono said. "They were friends."

"I'm sorry for your loss. Okay, we should do a more formal interview, then." Lei cut a glance over to Pono. "Why don't you get him set up in an interview room and I'll get the photos we want him to look at on a tablet so we can go through them there?"

"Sounds good." The two men exited. Lei sat down, routing the GoPro pictures to a tablet device for them to review and finishing her notes from the phone call to Dr. Farnsworth. While she was at it, she called in a Be On Lookout for Ben Miller. The last thing they needed was for Danielle's stalker to slip off the island. Lei hoped they were in time to bring him in, even now.

She picked up the tablet and headed for the interview room.

The two men were already seated, and Pono had the recording equipment on. He added Lei's name and rank for the record as she took the third chair.

Nunes sat quietly, but there was an air of coiled distress about him. His dark eyes were red-rimmed and he blinked repeatedly. "I was shocked to hear Danielle is dead."

"Yes, it's a real shame. So how long have you worked for the Department of Land and Natural Resources?"

"Ten years."

"Then you've been through some lean times." Pono rubbed his mustache briskly. "I heard the furloughs were really tough a few years ago, when the state cut way back on resources."

"Yeah. The economic crash of 2009 hit the state really hard. Teachers and all state employees were furloughed. We were cut back to just four days a week and lost all personnel who weren't permanent state employees. It was really hard to keep up back then. Still is. I've come to realize we can only do what we can do." Nunes held his hands open philosophically, and Lei spotted a carved hook pendant in the neck of his shirt.

"I just gave my husband a bone hook like that." She pointed to the necklace.

"Symbol of fishermen and providers." Nunes touched the pendant, a gesture that had a feeling of superstition about it, and Lei smiled.

"So you do some fishing yourself?"

"Of course. I love the ocean and all that's in it. I fish to feed my family, like so many do here on Maui. I'm proud to be with DLNR so we can make sure the reefs are healthy and there's food for generations to come."

"So tell me about Danielle Phillips and her relationship with DLNR."

"Lani. She loved the ocean, too. She helped us with our investigations." Suddenly Nunes's clear brown eyes clouded, and he pressed the thumb and forefinger of one hand over his eyes. "I can't believe she's gone," he whispered.

"Tell us about your relationship with her," Lei said. Nunes seemed to be reacting personally to this. Could there be something more between the two?

"Relationship?" Nunes removed his hand, blinked his eyes, and sat up straight. "We were friends. I was her main contact when she handed over evidence. To issue a citation, we have to have hard evidence that a rule or regulation has been broken, such as ocean biologics taken from a protected area. She was in the ocean so much for her research that she was able to boost a lot of photos to us that helped us win cases."

"So not only do you have to bust people with the fish in hand, but you have to have evidence the fish were caught illegally?" Lei frowned. "That seems challenging."

"It is. But it's kind of like being a detective." Now Nunes's eyes gleamed a little. "I do a lot of stealth photography with a long lens or underwater, with a GoPro like Lani used."

"So did she do assignments for you? Like, follow so-and-so; we suspect them?" Lei asked.

"No. She wasn't an agent. She would just spot things, document them, and boost them to me when they came across her path."

"Okay. We need to know that you'll keep this whole conversation confidential, because this is a homicide investigation."

Nunes reared back a little in his chair. "Someone killed Lani? I just thought she drowned. Accidentally."

"No. It was a homicide."

"Oh God." He covered his mouth with a hand, eyes wide. "Whatever I can do to help."

"Yes, that's why we called you in. We found a GoPro on the bottom of Molokini's bay with a lot of photos on it. We're having trouble interpreting them." Lei woke up the tablet, moved her chair around the table to show Nunes. The agent and Pono both leaned in to look. "We can't tell where these locations are, but I think the opening shots are to establish location."

"Yes. This is the way I told her to do it. Put the location in context, then date and time-stamp the photos." They scanned through. Nunes pointed to the ones with the net. "That's illegal aquarium capture happening."

"Can you see anything identifying in the photos?" Pono asked. Several divers in snorkel, not scuba, gear were chasing fish into an underwater net. Nearby was a submerged white plastic drum, a ring of buoy around the top keeping it upright at the water's surface. Nunes pointed to it.

"They'll put the fish in that and ship them off-island in the same water they were captured in. Helps keep the fish from dying of shock." A few photos further on, Danielle had snapped a shot of the three divers rolling the white barrel up out of the water onto black volcanic rocks. "Looks like La Perouse Bay. And those are the Micronesians we've been busting."

"Micronesians?" Lei squinted at the grainy photo. All three men, wearing baggy trunks, had bushy black hair and darker skin than most Hawaiians.

"Yeah. They've been immigrating to Maui for years now under our agreement with their government. Because we nuked Bikini Atoll and it caused a lot of unforeseen damage, the native people can come live in the United States and get free health care. Every year there are more and more of them, and some of them fish like they do in their islands— no size or count limits. They don't respect our conservation laws."

"Oh, man," Lei said. "Talk about integration problems."

"Right. So this is an entirely different kind of fishing." Nunes tapped the screen, expanding a photo where two black-suited divers appeared to be retrieving an ahi tuna. "It's legal to fish or dive on the back side of Molokini, the part they call 'Ono Alley,' because there are so many pelagic fish over there. But not on the inside. Usually fishermen are using line gear for those fish, but maybe what happened was that these divers were chasing a fish and he came in shallower, to the protected area. They weren't willing to let him go. A fish like that is worth thousands."

They scrolled on.

"What can you see from these pictures?" Lei indicated the black hull of the boat overhead from the final photos on Danielle's GoPro.

"It's a Zodiac hard bottom, twenty footer or so. Quick and easy way out to Molokini on a calm day. Zoom in." They did. Nunes went on as he studied the photo. "Can't see anything. That's the difficulty. Lani had to find something we could track later that tied people to the photos and establish date, time, and location. She knew that, so she'd have tried to find something."

"I don't see any identifying marks on the Zodiac," Lei said as they all scanned the underside of the black boat.

"The motor in the water looks like about a sixty-horse outboard, but I can't see anything either. I know she'd have tried to get a shot of the registration number on the hull," Nunes said.

"This is the last photo on the GoPro. Maybe they killed her before she could get that identifying shot," Pono said. Lei gave him a sharp look. It wasn't a good idea to speculate in front of a witness.

"We try not to jump to conclusions," Lei said, addressing Nunes. "You can't talk about what you saw here. We'll turn these photos over to the DLNR after the investigation."

"Where's that list of people cited for illegal fishing I asked you for?" Pono said.

Nunes produced a typed list from his pocket. "Here. These are poachers and fishermen cited for various infractions in the last six months."

"Thanks for pulling that together so quickly."

Nunes shrugged. "All in the database. Is that all for now?"

"For now." Pono let him out of the room as Lei switched off the recording equipment. She walked to join her partner as he held the door ajar. "Let's do a quick comparison of the murder weapon with the spear these divers had in the last photos on the GoPro."

"Don't you want to go pick up the stalker?"

"I called in a BOLO to get things started. I want to follow up on a slew of search warrants next, but if we know what kind of speargun we're looking for, so much the better."

They were headed down the hall toward the evidence room as they talked, Lei carrying the tablet. "So I'll get on the horn and get a search warrant for Ben Miller's place, too," Pono said. "Already got the ones for home and office."

He thumbed his phone open as Lei stopped at the half door to the evidence room. "Sergeant Lei Texeira checking an item I dropped off earlier."

Officer Clarice Dagdag was a short, plump woman whose legs made a *whisk*ing sound in her crisp uniform as she bustled off to retrieve the spear for Lei. Lei gave the spear, still in its paper wrapping, to Pono as she signed the logbook. "Thanks."

Clarice inclined her head, her glittering rhinestone cat's eye glasses already aimed back toward a tiny television monitor on her desk, where a soap opera played out a muted drama.

They carried the spear to one of the workrooms with a computer and an evidence processing table. Pono unwrapped the spear shaft as Lei pulled up the photos on the tablet and scrolled to the ones of the divers at Molokini.

When Lei had the right photo, one that showed a diver holding a trigger speargun, she looked at the shaft Pono had taken out.

The shaft looked like hardened steel. Pono picked it up and looked at the flat end. "Eight-millimeter diameter by sixteen-point-five length." There was a hole in the end of the shaft and a double-barbed head. The metal flanges of the barbs slid open or closed easily. "I can make out 'Mares' here on the shaft. Almost worn off. But this is definitely a pneumatic gun."

"A what?"

"A compressed-air speargun that fires the shaft using air pressure and a trigger. Someone removed the nylon cord that connects to the speargun body." He tapped the empty hole in the shaft. "Mares is a popular brand. We just need to look through their catalog to find the types of guns that fire this shaft to know what was used."

"Okay. I'll pull that up." Lei didn't bother turning on the ancient computer in the corner, instead opening a search window and punching in the Mares brand on the tablet. She keyed in the shaft specs.

"Looks like the smaller model of the Sten Pneumatic Pro." She pulled up a window with the photo from the catalog, dragged the GoPro shot of the diver holding the gun, and positioned the photos side by side. Pono leaned in close as they eyeballed the photos.

"Just visually comparing, it does look like it could be this size." Pono pointed to the Mares catalog. "This little Mares gun would have to be pretty close to the victim to drive the spear as deep into the body as the shaft went into Danielle. I can't see clearly enough to check if there's a rubber band on the diver's gun in the photo. Can you zoom in?"

"Why would there be a rubber band on it?" Lei used her fingertips to open the photo further, and though the resolution got fuzzy and grainy, they could see a faint line at the top of the speargun in the diver's hands.

"Different type of weapon. That's definitely a rubber band gun. I was going to tell you I didn't think a pneumatic had the juice for big fish. Deep-sea spear fishermen tend to use longer guns with multiple rubber bands to get more torque."

"So that's not the murder weapon in the photo."

"Correct."

"But it could be one of the other divers, or someone not pictured."

"I guess. Still, diving at that depth—they wouldn't have brought only a small gun like that Mares pneumatic."

"Okay. But at least we know what we're looking for when we go out with the search warrants." Lei rewrapped the spear shaft, trying not to remember how it had looked protruding from Danielle's body. "Since it was a smaller gun and it had penetrated her deeply, wouldn't the diver who shot her have to be pretty close?"

"Probably. That sounds like some fun research." Pono grinned, rubbing his hands together in anticipation. "I'll see if my buddy who owns a dive shop can loan us a Mares gun and we'll figure out exactly how close we'd have to be and in what position to get the shaft into a body like what was done to our vic. Dr. G will love helping us reconstruct the scene."

"Yuck." Lei shook her head. She found her imagination was sometimes her enemy on projects like those. "It's enough for right now that we know the other diver had to get pretty close to Lani. That could mean she knew the shooter."

Download *Bone Hook* and continue reading now!

ACKNOWLEDGMENTS

Aloha dear Readers,

If you've been with me awhile, you know this is one of my favorite points in writing a book: that moment when I get to address you directly and say a few words.

First of all, THANK YOU. Thank you for your wonderful enthusiasm, reviews, sharing the books with friends and family, and for being a very real reason for me to keep coming to the page every day. I love you guys and gals, especially those I'm lucky enough to interact with through social media. If you haven't already, join the party! I'm on Facebook, Twitter, Instagram, andPinterest, and love to interact with readers on all platforms.

Second of all, thanks to our photographer friend Reis Shimabukuro, who tried his best to get me into one of the team houses at Pipeline, and while then claiming not to know much, gave me lots of inside scoop into how the team houses are run. I made up stuff and probably got a lot wrong, but hey—the surf industry people should have answered my calls and e-mails asking for a meeting if they wanted me to get it right!

This book was also a real return to police work, and as such I owe special thanks to Ret. Captain David Spicer, who keeps my procedure at least mostly in the ballpark.

Surfing is close to my heart. I come from a surfing family, three generations of wave worshippers in Hawaii, and I married a surfer. I still take my boogie board out on occasion, and it was past time I came up with a way that I could use a mystery to share that world with a broader audience.

An aside about the title, *Rip Tides*: I titled the book that because it's a common usage term though not technically correct. I'm actually referring to the phenomena of *rip currents*, which have nothing to do with tides. Rip currents occur when waves expend their traveling energy as they hit the beach. That energy is only partly dissipated by the breaking wave. The remaining energy collects alongside wave peaks in fast-moving "rips" that suck back out to sea and many times, cause drowning for inexperienced swimmers who may be caught in them and panic. Surfers can read the ocean and use rips to their advantage, for quick transport out to a peak or to end a ride.

Book research for *Rip Tides* took me back to the North Shore of Oahu. Our family had lived on the beach in a cottage between Sunset and Pipeline from 1969–1970, with my dad surfing those breaks every day until we moved to Kaua`i when I was five. This winter, I was exhilarated by almost a week in a beach house on that famous stretch of golden sand, hearing the thundering of the breaking waves through the night, watching the most amazing surfing in the world during the day. I think my descriptions are particularly rich because I went there and immersed in the scene. I even found the beach house our family lived in, hardly changed at all. (I am also gathering material for my memoir, **Freckled,** so locating it was exciting!)

If you enjoyed the story, please leave a review! It's the best thanks you can give any author.

Much aloha,

FREE BOOKS

Join my mystery and romance lists and receive free, full-length, award-winning novels *Torch Ginger & Somewhere on St. Thomas.*

tobyneal.net/TNNews

TOBY'S BOOKSHELF

PARADISE CRIME SERIES

<u>Paradise Crime Mysteries</u>
Blood Orchids
Torch Ginger
Black Jasmine
Broken Ferns
Twisted Vine
Shattered Palms
Dark Lava
Fire Beach
Rip Tides
Bone Hook
Red Rain
Bitter Feast

Paradise Crime Mystery
Special Agent Marcella Scott
Stolen in Paradise

Paradies Crime Suspense Mysteries
Unsound

Paradise Crime Thrillers
Wired In

Wired Rogue

Wired Hard

Wired Dark

Wired Dawn

Wired Justice

Wired Secret

Wired Fear

Wired Courage

Wired Truth

ROMANCES

The Somewhere Series
Somewhere on St. Thomas

Somewhere in the City

Somewhere in California

Standalone
Somewhere on Maui

Co-Authored Romance Thrillers
The Scorch Series
Scorch Road

Cinder Road

Smoke Road

Burnt Road

Flame Road

Smolder Road

YOUNG ADULT

Standalone
Island Fire

NONFICTION

Memoir
Freckled

ABOUT THE AUTHOR

Kirkus Reviews calls Neal's writing, *"persistently riveting. Masterly."*

Award-winning, USA Today bestselling social worker turned author Toby Neal grew up on the island of Kaua`i in Hawaii. Neal is a mental health therapist, a career that has informed the depth and complexity of the characters in her stories. Neal's mysteries and thrillers explore the crimes and issues of Hawaii from the bottom of the ocean to the top of volcanoes. Fans call her stories, *"Immersive, addicting, and the next best thing to being there."*

Neal also pens romance, romantic thrillers, and writes memoir/nonfiction under TW Neal.

Visit tobyneal.net for more ways to stay in touch!
or
Join my Facebook readers group, *Friends Who Like Toby Neal Books,* for special giveaways and perks.